Praise for *Lazarus is Dead*

'As gripping as a thriller and endlessly thought-provoking
... Surprising, spellbinding, witty and utterly original'
Sunday Herald

'A brilliant reimagining of the Lazarus story...wry,
incisive and surprisingly moving'
Irish Times

'He can stir emotion quickly and simply... His essayistic
digressions temper the mythic luminosity of his subject'
Times Literary Supplement

'A thoughtful, enjoyable book'
Spectator

'It is the narrative voice – cultivated, wry, yet not too
knowing to sustain a note of wonder – that makes this
novel so compelling'
Sunday Times

'Beard strikes just the right tone... Enough flesh and blood
is added to the bones of Lazarus's story to make you care
about his eventual fate... *Lazarus is Dead* is a delightful
falsehood – a brilliant novel and a shining example of
the gospel untruth'
Guardian

RICHARD BEARD

Lazarus is Dead

A Biography

VINTAGE BOOKS

London

Published by Vintage 2012

2 4 6 8 10 9 7 5 3 1

First published in Great Britain in 2011 by
Harvill Secker

Vintage
Random House, 20 Vauxhall Bridge Road,
London SW1V 2SA

www.vintage-books.co.uk

Addresses for companies within The Random House Group Limited
can be found at: www.randomhouse.co.uk/offices.htm

The Random House Group Limited Reg. No. 954009

A CIP catalogue record for this book
is available from the British Library

ISBN 9780099554349

The Random House Group Limited supports The Forest Stewardship
Council (FSC®), the leading international forest certification
organisation. Our books carrying the FSC label are printed on FSC®
certified paper. FSC is the only forest certification scheme endorsed
by the leading environmental organisations, including Greenpeace.
Our paper procurement policy can be found at:
www.randomhouse.co.uk/environment

Designed and typeset by Dinah Drazin

Printed in Great Britain by Clays Ltd, St Ives plc

'Our friend Lazarus has fallen asleep, but I'm going to wake him up.'

John 11:11

7

7

Lazarus is dead.

There is no room for doubt. He died, he came back to life, but then he died again. If he were alive today, we would know. I think.

Other certainties are harder to come by. The earliest reference to Lazarus is found in the gospel according to John, whose reliability as a historian is questionable. Among the gospel writers Mark is considered the most factually accurate. Matthew and Luke base their accounts on Mark, while John is closer to the type of writing known today as creative non-fiction.

For structural reasons, John selects seven of the best Jesus miracles and uses them to shape his narrative. He starts with the water-into-wine. Then some healing miracles, the feeding of the five thousand, the walking on water, as each miracle builds towards the climactic seventh event, the death and resurrection of Lazarus.

This is the sign that announces the arrival of the messiah.

Jesus turns water into wine at a wedding in Cana, and the next morning Lazarus opens his eyes and stares at the whitewashed ceiling. It is grey, and he has a nagging sense, this morning, of something amiss.

The feeling fades. He has too much to do, an arrangement to speak with his chief Bedouin shepherd, another trip to the city.

He leaves the house without eating, and is halfway across the village square when he hears the name of Jesus. A young man with bright eyes is balancing on a halved barrel, answering shout-out questions from a small group of villagers.

Yes, god's truth, he survived in the desert with no food or water for forty days. The river? He stands waist deep in the water and forgives the sins of the people. He is a lamb, a shepherd, bread, blood.

'Who was with him?'

The square falls silent. Lazarus is not like the rest of them. For an outsider, he isn't all bad, but no one expects him to stop what he's doing to listen to this kind of nonsense. He has his business interests, selling sheep to the Temple, and his powerful contacts in Jerusalem. His life is ordered, successful, unusual; he has no need of enlightenment.

The bringer of news smiles and opens out his arms. 'Everyone is welcome at baptism.'

'I mean, who's helping him? He'll have had someone with him.'

'John the Baptist.' The messenger is confident again, now that he's safe with the facts. 'John the Baptist and Jesus standing side by side in the river.'

'Thought so. Someone else always has to go first.'

Lazarus sees his shepherd Faruq at the edge of the crowd. He takes the Bedouin by the elbow and leads him away, lowers his voice. 'How was Jerusalem?'

Faruq looks back over his shoulder, but not for long. Lazarus pays the best prices, and always finds buyers. He has Faruq's future in his hands.

'They've reduced the quota of animals again.'

'Again?'

Lazarus winces, rubs the back of his hand across his lips.

'They still need sheep,' Faruq shrugs. 'It could be worse.'

'I'm thirsty, don't know why. Go and sort out the best of the lambs. It's time we took the initiative.'

Lazarus appears in only one of the four gospels, and at first John provides a minimal amount of biography: *'A man named Lazarus, who lived in Bethany, was ill'* (John 11: 1).

The village of Bethany survives to this day, about three miles from the city of Jerusalem. It spreads over the last of the high ground before the fall of desert to the salt Dead Sea, the lowest point on earth. From Bethany on a clear day tour guides can point out, in the far distance, the leaden glint of heavy water.

Bedouin herders scrape a living from these down-
lands, their sheep grazing the *natsh* (poterium thorn)
and sage plants that survive the slopes of rock and sand.
The shepherds supplement their income selling camel
rides to coach-class tourists at the service station midway
between Jerusalem and the sea.

Before highways and petrol pumps, in the time of
Lazarus, the Bedouin roamed this vast desert area. At
Passover and other festivals they traded sheep at border-
land villages like Bethany.

John does not identify the exact nature of Lazarus's
illness.

Lazarus bangs open the gate. In the middle of the yard
there is a bay tree with a circular bench around the
trunk. His sister Martha is standing on the bench and
picking dark green leaves for the pot. She is surprised to
see him back so early. At last, she thinks, an opportunity
to talk about money.

'Not now.'

He goes inside the house, grabs a jug and plunges it
into the urn of water against the north-facing wall. He
upends the jug into his mouth, spills some, drinks some,
shakes his head. He feels drowsy. He splashes water onto
his face, blinks hard, searches for the centre of a vague
headache.

Martha watches him from the doorway. She'll give
him 'not now'. If he wants to be ill he can set aside a
day later in the year, in the summer. Passover is their
busiest season, when honest believers decide how much
they can spend sacrificing a sheep to absolve their sins.
Lazarus will persuade them to spend slightly more.

'Watch what you're doing!' Martha says. 'You're spilling water over my floor.'

She's nearly forty, too old for a wife's work. Lazarus should be married by now.

Out in the courtyard the gate creaks.

'We never get a minute.' Martha turns and wipes her hands on her apron. 'Absalom, how good to see you. You're looking very well.'

Lazarus lives in Bethany, and he is ill.

John records no specific symptoms, nor any indication of how long the sickness lasts. This suggests that the details are unremarkable, and the most common and therefore least noteworthy illnesses in the ancient world are tuberculosis, eye diseases (glaucoma, trachoma, conjunctivitis), scabies, smallpox, shigellosis (dysentery) and malaria. There is also widespread malnutrition — xerophthalmia and other deficiency disorders.

Whatever Lazarus has, we know it was fatal. It is not, however, infectious. He lives with his two sisters: *'Now a man named Lazarus was sick. He was from Bethany, the village of Mary and her sister Martha. This Mary, whose brother Lazarus now lay sick, was the same one who poured perfume on the Lord and wiped his feet with her hair'* (John 11: 1–2).

Their brother is falling ill, and towards the end of his illness the sisters will send for Jesus, and run to the gate when he arrives. Even when Lazarus is dying they will be healthy and able to make decisions. They are not sick at his deathbed, nor four days later when he comes back to life, nor in the brief time after his resurrection before Jesus leaves Bethany for Jerusalem.

Martha and Mary's evident vigour eliminates tuberculosis and smallpox, diseases that are highly infectious.

Lazarus gestures Absalom, the Rabbi and chief Elder of Bethany, to settle himself on a stool. 'Our door is always open.'

Absalom has flyaway eyebrows that frighten children, but in the house of Lazarus he sits and squeezes his hands between his knees. He is no stranger here because Lazarus has a gift for friendship, and he makes Absalom welcome by despairing of the shocking weather – not a cloud in the sky – then bemoaning the price of sheep.

Lazarus is an incomer, but in his thirteen years in Bethany he has brought trade to the village and proved his loyalty by investing in a family tomb. Bethany is where he plans to die. 'I'm sorry about your mother.'

Absalom's eyes moisten. 'It was a blessing.' His eyebrows lower, hiding his grief. 'Water, wine,' he says, then abruptly looks up. 'You'll have heard about this wedding in Cana. What do you think?'

'I think we have enough excitement of our own. The Temple priests are buying fewer lambs than they promised. We have to make sure that any lambs they do take are ours. That's why today we're going to see Isaiah.'

Malaria? Bethany is a village at the top of a hill. The wind blows, water is scarce and mosquitoes do not flourish. Lazarus owns his own tomb, so he is not poor, and therefore unlikely to suffer from malnutrition. Dysentery is caused by inadequate domestic hygiene, and Lazarus has his two sisters to cook and clean for him, with Martha famous down the ages for her commitment to housework.

Eye diseases are rarely fatal. As for scabies, it doesn't kill unless the victim is incredibly unfortunate.

Whereas Lazarus was born lucky. In another piece of vital information offered by the Gospel of John, Lazarus is the friend of Jesus.

Among all the people Jesus knows, and all the people Jesus meets, Lazarus is unique in the Christian New Testament. Not in coming back from the dead (there were others) but in being named as Jesus's friend. Jesus has disciples, some of whom he loves, but Lazarus is his only recorded friend.

And famously, unforgettably, in the shortest verse of the bible, Lazarus can make Jesus weep.

6

Friendships have to start somewhere; a definite place, a specific time. Lazarus and his sisters live in Bethany, in the south of Judaea near Jerusalem. Jesus grew up a hundred miles north in Nazareth. There is no biblical explanation of where or when Lazarus first became friends with Jesus.

There are, however, sources of information other than the gospels.

In the informal record Lazarus is everywhere. He appeals strongly to the imaginative mind, a recognisable figure on frescoes and marble reliefs throughout the ancient world. He and Jesus are the two characters most frequently depicted on the monuments of the Christian necropoli in Rome.

The story of Lazarus spreads by ripples and echoes: he appears in mosaics and sculptures, on ancient crockery and early Christian lamp covers. The iconographers of the early Church make him gleam with precious metals and, later, the painters of the Renaissance adore him.

In literature, as in the visual arts, Lazarus is remembered out of all proportion to his brief appearance in a single gospel, his name more familiar than any but the closest disciples. In the course of two thousand years Lazarus has featured in medieval hagiographies, in mystery play cycles and illustrated manuscripts. He attracts the attention of French philosophy and the American stage, English poetry and the Russian novel.

These are the sources other than the bible that can enlighten the biography of Lazarus.

'Fine,' Lazarus says. 'Now. But make it quick. We're leaving for Jerusalem.'

Martha his sister is a local touchstone, instantly recognisable to writers native to the region: 'Martha was the very embodiment of work,' says the Israeli writer Sholem Asch in *The Nazarene* (1939). 'I can still see her standing in the yard, in the cool damp of a winter's day, washing clothes in a pail, or stooping over the open oven baking flat cakes, or else boiling lentils and greens in a great earthen pot: her squat, thick body wrapped in a sackcloth dress, her legs, red and swollen, showing beneath the skirt, which was too short...if she was not cooking, she was scouring vessels; if she was not washing clothes, she was in the garden tearing out weeds.'

She also takes care of the money, and is therefore the first to notice when trade falls off.

Lazarus is selling fewer sheep into the Jerusalem Temple. Martha has heard about his 'distractions', of course she has, just like everybody else, but this is more serious. His regular customers are leaving the city to get baptised in the River Jordan, where the atonements offered by Jesus are free. Sacrificial lambs on the other hand, like the ones sold by Lazarus, don't come cheap. Nor do they cancel out sins to the apocalypse and beyond.

Even the sick, until recently a captive market, have started to look elsewhere. Instead of offering sacrifices at the Temple they gather outside the city walls, hoping to be first into the Bethesda pool when the surface of the water trembles.

Something out there is changing, something is wrong.

'You have to make more of an effort, brother. You're not as young as you used to be.'

'Martha, stop worrying. For as long as there's a god, sheep will be needed for sacrifices. That's how it's been since the time of Abraham. And anyway, I have a plan. I always have a plan, and if this works out we'll be settled for life. All three of us.'

'We need Isaiah at the Temple to like you. Don't push your luck.'

'I always push my luck,' Lazarus says. 'And he's going to like me very much indeed.'

The question about when Lazarus befriended Jesus is partially answered in a book by the Portuguese novelist and Nobel prize-winner José Saramago. In *The Gospel*

According to Jesus Christ (1991), Saramago identifies a moral flaw in the popular story of the nativity. Come and take a closer look at Bethlehem, Saramago says, where 'the ashen shadows of twilight merge heaven and earth', and from where construction workers travel daily to the site of Herod's new Temple in Jerusalem.

Joseph, husband to Mary and father to Jesus, is cutting scaffold at the Temple when he overhears soldiers discussing an imminent massacre of children. He is horrified. Even more so when he learns where the slaughter will happen. Bethlehem, his own village, where he left his wife and child safe among other wives and children.

In the gospel according to Matthew, Joseph is forewarned by *'an angel of the Lord'* (Matthew 2: 13), who appears to him in a dream.

Either way, angels or soldiers, Joseph and Mary know in advance about the massacre. They need, urgently, to flee into Egypt so that one-year-old Jesus survives. It is his destiny.

Saramago dwells on the moral implications. Joseph and Mary escape into the desert. They knowingly leave the remaining Bethlehem children to die.

For Saramago, it is unthinkable that Joseph should save himself and his family at the expense of his neighbours' children. Joseph's moral cowardice benights his life from this point onward. He will not recover from the guilt of failing to alert the others, and is never again at peace.

Saramago is a communist atheist: he underestimates the human capacity for compromise. Joseph would have wanted to save every child in Bethlehem. Of course he would. He knew the slaughter was coming. Saramago correctly identifies the immorality of not saving even one other child, and remember that Joseph was close to perfect – he was the husband of the mother of god. If he couldn't save every stranger, he could at least save a friend.

In Bethany Lazarus has invested in a double-chambered tomb, one of several in a long row cut into a low escarpment outside the village. This is where the richer inhabitants of Bethany go when they die. On the open land facing the entrances Faruq has penned his Passover lambs, because as a tomb-owner Lazarus has grazing rights. On this particular morning his resourcefulness fails to please him as it should.

His left eye hurts, and a chorus of out-of-town women are bewailing Absalom's mother, buried the day before yesterday. Lazarus has paid his respects. He said more than once that she was a lovely old lady, and donated generously for the three-day wail. Which is now tuned perfectly to scrape against the pain in the left front side of his head.

Absalom thanks each of the mourners individually, on behalf of his mother. He hands out more coins, as if the wailing should never cease.

Lazarus assesses Faruq's lambs. The air above them hazes with ticks, and their skittish orange eyes shine brightly. The Jerusalem priests will reject any animal with blemishes, a cut foreleg or a snout grazed in a fall. By themselves, the sheep tend to get stuck in gullies or eaten by wolves, which is why Lazarus chooses not to abandon them to god's mercy. He prefers to think ahead, to shape the future until it fits him best. He distrusts the hand of god, and employs experienced shepherds, desert Bedouin like Faruq.

Knee-deep in the flock, Lazarus picks out a trembling lamb, lifts it to his chest where the tiny heart flutters just above his own. He closes his eyes and crushes his nose against the dark velvet of the animal's head. Someone ought to save it.

The lamb has an eye infection. Lazarus drops it back in the pen.

Physically, the information we have about Lazarus comes mostly from the moment he emerges from his tomb, four days after his death. I can therefore say with confidence that today, on the morning after the first miracle performed by Jesus at the wedding in Cana, as Lazarus sets out for Jerusalem with Absalom and a couple of selected lambs, he is probably clean-shaven.

In any biography, which is an attempt to bring someone back to life, the facts will generate patterns of evidence. There is a coherence to the visual memory of Lazarus: in the portrayals that survive, mostly paintings made between 1300 and the end of the eighteenth century, Lazarus is consistently free of facial hair.

For a representative image, look to the Spanish painter Juan de Flandes. In *The Raising of Lazarus* (1560), we see a well-made man (clean-shaven) in his early thirties with short hair greying at the temples. He has shocked eyes in a face drawn tight after four days entombed in a cave, but the point is that before he died he was already different. He shaves. He does not resemble the massed ranks of heavy, bearded men who watch him rise from the dead.

This attention to detail is respected throughout the pictorial record − it remains artistically true because it *is* true. From Giotto in 1304 to Rembrandt in 1630, Lazarus is clean-shaven. Van Gogh (1891) gives him a wispy ginger beard, but only because he sees himself as Lazarus, and Lazarus as him, as followers everywhere do for whichever Christ they choose.

Can we be more precise? Bethany is an outlying village, and Lazarus is fit from regular trips into Jerusalem, with firm buttocks from the uphill tramp back home. He has a watchful look in his eyes. He never forgets that he's a Nazarene despite his thirteen years in the south.

And his age: he is thirty-two years old, the same age as Jesus, a man in his physical prime.

In the darkest hour of the night, Joseph the father of Jesus barges into his best friend's house, and hurries both families out to a waiting cart. He has an assertiveness about him, an absolute seriousness with which there is no arguing.

'I haven't got time to explain.'

They must have been friends for Eliakim to trust him. Joseph and Eliakim are Bethlehem neighbours, workmates who travel daily to the Temple building site, and both from the line of David. Eliakim the father of Lazarus wouldn't have bundled his family into the darkness for just anyone.

Eliakim's wife Sarah is pregnant again, and in the cart she bumps and shudders over the desert stones along with the toddlers, Jesus and Lazarus. The older girls Martha and Mary sometimes walk and sometimes ride, but Joseph and Eliakim trudge forever at either end of the cart, their emigrant convoy propelled by hope ahead and disaster behind.

On the first day, or perhaps the second, the news of the massacre in Bethlehem overtakes them. Joseph doesn't know what to say.

'The children. They are very special.'

'I know that.' Eliakim understands instantly that they can't go back. 'Every child is special.'

'The boys needed saving. Our boys.'

'How did you know the soldiers were coming?'

Joseph remembers the angel from his unbelievable dream.

'I overheard some talk at the Temple.'

Neither man stops walking.

'Thanks,' Eliakim says, eventually. 'For everything.'

'That's what friends are for.'

5

All the sources suggest that Lazarus was rich. By the time information begins to resurface in thirteenth-century Spain, in the *Legenda Sanctorum*, or Golden Legend, of 1260, Lazarus and his sisters live in separate opulent castles each with a view over Jerusalem.

Not true (archaeologists have uncovered no remains of castles directly outside the city), but even in John's pinched account there is convincing evidence of money. Lazarus owns an expensive tomb, with two separate chambers and a sliding door. As a dead man he is wrapped in linen, the finest textile available for shrouds. There is at least one bottle of three-hundred-shekel perfume in his house, later used by Mary to wash the feet of Jesus.

This ability to generate wealth supports the view that Lazarus has connections with the Jerusalem Temple. And the village of Bethany, between the desert and the city, is perfectly placed to satisfy the Temple's demand for sacrificial lambs.

The numbers are astonishing. Each and every synagogue will expect to slaughter a thousand lambs a year. At new moons and the seven annual festivals, sinners make additional offerings of repentance. Many of these supplicants are the ill and sick whose prayers for forgiveness are the same as prayers for health – killing a sheep is ancient medicine.

The rock-cut tomb, the expensive perfume, the shroud: Lazarus is an overseer. He makes a healthy living from underpaying the shepherds and overcharging the priests, an expert at the feints necessary to realise a profit, to get more for less, or something for nothing.

His ambition to get on in the world may, possibly, have inhibited his spiritual growth, but he doesn't care. Not caring gives him charisma, a self-reliance the Temple priests have learned to trust. He is weak on god, but gets things done. He's an individualist before his time, a fact as biographically persuasive as his shaven face. Raised in small-town Nazareth, as a young man he moved the length of the country to live and work within walking distance of Jerusalem. He is enterprising and economically mobile. He is not like anyone else.

*

15

From the Bethany cemetery to Jerusalem, Lazarus pulls two lambs behind him on a length of red rope. Small brown hooves skitter on the path as Lazarus lengthens his stride down the slope of the first valley. Within minutes, his clothes are drenched in sweat. He climbs hard up the next hill, hands pushing down on his thighs.

Unusually, Absalom easily keeps up with Lazarus and the trotting lambs.

'They believe it happened,' he says. 'They're calling it a miracle.'

'Must make it almost worthwhile getting married.'

Lazarus would prefer to conserve his energy, but this is a conversation that Absalom is determined to have.

'They swear on their mothers' lives. The water turned into wine.'

'They were drunk. It was a wedding. I know what they're like in the Galilee. The water was poured into old jars, and peasants drink straight from the jar. It was dark and late. They smelled the old wine on the rims and tasted what they wanted to taste.'

At the crest of the hill, Lazarus has to stop and rest. Today, for some reason, he is struggling to walk and talk at the same time. He blows hard as he catches his breath, his hands braced on his knees.

'Anything wrong?'

'I'm fine.'

The lambs jump past him and he pulls them back, then lifts his head.

On the far side of the second valley is the shining city. From a distance, from above, red in the midday sunlight, the walls of Jerusalem never fail to impress him.

'I thought Jesus was your friend,' Absalom says.

'He is my friend.'

'Maybe this isn't a good time.' Absalom walks on ahead. 'You have a lot on your mind.'

Lazarus straightens up, wipes the sweat from his eyes. Nothing wrong with him that a brisk walk in the fresh air won't cure. The story about Jesus at the wedding has upset him more than it should, because they aren't in competition, not any more. Lazarus had forged ahead years ago. He was the one succeeding in Jerusalem, the capital city his second home.

Inside the walls the streets and alleys of the city are alive with people, animals, noise.

Lazarus is easily recognised by his cheekbones, the open curve of his lips, his jaw. There is a shine on the shaven skin of his face, and he stands out from the crowd like a foreigner. A boy tugs at his clothes.

'Can Jesus make me a faster runner?'

Lazarus growls and the boy runs away, laughing. Lazarus licks sweat from his upper lip and snorts at a shouted joke he doesn't properly hear. Ishmael the baker stands outside his shop. He steeples his hands in front of his face, makes a little bow.

'Lazarus,' he says. 'You're looking well.'

Along the narrow streets, sunlight spills off the overhead canopies and breaks on the paving stones into spikes. Lazarus carries his lambs one under each arm, protecting them from the shouting, begging, the hooves of beasts and the stench of daily sacrifice. Down the smoke-filled alleys barefooted boys run errands. Servant girls carry baskets of bread and a military patrol goes by, dark scarlet and tarnished metal, high-laced sandals slapping the warm worn pave-stones.

In doorways and on corners sit the poor and crippled, but bad luck can happen to anyone. Lazarus is thinking ahead to his meeting with Isaiah, who is famously devout but whose daughter, alas, is one among the unfortunates. However high Isaiah rises in the council of priests, his daughter Saloma is there in his house as a penance, a reminder of the good left undone.

'Come on,' Lazarus says to Absalom. 'Let's not keep him waiting.'

The Lazarus family and the Jesus family had been Bethlehem neighbours, the fathers close friends, two young Davidians on the work gangs of the second Temple. Joseph would splice the wooden joists, Eliakim cut the stones for the walls. The stones were rougher work, but then Eliakim was the stronger of the two.

Eliakim had named his second daughter Mary, after the serenity he admired in the wife of his friend. His own wife, Sarah, was a worrier. She suffered at the birth of each of their children, but for her fourth, after Martha, Mary and Lazarus, the conditions had been impossible. She used up the little strength she had on the exhausting journey into Egypt.

Sarah died but the baby lived. It was a boy. Eliakim remembered the flight across the desert and chose not to name him Joseph.

His second son and fourth child he named Amos, and as soon as Amos could walk he tagged along with Lazarus and Jesus. When they ran from the local Egyptian children, Amos ran too. The women forgave the older boys much for that – for their softness of heart. They allowed Amos to feel he belonged.

They did the same when Herod died and the families moved back across the desert to Nazareth. The Galilee region was safer than Bethlehem, but unlike Joseph, Eliakim never warmed to life in the provincial north. The site work in the nearby town of Sephoris was less rewarding than god's masonry at the Temple in Jerusalem. He was bringing up four children on his own, and constantly had to ask Joseph and Mary for help.

Every evening Eliakim would walk home from a day's heavy stonework and idealise his dead wife, who'd lived the last weeks of her pregnancy on a jolting cart in the baking open desert. He'd drink wine, and on bad days mutter and grumble about Joseph.

'Should have kept his mouth shut.'

He and his wife and children could have stayed behind in Bethlehem. The soldiers would have found Lazarus, he knew that, and Herod's soldiers spared no one. Lazarus would now be dead, but children die all the time.

His wife Sarah would have lived. Within two months the new baby Amos would have gone some way to replacing their poor lost Lazarus. They could have had more children, many more. Lazarus was replaceable but his wife was not. Lazarus wasn't the one who should have been saved.

The Sanhedrin, the ruling council of Jerusalem priests, insists on its place in any story of the life of Lazarus. Again, the Gospel of John provides valuable information. After his resurrection, *'the chief priests made plans to kill Lazarus'* (John 12: 10).

That decision is a year in the future. In the meantime his job and his geographical closeness to Jerusalem suggest that Lazarus already has the Sanhedrin's attention. Every year he sells the Temple as many sheep as he can, and Isaiah is the Temple priest charged with regulating the sale of beasts in the open-plan Court of the Gentiles.

Up close, the marble cladding of the Temple is cracked, and in many places stained with soot from ceremonial torches. Doves crash against the sides of tight wicker cages. Lambs bleat in confusion, while behind their tables the currency changers sit with blank faces as they perform intricate sums in their heads.

Lazarus acknowledges dealers and junior priests as he makes his way amongst them – they are his future, and friendly hearts are a reliable source of profit.

Isaiah has taken over a recess in Solomon's Porch, sheltered from the hustle of the main Temple courtyards. He has what they call in Jerusalem a 'clean' forehead, shawl wrapped tight over his receding hairline, a look much favoured in the city for its suggestion of honest intelligence. He is flanked by priests and guards as he centres himself on a formal high-backed chair. He glances at Absalom.

'As a mark of my respect,' Lazarus says, holding up the rope attached to the lambs, 'and to bless our future dealings.'

Lazarus has been working towards this meeting for some time, but the formality of Isaiah's reception surprises him. The chair is not an encouraging sight, nor are the Temple guards. Lazarus adapts quickly, pulls his lambs forward, makes his eyes smile.

A guard takes the lambs to one side. They bleat.

Lazarus covers his heart with his hand in the sign of greeting. Isaiah waves the courtesy away, but Lazarus quickly completes the gesture, heart lips forehead. His skin is hot. He touches his forehead again. He's burning from the inside out.

'I trust your family is well,' he begins.

'My family is a gift from God.'

'God has been generous.'

'Lazarus, enough. We know each other better than that, but not as well as we might, it seems. We the priests are concerned about the rumours from Cana. You can help us, Lazarus. Tell us about your friend from the Galilee.'

A chill descends on the room. Lazarus stifles a cough. He regrets ever mentioning it, but today's water-into-wine isn't the first that's been heard of Jesus. There were the weeks in the desert, then the public baptisms at the river. People in Jerusalem took notice, and after one interested comment too many, Lazarus had been unable to resist.

Yes, he and Jesus had once been friends. Good friends, actually. We grew up together. Now he curses himself for coveting the reflected glory.

'At every festival there are fewer sacrifices,' Isaiah says. 'We both know who is responsible.'

'That's partly why I arranged to see you.' Lazarus changes the subject. 'These are unsettled times. We need to look to the future, we all do, in the interests of those we love. As Absalom the Rabbi of Bethany is my witness, I would like to marry Saloma your daughter.'

*

In Eliakim's honest opinion, his family would have fared better staying where they were in Bethlehem.

Late each night he used to collapse on the floor, the handle of an empty wine jar twisting back his fingers. He groaned, wished he was dead. It was finished for Sarah, and she'd been lucky to die knowing her children were safe. Lazarus above all others was safe, and once clear of Bethlehem Sarah had gleamed with joy as if disaster had been forever defeated.

Eliakim knew better. Children needed saving in Egypt, and in Nazareth, and would do until the end of time. There was no single day when the children didn't need protecting.

There were good times, too. Eliakim amazed the children with his stories about Jerusalem. A week in the big city, he said, especially at Passover, was worth a lifetime in a village like Nazareth. The Temple was a mile high and every massive stone was clad in spotless white marble. It was the home of the almighty that he and Joseph had built beam by beam, stone by stone. They were tradesmen by appointment to god.

Eliakim could have been happy there, anywhere close to the city. They all could. Then he'd drink wine and remember to wish he was dead.

Eliakim died when Lazarus was seven. He was working on the roof of the Roman theatre in Sephoris when a wooden scaffolding pole snapped beneath him. He fell twenty metres onto a pile of plasterer's straw – instead of dying he broke his hip. He was carried back to Nazareth, and was recovering well. Then he caught pneumonia.

Joseph stood last in line to make some farewell gesture to the body. The old fool was dead. His friend Eliakim, father of Martha, Mary, Lazarus and Amos, was dead. With the heel of his hand Joseph pushed a tear back towards his eye. Push it back. Death should never happen, for any reason, to anyone.

4

Mary, the sister of Lazarus, is unmarried, but she is generally considered better looking than Martha because she does fewer domestic chores. *'"Lord, don't you care that my sister has left me to do the work by myself? Tell her to help me." "Martha, Martha," the Lord answered, "you are worried and upset about many things"'* (Luke 10: 40–41).

Mary and Mary, the mother of Jesus and the sister of Lazarus. The number of Marys in the bible can seem clumsy, and a fiction writer would have edited out the confusion – the mother of Jesus and the sister of Lazarus (and also Mary Magdalene) should have different names so that readers can tell them apart.

In fact there are two Marys for a simple reason: the sister of Lazarus is named after the mother of Jesus, and as a clue to her character the Mary connection is useful – the Lazarus Mary is a younger version of the Virgin Mary, and equally devoted to Jesus. Before too long, she will be washing his feet with her hair.

'You are unbelievable,' she says to her brother. 'Of

course Isaiah said no. He's more worried about Jesus, like every other Jerusalem priest. They're so frightened by the truth they can barely breathe.'

Mary is famously impractical. She doesn't appreciate how Lazarus has planned it all out.

He goes outside to think, stops at the bay tree and snaps off a leaf. He has a metallic taste in his mouth. He chews the leaf, spits it out, picks another which he slides between a gap in his teeth. The edge slices his gum. He swallows blood.

At yesterday's meeting he'd promised Isaiah that Saloma would want for nothing. Martha and Mary would care for her in Bethany, and the more lambs Lazarus traded in Jerusalem the more comfortable both she and Isaiah would be. It was a future any loving father should have grasped for his only daughter, especially if she was over the age of twenty and still unmarried because she had something wrong with her that nobody liked to mention.

Isaiah had ignored this reasonable offer, and insisted on talking about Jesus.

Lazarus feels his headache shift. It moves from behind his left eye to the centre of his forehead. He coughs once, twice, spits on the ground by the tree.

'It's absurd,' he says to Mary, 'Jesus and I haven't been friends for years.'

As adults, Lazarus and Jesus are easy to distinguish. One lives near Jerusalem and the other in the Galilee. One is clean-shaven, the other typically remembered as bearded.

But as children in small-town Nazareth, the boys

could barely be told apart. They were the same age, born within a week of each other in Bethlehem. They endured the same character-building trek across the desert, and lived side by side in Egypt (probably at Alexandria). By the time it was safe to return home, and they arrived in Nazareth, neither could remember a life without the other.

In Nazareth they were outsiders, and these are the friendships that survive. The local boys liked to taunt them, but Lazarus and Jesus rarely came to harm because they were lucky. Lazarus believed they were born lucky, the only two boys to escape the massacre in Bethlehem, and both from the line of David.

This meant that David begat Solomon begat Roboam begat Abia, forty-two generations back to Abraham, and that at some upcountry confluence both Joseph and Eliakim's families joined by a minor tributary into that principal river of distinguished names. Arriving from Egypt it also meant that both families could claim a tribal welcome in Nazareth, a proudly Davidian village.

Hard to get luckier than that.

Nazareth seemed designed for an idyllic childhood. Prosperous, agricultural, the region was neither too wild nor too civilised. To the north were bandits, allegedly, and Romans were garrisoned in the south. But in Nazareth itself it was easy to believe that if people were kind, life could be sweet and endless. Everyone would live forever.

For Lazarus and Jesus the world was figs and cold water, soft blankets at night and sunrise through half-opened eyes. On the best days of summer the sky filled with cloud, bringing shade and the promise of rain, and whatever Lazarus did, Jesus did next. They climbed the timber delivered to Joseph's workshop, scrambling up tree trunks and testing their balance. Lazarus climbed higher. Amos jumped up and down, scraped his knees when he tried to follow.

There were accidents. Lazarus and Jesus fell out of the same olive tree, one after the other, and had very similar bruises. Lazarus caught a cold and passed the sickness to Jesus. The boys always recovered, and Menachem the Nazareth Rabbi told them they were indestructible, as strong as mules. None of the native children had bones as solid or constitutions as strong.

Nor was anyone else as receptive at synagogue. Menachem had high hopes for both these boys, almost as high as they had for themselves. Between the two of them all ambitions seemed achievable. They spent long afternoons developing unchecked childish dreams: friends until the end of time, they'd wear golden sandals and have angels to buckle them.

'What was the last thing he said to you?'

'I can't remember.'

Jesus had promised to visit them in Bethany. He never had.

'What I dislike most is pretence of any kind. Including the kind they're calling miracles. How do these un-believable stories spread?'

'I don't know, I'm not involved.' Lazarus could see that Isaiah was sceptical, and at that moment he wished he and Jesus had never met. 'He was a small boy with scabs on his knees. Like the rest of us. He couldn't even swim.'

'God is not whimsical,' Isaiah had said, and the massive columns of Solomon's Porch appeared to support this opinion. 'He doesn't visit his chosen on earth to play games, to point his finger and pick out this one and then that one for the better portions of luck. You need to think clearly, Lazarus. Jesus is not universally liked.'

'I know, I *know*. He creeps round those tiny villages. The stories aren't remotely credible.'

'And if he comes to Jerusalem?'

'He wouldn't last a minute, I promise you. He's a provincial nobody. He has no idea how the world works.'

'And you'd teach him a thing or two about Jerusalem, wouldn't you, Lazarus? How to overprice sheep and hide their blemishes. The secret short cut to Lydia's house. Are you trying to protect him?'

'I haven't seen him for years. But I'd advise him to trust no one.'

Lazarus had then registered what Isaiah was saying. How did he know about Lydia? He decided to carry on regardless, because his headache made him irritable. 'Not even his disciples, not in Jerusalem. Trust no one here but me.'

'Yes, Lazarus, talk to me about the disciples. You're his friend. Explain how it is that you're not included in the twelve.'

Lazarus had confessed to their childhood friendship out of vanity. Not long after, Jesus had selected his disciples.

'I'm sure he knows what he's doing.' Mary was perfecting a wide-eyed look born of too much hope and not enough attention to housework.

'He's making me look stupid.'

'Maybe he'll pick you later.' Jesus had chosen twelve, like the tribes. Lazarus was excluded, barely a friend of Jesus any more, and everyone now knew that and it hurt.

'Some people say he's the son of god,' Mary added.

'He's the son of Mary. We grew up in the same house. You were there, remember?'

The disciples were practically strangers to Jesus. Also, they were incredibly slow. They needed every story repeated, every lesson explained with exemplary images from their simple peasant lives.

'Fishermen,' Lazarus said. 'They carry around that smell. Rotting fish. In the webs between their fingers.'

Lazarus was more worthy as a friend and ally. After synagogue he and Jesus used to play David and Goliath. Lazarus was Goliath so Amos could be David while Jesus did both the armies. At the climax of an epic battle, involving whatever weapons came to hand, Lazarus could die quite brilliantly.

Death was always a shock to him, a slingshot out of nowhere right between the eyes. He stared blindly, appalled. His hands clasped his forehead, his body stiffened and revolved until, rigid, he keeled stone dead to the ground.

They sat together, knelt together, ate together. The other Nazareth children were dullards, or girls. Unlike Lazarus and Jesus, none of them could appreciate the living excitement of the scriptures: there was always one hero missing, the one yet to come.

'Isn't that right, Rabbi? The prophets know the story isn't finished.'

'They know the future is more interesting than

the past,' Menachem replied. 'Even when the past is fascinating.'

The Rabbi was delighted by their application to the Torah. His eyesight was failing (glaucoma, trachoma, conjunctivitis), but he liked to bring his face close to theirs to feel whatever was exceptional about these two exiled boys from Bethlehem. He could never quite decide what it was.

Lazarus felt he was special. It was common knowledge that he'd been reprieved from the massacre of the innocents, and around the time of his birth a star had shone brightly in the sky. Lazarus could run faster and swim further and climb higher than any boy in Nazareth, and he knew by heart the heroes from scripture responsible for making yesterday become today.

He believed in heroism like he did in living forever. The great prophets of the bible were undeterred by obstacles. They rarely fell sick, but he was sure that sickness would barely intrude on their working day.

Lazarus, however, has not lived the life of a prophet. As a young man he left Nazareth to work as a sheep trader to the Temple, but somehow he has stalled as an overseer living with his sisters in a semi-rural village. He had expected more of himself. At the age of thirty-two he has mislaid his imagined greatness, but he still feels able to perform a great task. Only none has so far presented itself.

3

A man destined to be a disciple would have stayed put in the slow sure village of Nazareth. He'd have trained as a stonemason like his father before him, married and had many children he'd apprentice in their turn as masons.

Lazarus had never been much of a follower, so his friendship with Jesus presupposes some other purpose. It was widely known at the time that they were friends, a fact reported in the Gospel of John. If nothing else, their friendship can clarify time lines in this decisive period of the Jesus story.

In Matthew, Mark and Luke, Jesus is active for about a year between his baptism by John the Baptist in the River Jordan and his death by crucifixion in Jerusalem. John lengthens this period to three years, but the respected biblical scholar E. P. Saunders, in *The Historical Figure of Jesus* (1993), supports the consensus that the earlier three gospels are probably correct.

I agree. Lazarus falls ill at the time of the first miracle at the wedding in Cana. Surely he wouldn't have been made to suffer for three full years? Not if he was truly a friend, not if New Testament friendship is to mean anything. The illness of Lazarus therefore lasts about a year, from Passover to Passover, from the water-into-wine until his predetermined death ten days before the crucifixion of Jesus.

He has less than twelve months to live, and counting.

Over the next few weeks, after his inconclusive meeting with Isaiah, his illness makes itself known in the usual way: Lazarus has flu-like symptoms. He has a dry mouth, an ongoing headache and a general sense of fatigue. His teeth hurt.

Also, his eyes can water when he thinks kindly of other people. He finds himself feeling sorry for the poor defenceless lambs Faruq brings in from the desert, and for himself.

Obviously this can't go on, so he makes a survey of his sins that need forgiving. There's the Sabbath, which he doesn't always respect, and the truth, which he doesn't always tell. But business is business. There's Lydia. He hasn't married her when he promised he would, though not recently and never in the presence of witnesses. He shaves and he cuts his hair short, even though the Book of Leviticus clearly states (19: 27) *'Do not cut the hair of the sides of your head or clip off the edges of your beard.'*

Lazarus brazenly flouts this scriptural law. We must imagine he is as careless with others, especially as disobeying biblical laws hasn't done him any apparent harm. At thirty-two years old he is accepted and respected in his adoptive village of Bethany. He has profitable working relationships and his skilful trading has made him rich. Lazarus does not truly believe that an almighty god cares whether or not he shaves.

It would be too strong to say that Lazarus doesn't believe in god. At the time this would be like not believing in bread, or the sky. More accurate to suggest that as well as praying he likes to plan. He gets better results that way.

He intends to continue the upward curve of his life by marrying the daughter of a serving member of the Sanhedrin ruling council. In order to achieve this, he needs to demonstrate to Isaiah the transience of his friendship with Jesus, who has only himself to blame. He should have visited Lazarus in Bethany. He shouldn't have betrayed their ambitions by staying behind in Nazareth, doing what his father did.

Lazarus can almost convince himself that the correct way to behave is to do the opposite of whatever his former friend would advise. He decides to follow standard religious procedure, thereby showing his disdain for new ways of thinking. He will offer lambs for sacrifice at the Temple.

God can then feel free to grant him his wish to marry Saloma, Isaiah's daughter. At the same time he can cure Lazarus of whatever illness is slowing him down. Or, more accurately, out of gratitude for the sacrifice, god will stop punishing him with illness for the sins he keeps committing.

Isaiah will be impressed. And as a remedy for sickness, there is evidence that sacrifice works. On a previous occasion, when his flu-like symptoms developed into flu, Lazarus offered up a sacrifice and recovered within a week.

They used to play hide-and-seek. It was more fun if Amos did the finding. At the age of four or five Amos would doggedly search in every obvious place, then start again from the beginning. The older boys shouted out 'Here I am!' and then pretended they hadn't said anything, as if the message had descended from the sky.

Lazarus kept score, and at this, like every other game, he won more often than he lost. He even competed at sunsets, sitting beside Jesus on the hill behind the village. The two boys looked out over the plain below, arms up, waiting for the exact moment the sun dipped finally beneath the horizon. They always missed it. It was light, then dark. The plain was a visible blackness, and then it was simply black, and night had stolen in.

This made them late getting home, where Martha and Mary would rush to the gate to scold them. Lazarus didn't care, because among ten-year-olds in Nazareth he was the brightest star in the sky. In the fresh upland air he grew strong and quick, sharp and solid, ready for the buffeting of the world.

Jesus as a child was unremarkable. This must be so, because from his childhood he leaves behind no significant trace – the gospels contain a solitary reference, in Luke. At the age of twelve Jesus visits Jerusalem with his parents. He gets lost.

Elsewhere there are attempts to fill the gap, notably in the Apocryphal Gospel of Thomas (about 150 CE). In this imagined childhood Jesus can purify drinking water, as if by magic, and mould clay into twelve living sparrows. He 'withers' a child for no good reason, and kills another for barging him in the street. He heals a man who drops an axe on his own foot, and brings a child back to life who falls from a second-floor window.

Thomas validates these miracles by specifying that 'there were also many other children playing with him', and these childhood friends presumably act as witnesses. If this were true, then Lazarus must have been one of the watching children, because he and Jesus were always together. That's how everyone knew they were friends.

Yet the failure to name Lazarus in these stories is

not the only reason the Gospel of Thomas is sidelined as Apocryphal, meaning 'of uncertain authenticity'. Thomas is omitted from the canonical books of the bible because he makes a basic theological mistake, known as the Docetist heresy. If Jesus can perform miracles as a child, then his earthly body only *seems* to be physical. If he has divine powers from the outset, he is never truly human. He wouldn't have missed food or sleep. He wouldn't have needed friends.

The Bethany road to Jerusalem enters the city at the Sheep Gate, close to today's Lion Gate. Leave the village, walk past the cemetery, down and up the first valley, over the ridge and descend the Mount of Olives to the narrow Kidron stream. About a hundred metres short of the city walls, climb the steep paved approach. On the right-hand side, the road overlooks the pool of Bethesda.

Lazarus trades twelve months a year with the Temple. He therefore looks down at the Bethesda pool on a regular basis. Archaeological findings have since confirmed that the pool is a double rectangular reservoir, with colonnades along five of the eight sides. From his elevated vantage point on the Bethany road, breathing deeply and shading his eyes, Lazarus can pick out the sick and dying gathered in the covered porches. This is where they come when they lose the ability to reason, and their only hope is a miracle cure.

Over the years Lazarus has witnessed some spectacular demons. At Bethesda, contortions can be good entertainment, as is public nakedness and random cursing at the skies. There's always the chance of seeing the water tremble as an angel passes by, which is the signal for the sick to rush madly towards the water. It is a race, because first into the pool will be cured.

As a divine provision for helping those genuinely in need, this is blatantly unfair. The least sick have the vigour to jump in first, and they are the ones who are healed. Lazarus has always wanted to haul someone forward from the back, but life isn't like that. The first will be first.

However fragile he feels, Lazarus now makes regular trips to Jerusalem and ensures that Isaiah sees him handing a pair of his finest lambs to the Temple guards, one for the priests and one for god. The lambs are a public apology for being friends with Jesus, and therefore for causing Isaiah and his daughter embarrassment, and Lazarus looks a convincing penitent. He is pale, sometimes shivering. When he leaves the Courtyard of the Priests, he smothers his cough in his hand and wipes his eyes, which water constantly as if he's crying.

Lazarus endures.

For two months he is a man with a headache and the sweats who sets a solid example, sacrificing a pair of sheep every other day at ruinous prices. Sometimes he offers up a lamb with an eye infection or a scar on the muzzle. An imperfection or two is neither here nor there, whatever the priests say, and the sacrifice is for his own benefit so he's prepared to take the risk. He lets his hair grow. He doesn't shave.

Eventually Isaiah approaches him as he leaves the inner Temple.

Lazarus bows low. He coughs, hacks it out from the

centre of his chest, his tongue a deep gully to channel the phlegm. He spits to one side, puts his hand to his flitting heart.

'Your remorse has been most impressive,' Isaiah says. 'Almost worthy of a son-in-law. You are a lucky man. I've found a way you can make amends.'

Lazarus bites his tongue. He's doing as much as he can.

'Be here tomorrow after dawn prayer. The Sanhedrin have new questions about Jesus. Don't be late.'

2

The priests will want to know if Jesus is capable of performing miracles. The answer is: he wasn't even best at synagogue.

Not always.

He was the best at laws. Jesus learned by rote from the books of Solomon and Maccabees, and at classes in the Nazareth synagogue he could discuss texts like Daniel 12: 2–3 (*Your dead shall live, their corpses shall rise./O dwellers in the dust, awake and sing for joy!*).

When it came to scriptural law, Lazarus conceded defeat. The laws bored him. He preferred the lions.

Here they come. Their yellowed teeth are deadly as they stalk their den towards Daniel.

Lazarus was best at stories and heroes, the first with every answer as if he were actually there. Here comes the whale. Throw Jonah over. The bad luck he brings to the ship will sink, but the man himself will live, three days and nights in the belly of the beast.

Here comes Delilah. She cuts his hair and he loses his strength, but that comes later. Samson's weapon of choice is the jaw of an ass. Ask Lazarus. Ask him about Saul back from the dead to visit King Samuel: *'Why have you disturbed me?' he said. 'Why did you make me come back?'* (1 Samuel 28: 15).

And beyond the synagogue it is Lazarus who knows what boys should do. They run up hillsides shouting out loud. They climb into olive trees, throw stones at birds but always miss, look north to Mount Hermon and vow that one day they'll climb to the top, if it's the last thing they ever do.

He and Jesus make a thousand promises. They will never desert each other, however great the danger.

A Sabbath when Lazarus and Jesus are thirteen or fourteen years old. The Nazareth sky is bruised and moody, clouds covering the sun, a perfect day for an excursion: into the fields, down the hill, Amos lagging behind. The city of Sephoris is a two hour walk, no more, but Jesus needs convincing — on the Sabbath they should stay at home. This is typical. Jesus looks before he leaps. Lazarus likes to leap.

'See that axe by the tree? No, further down. Race you!'

They career downhill, arms freewheeling, the world empty except for them. Lazarus makes it first. He picks up the abandoned axe and swings it two-handed into dry soil. Jesus prises the axe loose and does the same. Then Amos catches up and they fling the axe into long grass and wipe their hands and run again.

The city is deserted. Sephoris is a grand Herodian

project, a long-term building site, but on the Sabbath no one works. Even the new amphitheatre has to wait, and the three boys stand awed in the curved shadow of the nearly completed building. They look up at the racks of wooden scaffold rising like the sides of a basket.

'I'll go first,' Lazarus says.

'You're not allowed.' Amos is twelve years old and brown as a walnut. He increasingly has an opinion. 'Someone might see us.'

Lazarus steps onto the lowest rung. 'They're all at home praying their children stay safe. You wait here. Keep a lookout.'

Lazarus is scared but he starts to climb, like boys any-where. He imagines himself as a biblical hero, someone who isn't scared.

The wooden scaffold is designed for craftsmen to climb from the inside, in the gap between the building and the poles. From the outside, each level slopes away from the walls, so Lazarus has to climb out as well as up. At the top of each level he lets his legs swing free and hauls himself over onto the next narrow platform.

He looks down from the first level, assuming Jesus will follow.

'Watch where I put my hands and feet. If I don't kill myself, copy me.'

'Come down!' Amos shouts. 'You'll fall!'

'Give me a proper funeral!' Lazarus is moving upwards again. 'Make sure everyone cries!'

Jesus follows, and through the wooden poles Lazarus can feel his friend climbing up behind him. The vibrations are in his toes, in his legs, all the way through to his fingers.

The scaffold creaks like fishing boats.

It starts to rain. The boys are halfway up the side of the amphitheatre, on the outside of the scaffolding. From the ground, and also from a distance and safely from far far above, they may appear very small.

Lazarus's hand slips, but he catches himself with the crook of his elbow. He blinks grey rain out of his eyes, checks back down on Jesus.

If he falls, he'll take his friend with him, and no one in Sephoris will be able to save them. Beyond Jesus down on the ground Amos is waving his arms, the rain on his upturned face like tears.

Lazarus makes a last big reach for the safety of the roof. He grunts, pulls himself up, swings his body over. His arms and legs ache with the effort but he is safe. He shuffles round on his belly and peers over the edge.

Several feet below him, Jesus is clutching a pole and refusing to move. His eyes are clamped shut and his body is shaking, his wet face jammed against the scaffold to stop his teeth from chattering. A sparrow flies close, hovers, darts away.

'You're nearly there,' Lazarus shouts. 'If I can make it so can you. Grab my hand and I'll help you up.'

Jesus clenches his lips together, slowly ungrips a hand. He slips, grabs on hard.

'Come on!'

Lazarus leans out further, as far as he can go.

'Take my hand. It's great up here. It's easy.'

Jesus reaches up but not far enough, and he falls. His hands and his arms and his body detach from the scaffold and out he goes, into the air, clear space all around him. Lazarus swipes at his clothes and clings on, hauls him up and over and onto the safe flat roof. It is an impossible achievement, an unbelievable rescue.

They roll onto their backs, panting, swallowing rain, laughing, their doubled heart hammering a hundred times before ordinary breathing resumes. On their hands and knees they look over the edge and wave to Amos below.

He shouts at them to come back down. They cup their ears and shrug, then take in the godview from the highest building in Sephoris, the damp spread of the city, the big rich villas, fields, a glinting river, brown-black mountains. Swathes of heavenly light cut through the distant rainshadow, and Lazarus feels an exhilaration so powerful he imagines there is nothing he and Jesus will not do together, nowhere they will not go.

'I can fly,' he says. He has already saved Jesus, so why not another miracle? 'I'm going to jump.'

He kneels upright, arms out like wings.

Jesus heaves him back and they tumble laughing into the warm rainpools glistening across the roof.

'We should go back down,' Lazarus says. 'Before Amos tries to follow.'

They lie on their backs, hair wet with rain. Jesus turns his head, asks if Lazarus can keep a secret.

'I don't know.' He isn't old enough to know if he's trustworthy. 'Tell me and we'll find out.'

But Jesus pretends to lose interest, or decides it doesn't matter.

Lazarus closes his eyes for the touch of raindrops on his eyelids. They will do anything for each other. There is no other secret, and nothing else needs to be said.

*

In the Temple before sunrise the enclosed Courtyard of the Israelites glimmers with oil lamps. The light is diffused by incense and the dawn, flames reflecting from the rounded gloss of marbled pillars. A bench is built into one wall, reserved for the old and frail. Their voices merge with those of the younger priests, standing and rocking on their heels, closing their eyes and reciting cautionary scriptures.

The priests have black leather boxes bound to their arms or foreheads, phylacteries containing extracts from the Psalms or the Book of Judges, reminding them of the supremacy of priests or the promise of the One to come. *Those who are wise shall shine like the brightness of the sky.*

Lazarus stands in the centre of the room, and the nearer priests wince, and draw back. Lazarus has walked from Bethany in the dark, before the heat of the day, but there is a smell around him which is both distinctive and hard to place. It is not a pleasant smell.

The Sanhedrin ruling council has seventy-one members. Lazarus estimates that most of them must be here. The room grows quiet. Isaiah steps forward.

'For you, Lazarus, this is a great honour,' he says.

'And a great responsibility,' someone adds.

'But for us this is a solemn duty. As you know, the penalty for blasphemy is death.'

Lazarus is uncertain of his scripture – as a child he'd been busy making other plans – and he isn't sure what counts as blasphemy. He knows he isn't perfect, but shaving and cheating are minor offences at worst.

'Your friend in the Galilee is becoming a disruptive influence,' Isaiah continues, 'and we the Sanhedrin are

41

committed to keeping the peace. There is a problem. Jesus has staged an event that some witnesses are calling a miracle. The news spreads. The more impressionable believers claim him as the messiah, the king of the Jews. That's dangerous. The Romans don't like the idea of an unofficial king, and the Romans can be oversensitive. Like ourselves, they're always alert for impostors. When was the last time you saw your friend?'

Lazarus looks at different faces, but in the lamplight expressions are difficult to read. He sees many earnest men with beards. 'Not so long ago. Quite recently, in the grand scheme of things.'

He'd like to please them so they buy his sheep. He wishes he knew what they wanted to hear. 'Though at the same time, in human terms, I haven't seen him for ages.'

'Thirteen years,' Isaiah reminds him. 'Not since you arrived in Bethany. Is Jesus planning to visit Jerusalem?'

'I don't know. Is he?'

A blind priest seated along the wall taps his stick against the flagstones, insists on being heard. 'I saw him once. Years ago, a child. He sat on the steps outside and we talked with him. He had an astonishing grasp of the scriptures.'

'He was lost,' adds another voice. 'I was there too. How could a genuine messiah get lost?'

'Because on his own he's hopeless,' Lazarus says. 'I wasn't here to watch out for him. He was twelve years old and lost in Jerusalem. Anything could have happened.'

'He did know his scriptures, though.'

'Yes, so I heard a million times from Joseph when they arrived back home in Nazareth.' Lazarus senses he is talking out of turn, but these are resentments he has never been able to express. He wants his opinions about Jesus heard. He knows the man better than anyone, and he remembers Mary telling him again and again how wonderful Jesus was for speaking so confidently with the priests. 'She overreacted. So did Joseph. They were anxious parents relieved their son was safe. If you want the truth, these days I rarely think about him. We lead very different lives.'

Lazarus doesn't add that his is more impressive. At an early age Jesus had lost himself to the what will be will be. He'd sunk into the rut of doing what was expected, doing what his father did. Lazarus had escaped Nazareth. He worked hard. If Jesus had ever made the effort to visit Bethany he'd have found his friend rich and respected beyond reproach. Only Jesus never came.

'He had a good touch around animals,' Lazarus adds. He doesn't want to sound unkind. 'But honestly, as a boy he cast a shadow. When he was scratched by thorns he bled. He got scared. I know. I was there.'

1

There is no gospel according to Lazarus, and if any such document suddenly came to light, scholars would question its authenticity. They would have encountered references or fragments before now in the many available texts from the early centuries after Lazarus died, was buried, and on the fourth day returned to life.

These references do not exist. We therefore have

no direct access to Lazarus's version of the story, but without a biographer's overview he is unlikely to have realised the significance of his performance in that slow dawn before the start of the Temple day. His answers to the Sanhedrin postponed the death of his friend. Probably. If Lazarus had remembered in the boy Jesus something divine, the priests would have acted quickly and without mercy. God on earth was blasphemy, and the most efficient way to disprove a messiah was to kill him.

After his interview with the Sanhedrin at the Temple, Lazarus is rewarded with an invitation to the largest downstairs room of Isaiah's house in the Upper City. Servants scuffle in and out.

'Look me in the eye,' Isaiah says. He puts both hands on Lazarus's shoulders. 'Marriage is a beginning, not an end.'

'I agree utterly,' Lazarus says.

Saloma has yet to make an appearance. Her mother and her aunts and uncles, all her family including Isaiah, are very polite about the smell. Lazarus washed when leaving the Temple, washed again before coming into the house, but even he can smell the rancid odour that persists on his skin. The smell may be connected to his cough, and the frequent headaches. By the middle of every day the whites of his eyes are pink.

'I cry a lot,' he explains to Saloma's mother. 'From happiness.'

Another symptom is self-doubt. He finds himself questioning his plan to marry, despite the virtue of his motives. He wants to establish the Lazarus family at the heart of Jerusalem life. Not for personal gain, but for the sake of Mary and Martha. He is about to remind himself of some further benefits of marriage when the aunts and uncles make way for Saloma herself.

She is heavily swathed in robes, a headscarf, a veil. This is unusual for the traditional viewing of the bride before an engagement. A chair is placed in the middle of the room. Lazarus sits on it. Saloma will walk around him seven times.

Her eyes, the only part of her face he can see, are soft and dark but slightly lopsided. One is bigger than the other. She walks once around his chair. She has a limp.

'Close your mouth, darling,' Isaiah says. He clasps his hands together and stands up on his toes. 'There's a good girl.'

An aunt detaches the veil. Saloma has a heavy jaw. Her mouth is twisted. One of her eyes, vivid with terror, skews to the level of Lazarus's chest. He coughs. She flinches.

'Sorry,' he says, then holds up his hands in apology for saying sorry. 'Sorry.'

Lazarus has a growing blockage of mucus in his nose. He puts his head on one side, to try and shift the load between nostrils, and this gives him the appraising look he uses when judging sheep. Saloma's mother nods her head, impressed by his serious approach.

The further benefits: he'll have an exclusive contract to deliver sheep at the Temple. His sisters will become part of an established Sanhedrin family, and if anything happens to him they will not be left abandoned. He glances at Saloma's lumpen face. She will live in comfort for the rest of her days. Everyone will be happy.

Saloma has two more tours of his chair to go, each

slower than the last. The foot on the end of the leg that makes her limp is now dragging on the floor.

Her father encourages her. Lazarus remembers Abraham and Job, husbands and fathers heroic for enduring dismay. Saloma grips the back of his chair to help with the last half of the last circuit. Then they will be engaged, exactly as Lazarus had planned.

When I get home, he thinks, I'm going to cut my hair.

6

The Romans know about Lazarus long before his return from the dead.

He is the friend of Jesus.

For at least a decade the Roman consul Sejanus has argued that knowledge should be treated as power. Legions alone will never be enough to control the empire, and Sejanus formalises the idea that information is intelligence. The Romans, for their own safety, need to collect and collate every available scrap of information.

Sejanus therefore invents two new categories of soldier, the *speculatores* and the *exploratores*, and he attaches these units to the army. The *exploratores* are scouts. The *speculatores* are more like spies. They are licensed to listen and to think freely. Often they work out of uniform, but always with a clear objective: to identify and prevent unrest.

High in the Antonia Fortress, Cassius pulls aside
a gauze curtain. He has flat blond hair and blue eyes,
into which this far south nobody can read any meaning.
Afternoon sunlight floods the mosaic on the floor of his
room — a woman carrying a basket of apples.

Below the fortressed walls he sees the roof of the
Holy of Holies, the Temple courtyard, then a drop to
Jerusalem's mazed houses and alleys. The Fortress is
the highest point in the city, and on its way to heaven
the smoke from burnt offerings rises past the garrison
windows.

The smell of blackened fat reminds Cassius that whatever the Romans provide it is never enough. These people want something more, and their prayers are insistent
with invocations, horns and trumpets, the howl of dying
beasts.

The Judaean people are waiting for the One. This
one, that one, anyone. He's coming and he'll save them
all, yet Rome, in truth, is the saviour. Messiahs pull
rank. They appeal directly to a higher authority, making
Cassius confident they register as trouble.

He has been tracking Jesus since his first move south
towards John the Baptist at the river.

'He's harmless,' the local informants said.

'And the crowds?'

'The man was a long time in the desert. He doesn't
talk much sense.' The riverside spies also reported that
Jesus had no obvious strategy. 'He'll run out of ideas.
He'll go back home to the Galilee.'

They were right. Cassius rewarded his informers with
tax exemptions and gifts of Spanish leather. The carrot,
as recommended by Sejanus, not the stick.

Now Cassius is wondering about Lazarus. In his Galilee backwater Jesus has disciples. He has followers, none of whom register as threats, but the one man he calls friend is dangerously local to Jerusalem and in regular contact with Sanhedrin priests at the Temple.

Cassius has not been commissioned to believe in coincidence.

After his engagement to Saloma, Lazarus stops taking risks with his health.

That was two months ago, but he sees no measurable improvement. During the day fatigue overcomes him, and his head can ache as if clamped in a carpenter's vice. He is sometimes cold, shivering in June daytime temperatures of up to thirty-five degrees. Or so hot in the chill nights that sweat slicks the backs of his hands.

He continues to offer sacrifices, not as many as when he needed to influence Isaiah, but often enough to harm his business. He picks out the best of Faruq's animals with the softest velvet ears, those he'd usually have reserved for Jerusalem's most penitent grandees.

'We can't afford this,' Martha warns. 'You're sacrificing lambs you should be selling. And we still have to pay Faruq.'

'I can't afford to be ill. I've got a lot coming up, and I have to look after you two. When I'm feeling better I'll earn the money back. Don't worry. All will be well.'

He develops a nasty rash.

It is safe to envisage the rash: the Book of Leviticus is a manual for acting correctly before the eyes of god, and two entire chapters are devoted to skin infections.

For a long time these skin diseases were collectively mistranslated as 'leprosy' (a disease of the nerves, not the skin), but Old Testament skin problems are more likely to have been caused by the widespread incidence of scabies. A visible rash also signifies the first phase of smallpox, which explains why Leviticus stipulates strict measures requiring prompt action: smallpox could devastate a community.

Lazarus has eight months to live. That much we know, but smallpox would have killed him quicker than that. His rash at this stage must therefore be scabies, caused by parasitic mites beneath the skin.

The mite *Sarcoptes scabiei* clusters on bedding, clothing and other household objects. Impregnated female mites wait for contact with human skin, then seek out the folds of the body. They make a home in the softness between fingers and toes, inside the elbow or behind the knee, between the buttocks or in the red heat of the groin. They start tunnelling.

Under the skin they burrow an S or Z shape, and inside this tunnel the mite eggs hatch. The larvae start to move, and their activity produces a vivid discoloration of the skin and intense itching. The itching is the worst part – 'scabere', Latin for itch.

Lazarus's most visible infestations spread a scarlet rash along the inside skin of his arms, and at night he lies on his back, eyes wide open, willing himself not to scratch. No need to panic. Leviticus specifies a procedure.

Cassius sends out frequent patrols to Bethany. Since Jesus returned from the Jordan to Galilee his friend Lazarus has rarely been seen in the city. Jesus has gone quiet, and

Lazarus has, too. Apparently he is ill, a feeble excuse if he has something to hide. Cassius looks for the connection – he assembles his information.

Several months ago Lazarus travelled to Jerusalem and appeared before a dawn council of Sanhedrin priests. Cassius has spies almost everywhere, but not yet in the Sanhedrin itself, and he suspects they were plotting, talking about Jesus and the Romans.

Since that meeting Lazarus has been spending money on sacrifices, sending in many pairs of sheep from Bethany. This is unusual behaviour for him. The animals could be a way of covertly delivering messages, but Cassius hasn't worked out how the system might function.

Either that, or the sacrifices are part of a broader ploy. Lazarus wants people to believe he's genuinely ill (thirty-two years old, regular walker, never a day sick in his life – the Roman informers have asked around), but Cassius is not so easily deceived. He senses there is some kind of plan in action, a longer-term design he can't quite decipher, and he is not entirely displeased. At some point in this scheme Jesus will come to Jerusalem. Cassius will be waiting, and he will take this chance to get noticed in Rome.

He needs to place a spy close to Lazarus.

Absalom examines his younger friend, first one arm then the other.

'You have a rash,' he says. 'But it could be worse. You're not dying.'

Absalom sighs for his departed mother. He still can't understand why she had to die, any more than he can conceive of an all-seeing god who creates bacterial parasites.

'You're unclean,' he says. 'You need to purify yourself.'

Medically, the cleansing procedure described in the Book of Leviticus remains sound. Lazarus must wash his clothes and his bedding and not leave his house for seven days except for ritual immersion in the village bath.

He wraps himself in a blanket and shambles across the square. For a few seconds the fury of the sun blinds him. It is high summer, with unforgiving sunshine day after day, but slowly the village buildings emerge from the light. A Roman patrol rests and drinks by the well, the soldiers hazed and floating in the heat. Lazarus shivers and heads for the *mikveh*, a carved pool inside a cave below the village.

He feels his way into the gloom, drops his blanket. Water drips and echoes. Steps are cut into the rocks, and the tepid water soothes his ankles, his shins, his knees, slaps against his thighs. There is a raised shelf to his left for the inflow, and to his right a flat overspill. The water is always gently moving, slowly refreshing itself from a higher source.

Lazarus walks to the far wall, swishing the water with his thighs and hands. He turns and lowers himself onto the smooth stone floor, the water reaching his chin. He breathes out, setting off a skin of ripples, works his arms one way and then the other, checks himself over. The rash spreads down both inner arms, it discolours the top of his legs and his feet. He flexes his toes and fingers. The water eases the itching.

He can see his ribs. Is he getting thinner?

Lazarus loves his body. He does not want it to perish.

He stretches out, rests his head on the ledge behind him. He pictures Lydia naked.

This is not so much a question of why, as why not?

Few men admit to visiting prostitutes but that doesn't mean they don't exist, either the women or their clients. *Strong's Exhaustive Concordance of the Bible* lists two prostitutes, fifteen whores and forty-two harlots. There are more harlots in the bible than tax collectors, more whores than doctors.

Lazarus is unmarried. He lives in Bethany with his sisters, but is frequently away on work in Jerusalem. He is making decisions in an era before the influence of Christianity — good men are not yet finding their goodness by striving to imitate Jesus — and paying for sex escapes the sanction of divine punishment. Or so Lazarus believes. It must do, or he'd have fallen ill long before now.

If anything, he feels blessed. Jerusalem is a city of eighty thousand souls, and the traffic in slaves and soldiers brings in every latest disease. Within living memory (as reported by the Jewish historian Josephus) an epidemic has decimated the city, probably smallpox. This among other invisible demons is always creeping from house to house, and every illness is lethal. And also not lethal. Some people are struck down and die, and some are struck down and do not.

Lazarus, so far, has remained untouched — even god, it seems, approves of Lydia.

He sinks his head underwater, and hears his beating heart loud in a pulse behind his ear. By following religious procedures he is giving god a chance to make him

53

well. He is a reasonable man.

He lets his face up for air, scratches an itch on the outside of his ankle – not the scabies but a mosquito bite. He takes the skin off the top. Sinks again, waits, rises up, breathes. His nails are too long. He picks off a fingernail and flicks it away into the slowly moving water.

Overhead, on the greenish roof of the cave, moisture gathers in blisters. One of these fills out, elongates, detaches and aims with focused intention directly at the centre of Lazarus's forehead. He blinks at the last moment and it hits him below the eye.

5

Leviticus works. If it didn't, the rules would never have been written down.

By the end of a seven-day quarantine his scabies rash is fading. His groin sometimes itches, and his head can hurt, and he hasn't sold a sheep in a week, but Lazarus feels sufficiently recovered to attempt the walk into Jerusalem. He has a question to ask Isaiah about the betrothal ceremony, now only a month away. He wants to know if Isaiah will pay for the wine.

At the tombs Faruq is dismantling a sheep-pen. Lazarus greets him and the two men squat on their heels. They face each other silently, and this is business so neither rushes to speak.

'Faruq, are you my friend?'

'Everyone is your friend.'

Lazarus leans his weight forward, elbows on knees.

His fingers brush the fading rash along his inner arm.

'My cousin knows a healer,' Faruq says. 'At Jericho.'

'I'm fine. The worst is over.'

Lazarus glances at the pens. Faruq has sold half his midsummer stock, but not to Lazarus. Like everyone, Faruq needs to live – friendship can only go so far.

'I'll negotiate higher prices,' Lazarus says. 'I haven't been well.'

Faruq's eyes are orange like those of his sheep, his face the colour of hardwood scratched and polished by every outdoor season. He nods his head. He watches Lazarus stand up, turn, walk past the tombs and round the corner. Slower than he used to be. Faruq detaches a rail from a fence.

We've established that Lazarus's illness is so familiar that the bible doesn't need to describe it. Also that Lazarus falls sick at the exact moment the water at the wedding in Cana becomes wine. None of the diseases common in the region at the time, however, fit the one-year interval between infection and death.

The incubation periods don't add up, and in this area the story of Lazarus needs some attention to make it credible. Even outside the story, beyond time, with the benefit of hindsight and foresight, it can be difficult to fit every factor together.

It is therefore worth searching out more detailed evidence of the disease that plays its part and will eventually kill him.

'Nearly all his life he suffered from a weak heart, then he was cured, as everyone in Bethany could testify, and now he was dead.' José Saramago claims that Lazarus had chronic heart trouble, and died peacefully in his sleep.

Equally absurdly, the Czech writer Karel Čapek (*Lazarus*, 1949) thinks Lazarus died of a chill – 'it was the cold wind that got me, that time when – when I was so ill . . .'

Not so. The story demands that Lazarus suffer. The more hideous his death the more impressive his revival. When the time comes, Jesus needs everyone to believe that Lazarus has truly come back to life. But they first need to believe, without reservation, that he died.

The most effective way to publicise his death in advance is to make his physical decline visible. His sickness should be horrific, definitive, undeniable. It should be both recognisable and worse than anything anyone has ever seen.

Yes, this is how it was done. Lazarus did not die from one of the seven prevalent illnesses of ancient Israel. Not enough. He has to contract them all.

In a small cell low in the Antonia Fortress, Cassius is questioning a young man stopped by a routine patrol at the Damascus Gate. He was leaving Jerusalem with a message for Jesus from the house of Lazarus.

Lazarus is too clever to have sent the message himself. It is an appeal from his sister Mary asking Jesus to pray for his sometime childhood friend, who is ill. He has been ill for months and is not getting better.

With a little Roman encouragement, the messenger is persuaded to continue on his way to Sidon without stopping off in the Galilee.

'We will know,' Cassius warns him. 'We will be watching. There is nothing we Romans don't see.'

Cassius, like any ambitious *speculatore*, tries to identify a pattern. Lazarus is either ill or pretending to be ill. He is in contact with his friend Jesus, who has a talent for drawing crowds. This is a situation with potential, because for some time Cassius has been developing an idea to impress the consuls in Rome. He's searching for a Roman client messiah.

Romans everywhere make life better for foreigners who have yet to become Romans. In Palestine it will be no different, and the secret to this corner of the empire is hatred. The rich hate the poor and the poor hate the rich. Cassius has studied their scriptures. The smooth men hate the hairy men. The Judaeans hate the Galileans who hate the Samaritans, and everybody hates the Idumeans. Periodically, they come to hate how much they hate each other, making them hungry for a messiah who can teach them how to love.

Their hope is their weakness. Rome allows them self-government, as long as Rome can select their king. Now Cassius wants to take this imperial principle one step further. A messiah is the future that Judaeans expect and a messiah, like a king, can be compatible with the Roman project. As long as Rome decides who that messiah shall be.

Standard pathology, on this occasion, will not apply. Remember that Lazarus is fated to come back from the dead. If there is divine intervention on the frontier between life and death, then natural law can equally be suspended elsewhere. Lazarus can have all seven diseases at the same time, but the progress of each will depend on his special circumstances.

Return again to the sources.

There is a thriving folk memory of a sick and diseased Lazarus, usually attributed to the moment he reappears from his tomb. He has a greenish tinge to his head, among other gruesome details. Sholem Asch remembers 'a skeleton...the skull was covered with a sort of skin, but the colour of it was neither human nor animal: ashen, bluish and lifeless...the naked, bony throat and neck'.

The parchment skin, a strange-coloured head, recessed staring eyes – over the years this description of the living Lazarus has migrated (as in Asch) to the time after his death. It is as if the resurrected Lazarus were only half alive, half brought back. The horror is vividly remembered, but incorrectly placed. The recollection of an agonised Lazarus comes not from after his resurrection, as Asch mistakenly assumes, but before.

'We saw two yellow arms,' Nikos Kazantzakis writes in *The Last Temptation* (1961), 'cracked and full of dirt; finally the skeleton-like body.'

Before, not after. Lazarus in the last months of his life will become quite a sight. His ruined body will become a public curiosity, his illness a combination of the harshest symptoms of the worst illnesses sent to try the Israelites.

This solution makes divine sense. Lazarus is about to die. To his family, and to all his friends except one, his suffering will seem to come from nowhere, with no obvious cause. This makes him the same as everyone else.

Nature is indiscriminate. It can warp the human body in terrible ways and at any time, and remember that Jesus wept. In the bible he weeps on this one occasion only, and there must be a reason for Jesus weeping, which has never been adequately explained.

Lazarus must suffer extremely. Though not suspiciously so. Nobody should guess that divine forces are at work, because that would lessen the impact of the eventual miracle. As far as possible the rules of cause and effect must apply. However abrupt his deterioration may appear, every change will have its clearly determined catalyst.

Though not yet, even if on his latest journey to Jerusalem the city has never seemed further away.

Lazarus is light-headed long before he reaches the second valley, and only vaguely returns greetings from acquaintances he ought to acknowledge. He feels grey from his tongue through his innards to his anus. He doesn't stop to contemplate the Bethesda pool, not today, but stumbles forward, eyes fixed ahead.

He enters Jerusalem through the Sheep Gate, but ignores the most direct route to the Temple. He avoids the street that leads to Isaiah's house.

Lazarus has choices, and options. He is in charge of his own life, and amid the disorder of the city he changes his mind. Anyone can change their mind.

4

Lydia works in the Lower City in a narrow building
jammed between alleys. Her windowless room is beneath
a sloping roof, reached by a tapered ladder that rises to a
trapdoor in the first-floor ceiling. This is Lydia's idea. If
a man can't climb the ladder, if he's that tired or drunk,
she doesn't want his custom.

Halfway up the ladder Lazarus rests and swallows a
gulp of air, ignores the ticking in his inner ear, shakes his
head. The rash on his arms flares up. He climbs another
rung.

Lydia has beautiful feet. The soles of her feet are waxy
and clean, as if she never walks on common ground.
He sees her feet, then the curve of her lower legs. The
rest of her is wrapped in a length of purple cloth tied
beneath her arms, and the skin of her shoulders is bur-
nished by lamplight, the flames reflecting in the broad
silver bracelet on her upper arm.

'If it isn't Lazarus.'

She is unprepared for the paleness of his face, the
tightness of the skin across the bones. And the smell.
She hides her wince, tucks her legs beneath her, picks up
a cushion which she hugs to her chest.

Lazarus hauls himself over the rim of the opening. He
lies still, his cheek crushed into the softness of a heavy
rug, his staring eyes level with the cushions landscap-
ing the floor. He flops over onto his back. The walls are
softened by Persian drapes, and their swaying rounded
shadows.

'I've been ill,' Lazarus says, eyes open to the furnishings.

'I know. I've missed you.'

Lydia's room is like a version of heaven, somewhere Lazarus and other men would like to come instead of dying. He climbs onto his knees and tilts the trapdoor. It balances on its hinges, then falls shut.

I want to clear up the business of the smell. Lazarus will die and his death will confuse the issue, but for two thousand years the Lazarus story has been associated with an unpleasant smell. This is largely Martha's fault.

'*"But Lord," said Martha, the sister of the dead man, "by this time there is a bad odour, for he has been there four days"*' (John 11: 39).

Or as the smell is forcefully recalled in the Mystery plays (*The Raising of Lazarus*, the Hegge Cycle, 1451): 'He stynkygh ryght fowle longe tyme or this.'

The standard explanation for the smell involves Martha's pragmatism. Lazarus will die six months from now, in the Judaean spring, when seasonal temperatures begin to rise. Her brother's body is a body like any other. Inside the tomb the corpse will rot, and organic decay does not smell good.

This is not why Martha mentions the smell. She is confused by Jesus heading towards the tomb – she can't understand what he's doing, and gabbles the first thing that enters her head. She is buying herself time to think, because she prepared the body herself. Lazarus is wrapped in sweet-smelling herbs and perfume and linen, Martha having doggedly observed every ritual of cleansing, every bitter gesture of interrupted love.

Martha does not take short cuts. It is not in her character. Therefore the corpse of Lazarus will not smell, not if it was prepared by Martha, not after only four days. The memory of the smell, like the memory of his decaying body, comes from the period before the death of Lazarus.

He scratches a fresh mosquito bite on the bone of his wrist. He shivers, even though it is warm in Lydia's attic. The bite itches. He scratches. It bleeds.

It itches.

He sits back on his heels, sinks into a rug. He'd expected to feel more alive than this. He slaps the side of his neck.

'I hear you're engaged,' Lydia says. She hadn't meant to say anything. It was unprofessional. 'Was that because you were ill? Probably you weren't thinking straight.'

'We've set the date for the betrothal. Two months from now.'

Lydia takes another cushion and stacks it on the first. She finds a loose stitch. 'Nothing is set in stone.'

'I should have told you. I've been ill. You know that.'

'I heard the news at the Temple. Did you think I wouldn't be interested?'

'A man without a wife is incomplete.'

'That's what they say. Unlike a whore without a husband.'

'Don't. I didn't come here to argue.'

'I'm sorry. I know why you came. I'll find the best oils, to celebrate.'

'I don't do this with just anyone,' Lazarus says.

'I know.'

She knows what he wants, and out of habit they act out their roles. Lazarus has always insisted that they're special, both of them. He is Lazarus king of the Jews; she is his queen. Lydia unstops a flask of nard, one of the first luxuries for which they'd developed a taste together: Lazarus preferred it to the smell of sheep. So did she.

Lazarus unpeels the purple cloth and Lydia stretches out flat on her stomach on the rugs, hands limp above her head. He admires her back and buttocks, and instantly believes he feels better. Only he, Lazarus, has ever truly appreciated her stunning nakedness.

He takes the perfumed oil and rubs a handful into her back. She is crying silently, a tear trapped in the flare of her nostril, but she doesn't understand. With more money he'd have made her exclusively his.

'This is the last time,' he says. 'I'm sorry.'

He'll live a chaste life in return for his health. He'll stop making visits to Lydia, honestly he will. Anything to avoid living obsessed by sickness, like an old man scared of death.

'Whenever you're ready,' she says. She wipes the tear away with her knuckle, sniffs once, twice, rests her cheek on her hands.

Lazarus swallows a cough. He holds his breath with his fingers on his chest.

Lydia turns and reaches out to him.

He holds up one hand, his face turning red.

'I know,' she says. 'It's often the last time.'

He aims to fend her off but instead grabs her hair. He pushes her face away so she doesn't have to smell him, but then it overwhelms him, a coughing fit that sets Lydia free and has him bucking on his knees with his weight on his arms.

The effort exhausts him. He collapses onto his side and drops a forearm across his face. He is so hot, but the worst is over, is probably over. It hurts to close his eyes.

The Lazarus smell is possibly the only instance in classical painting of smell as a recurrent motif. It insinuates itself into image after image, such as a Limbourg brothers' illumination in the *Très Riches Heures* (1416). A clean-shaven Lazarus is shown emerging from the tomb, and of the fourteen bystanders four are covering their noses, three with their hands and one with the bunched front of his tunic.

The onlookers expect a man who has been dead for four days to smell. Martha has actively directed their attention to this possibility, even though the idea doesn't stand up to scrutiny. If Jesus can bring a man back to life he can erase the evidence of decomposition. If not, the miracle is half achieved – the work of a messiah with limitations, so no messiah at all.

Lazarus must emerge from the tomb free of the stink of death and decay.

The smell, however, cannot be ignored. The evidence of the ages strongly suggests that a nasty smell is part of the story, and indeed it is. It belongs with the descriptions of a rotting, half-alive Lazarus: from the time before his death and not after.

His living body is fizzing with a compendium of diseases awaiting their divine signal, but the timing has to be right. Instead of multiplying and overrunning the host organism, the viruses and bacteria in Lazarus mark time and fester, embittering the blood. The full symptoms of his illnesses are for now repressed, but this stench that seeps from his every pore is the stink of calamity on standby.

It is the smell of divine intervention. There are side-effects. No god can act directly in a world such as ours without unfortunate consequences.

3

Now is as good a time as any. Several months have passed since the first of the seven signs of Jesus, the water-into-wine at the wedding in Cana. A second sign at this stage will not be out of place.

Jesus's second miracle, as recorded by John, also takes place in Cana when Jesus is approached by a nobleman. The nobleman's son is sick, and Jesus is asked to leave immediately for Capernaum to heal him. This is a powerful display of optimism because Capernaum is about twenty miles from Cana, or a day's walk. Jesus stays where he is. He heals the boy at a distance.

Mary hears this story in the Bethany square, and rushes inside to share the news with Lazarus. He staggers outside to the cistern, stares at his clean-shaven reflection in the water, then plunges his head into the barrel.

The healing of the nobleman's son is the second sign that Jesus has been sent by god. Lazarus takes a turn for the worse, exhibiting the early symptoms of every common ailment of the age. He has a generalised rash from the scabies crawling beneath his skin, now accompanied by reddish spots on his tongue and inside his mouth. These spots contain the smallpox virus, *Variola*, and because Lazarus must suffer he has both deadly variants, *Variola Major* and *Variola Minor*.

From early-onset tuberculosis (*Mycobacterium tuberculosis*) he has chest pains and a wet cough that doubles him up, bringing the smallpox lesions on the top of his tongue into sharp contact with those on the underside of his palate. The aerobic tuberculosis bacteria have invaded his lungs, where they divide and replicate every twenty hours.

The nausea induced by the malarial parasite *Plasmodium falciparum* comes at him in waves. Often it competes with the abdominal cramps caused by the *shigella* bacteria responsible for bacillary dysentery.

Which Lazarus also has, and which provokes vomiting and acute diarrhoea.

'It's nothing,' he tells his sisters. 'Stop your endless fussing.'

For a certain amount of the rest of his life, his first life, Lazarus will be confined indoors, and it is worth providing a fuller picture of how his house may have looked. The pilgrim who visits Bethany today, probably by bus or coach, will be dropped at a dusty roadside on what was once the village square.

There is an official blue sign reading 'Pilgrimage Sights', and an arrow points to a narrow road leading steeply uphill. On the right-hand side of this road, before the tomb and the three churches commemorating the miracle of Lazarus's resurrection, just after the first gift shop, is a two-storey house with a hand-written banner: The Home of Lazarus Martha and Mary.

Accredited tour guides warn that this is probably not the house, but the two young men who sit inside the courtyard will accompany interested visitors past the bay tree and inside the disputed building. They show off the engraved brass teapot and matching set of goblets owned by Lazarus himself, and earthenware bowls possibly used by his sisters. Whatever the truth, this is the only house we have.

There are two large rooms, one on each floor. There is a bench built into the walls of both rooms, wide enough to lie down on and sleep. There are rugs and cushions on the floors, woven decorations on the white-washed walls, and circular brass trays set on wooden stands to make convenient low tables. The attentive young men hint strongly that the teapot and goblets may be for sale.

Otherwise, Coca-Cola is available from a glass-doored fridge in the courtyard outside.

Lazarus stays mostly in the upper room. It makes his urgent trips outside more difficult, but Martha is convinced that the air upstairs is cleaner. She and Mary move the hand loom upstairs, and take turns to sit with him while working on the betrothal gown and asking him questions about Saloma.

'What's her favourite colour?'

Lazarus rarely wants to talk.

'We should send for Jesus,' Mary says.

There are awkward silences, and Jesus himself concedes the negative influence he can have on family life:

'For I am come to set a man at variance against his father, and the daughter against her mother, and the daughter-in-law against the mother-in-law' (Matthew 10: 35). The Lazarus sisters are not immune. They too are subject to the pressures of the age.

'Leave him alone,' Martha says.

'Jesus is trying to tell us something.'

'You're not helping. Check the stitches on the wedding gown. He needs something to look forward to.'

'Jesus is healing people he doesn't even know. Complete strangers – the sons of noblemen.'

'He's in Galilee,' Lazarus says. He pulls his knees to his chest, wipes his hand across his mouth. 'I'm here.'

'That boy was healed at a distance.'

'Of about twenty miles. We're at the other end of the country.'

'Pray. If you believe he can heal you then he will.'

A smallpox lesion bursts inside Lazarus's mouth, filling his saliva with bacteria. He is sitting but refuses to lie down. He has vowed never to lie down during daylight hours, because he will not admit to weakness.

'I have a fever and a nasty cough. That's all. I don't want anyone to worry.'

Mary's lips move fast as she prays for her brother. Then she prays she won't fall ill, and that Martha won't fall ill. Most of her prayers are answered.

Lazarus will not send for Jesus, neither at this stage halfway through his illness nor later when his life depends upon it: *'So the sisters sent word to Jesus, "Lord, the one you love is sick"'* (John 11: 3). Instead, Martha and Mary will act on his behalf, and only at the very end, when their brother has barely a day or maybe two days left to live.

In the meantime, it is unthinkable that Lazarus does nothing. He has the rest of his life to lead. He will attempt to save himself in every conceivable way except for calling on Jesus.

He has offered penitential sacrifices at the Temple: his fever and his headaches remain unchanged. He has purified himself in the *mikveh*, but blames the failed cleansing on his lack of sincerity. He has given up Lydia, almost entirely.

Yet he still feels ugly and weak and smells like a one-man plague. Mary can barely speak without mentioning Jesus, and Lazarus torments himself by remembering the past. He wonders whether there was anything of importance he missed at the time, all those years ago in Nazareth. Jesus has extraordinary powers, and Lazarus had noticed nothing.

He doesn't think so. The proof is there in what happened to Amos, but the past can't be changed. Unlike the future, which can be whatever he is determined to make of it.

2

Yanav the Healer travels with a dog called Ezekiel and a brown, one-eyed donkey. He is welcomed in Bethany like news from the desert or the arrival of cut-price eggs.

He is an event. The idle gawp at the donkey, at the brass rings in its ears and the clatter strapped to the yellow leather tent on its back.

The healer is a small bearded man with no visible neck. His clothes are good quality but travel-stained, and he has a wary look as if there's danger in fully opening his eyes. His face is often turned at an angle to his body, but the eye furthest away is the one to watch. The nearer eye sees, but the one at a distance does the thinking.

We can't know this for sure. We do, however, know what a healer of the time, like Yanav, would have been carrying in the panniers and flagons jumbled across the back of his donkey.

Foliage from a willow tree, and the dried sap of opium poppies. He has a jar of milk deliberately exposed to the sun. Olive oil, oil squeezed from fish livers, salt, and a box of maggots kept separate from the leeches which travel on the other side of the donkey, next to a bag of locusts. A flask of honey, a pouch of earth scooped from the centre of a termites' nest, sharp thorns, chalk, flat stones, and a stoppered vial of 'Greek potion' which is his own urine mixed with dill.

He also carries astrological charts and a sheath of peacock feathers, but these are just for show.

Mary notes the arrival of the healer and the next day she leaves the village before dawn. She is Lazarus's sister and has similar notions about heroism, though he and Martha have never bothered to notice. Martha is the oldest and Lazarus is a man. They underestimate her, but with the help of Jesus she alone can save her ailing brother.

She believes this to be true, and in her mind it is already so. Jesus will heal Lazarus if Mary of Bethany demonstrates sufficient faith.

She also believes, quite sincerely, that Martha will feel no anxiety about where her sister is or when she's coming back. Mary believes she will come to no harm on the Bethany road, nor after that as a young, attractive woman alone in the empty wastes between Jerusalem and the lake in Galilee. Her faith will keep her safe, and with the aid of kindly strangers she'll arrive in Cana by tomorrow at dusk.

Mary prays for the sick at the Bethesda pool, but passes them by. She prays for the beggars who jostle her in the clamour of Jerusalem. She will not be deterred, because she recognises the blisters in her brother's mouth. She knows smallpox. The consumptive cough she has also heard before, and tended to the dying with similar malarial fevers. If she does nothing, Lazarus will die.

At the Damascus Gate a military checkpoint slows her progress, but she joins the queue to leave the city. Waiting, too, may be part of the celestial plan.

The soldiers block her path. The northern road is dangerous for an unaccompanied woman. Besides, she has no business outside the city. She is carrying nothing she can sell in the desert.

'I wouldn't say that,' but before the soldiers can start she turns and doubles back, believing god must mean her to leave the city by another route.

By the time she reaches Herod's Gate, Cassius is already there.

'You are Mary, the sister of Lazarus.'

She glances over her shoulder, then briefly at his face. His blue eyes mean nothing to her.

'How is your brother? I hear he's not been well.'

'He is about to make a recovery, thank you.'

'It's not catching, then, whatever he has?'

'Let me through, please. I have a long distance to travel.'

'To the Galilee, I expect. You'll have heard the stories about Jesus and his two miracles.'

Mary is better looking than Cassius expected, and she blushes nicely, though young women should learn not to clench their fists. 'Do you believe either of these miracles are true?'

She does. Cassius sees this straight away, because the Jesus believers have no talent for deception, as if concealing their belief were as bad as denying it. Her shoulders dip, and she picks up her skirts, as if she expects to have to run.

'I wouldn't wish that on my worst enemy,' Cassius says consolingly. 'Let alone my brother's friend. Jesus of Nazareth sent by god. Imagine the responsibility.'

Mary raises the bright and defiant eyes of a believer, and Cassius briefly thinks that she too may be ill. She believes in stories that grow more far-fetched at every step from Cana, and to a *speculatore* credulity looks like an illness. It needs stamping out.

'Now go back home. You will not be permitted to leave for the Galilee. Every soldier on every gate has orders that you and your sister belong with Lazarus in Bethany.'

1

Jesus is not the only healer in Palestine at this time. Yanav has travelled extensively, and he has a reputation.

Lazarus welcomes him into the downstairs room, sits his back against the wall. Then he clutches his stomach, apologises and staggers to the latrine behind the house.

Yanav has seen it all before. He accepts some modest hospitality. A glass of sweet tea, one of Martha's honey cakes, and yes very kind perhaps just one more half of a honey cake. Thank you.

Martha bustles about, checking the healer has everything he wants, then in the absence of Lazarus she asks him directly how much he charges. Her hand leaps to her throat, then settles on her racing heart. For that amount she'd expect him to work miracles.

Lazarus returns, misses the entrance and smashes his eye socket against the door frame. Glaucoma. As well as pain in and around the eyeball, he is losing his peripheral vision. He crouches down, holding his head, cursing his eyes, hitting out at the door for being so narrow. Feels sick, stands up. He's too hot or too cold, and hasn't eaten for days.

'I'll need most of my fee in advance. There may be additional expenses. Herbs, and so on.'

'We have the money,' Martha says. 'If you can make him well.'

Lazarus has a coughing fit which leaves him panting and exhausted. He ends up on one knee on the floor, but refuses to lie down.

Yanav leads him to the bench, helps him to sit upright. Whatever he was expecting, Lazarus is worse, especially as Yanav's favourite healings involve diseases that no one can see. He likes sick people with active imaginations who thrive on close attention. They may well believe in peacock feathers and astrology, in which case Yanav is confident that he can help.

With Lazarus there is the rash, the fever and the pinkness in the whites of the eyes. Yanav examines the welted tongue, the pustules in the mouth. He sucks his teeth. Lazarus is suffering from symptoms that Yanav has encountered before, many times, though never all at once in the same body.

There is also a distinct, unpleasant smell, either from Lazarus or somewhere close. Yanav has never smelled anything like it. Courage, he tells himself, this is the friend of Jesus whom Jesus the upstart healer, for reasons of cowardice and inexperience, has neglected to attempt to heal.

Yanav rests his hands on Lazarus's shoulders. He squeezes, feeling for the density of flesh and bone, for the will of the man to survive. He looks hard into Lazarus's inflamed eyes.

'As I thought.'

Lazarus is tough, wiry, the upcountry type that lasts for ever. He is also rich and unmarried, so his only concern is his health.

Yanav's reputation depends on successful predictions. If he examines a man and predicts he will die, and he dies, then his reputation remains intact. Better, of course, to see in advance that a dying man will live.

There is something about Lazarus – he looks frail and

he smells horrendous, but Yanav can sense survival deep within him.

'No need to panic,' he says, deciding to trust intuition. 'If you do exactly as I say, I'll have you as good as new.'

5

5

Jesus comes to Jerusalem.

The British author Robert Graves, deep in his novel *King Jesus* (1946), uniquely identifies the significance of this unexplained trip to the capital city:

> He [Jesus] spent the months of December and January at Jerusalem, secretly financed by Nicodemon, but never once visited the house of Lazarus...; and Lazarus, pained by this neglect, did not seek him out in the market places.

During the last six months of his ministry Jesus travels to Jerusalem but decides against a visit to Lazarus. They both have birthdays at this time of year – thirty-three years old – but Jesus fails to make an effort for his only friend who lives a short walk away in Bethany. He avoids the visit even though Lazarus is widely known to be acutely, perhaps critically, sick.

This is not a friendship without difficulties.

In Bethany there is no time to lose. For the sake of his reputation, Yanav likes to make his more exotic interventions in public where everyone can see what he's doing.

'Fine,' Lazarus says, 'as long as it works. Let's get started.'

He leads Yanav out to the courtyard, and Martha follows.

Mary is sitting, arms crossed, on the circular bench beneath the bay tree. No one will discuss her adventures in Jerusalem.

'Whoever he was, your Roman was right,' Martha had said. 'This is where we belong. Not left for dead on the Galilee road. You didn't even tell me you were leaving!'

Now Mary stares meanly at a crumb trapped in the healer's beard. Yanav locates the crumb, examines it, then pops it into his mouth.

'Everyone sit with Mary on the bench,' he says. 'Make yourselves comfortable. We're going to chase this demon out.'

Lazarus watches Yanav rummage through the saddlebags on his donkey, while Martha and Mary bicker in whispers.

'How much are you paying him?' Mary asks.

'Does it matter?'

'Jesus heals for free.'

'Yanav is a professional, not a carpenter.'

He comes back with a curved thorn as long as his thumb.

'This won't hurt a bit.' He opens Lazarus's mouth. 'Head back. Hold still.'

'Aaah.' Lazarus can't make himself heard.

'Tongue upwards. That's it. Don't move.'

Yanav locates a glistening pustule on the underside of the tongue. He lances the swelling and collects pus onto the thorn's sharpened point.

'Martha next,' he says. Martha's eyes go blank but Yanav is the healer. He has a reputation.

He asks for her left hand, palm downward. He clamps the hand between his knees and scratches the thorn between her knuckles, once, twice, three times, each time drawing blood. Martha shivers through her arm, shoulder, neck, all the way to her chin. Yanav goes back over the cuts, making sure the point enters deeply beneath the skin.

Mary absolutely refuses. She stands up and turns her back.

'Please,' Lazarus says. 'Trust him. For me. He says demons don't like to be spread about.'

'Thank you. I prefer to pray.'

'As you wish,' Yanav says. He's disappointed, but healing is a mysterious art — everyone might be right.

'I'm going to live,' Lazarus says. 'I promise you all. Give me a week or two and I'll be dancing at my own betrothal.'

Days pass, and Bethany neighbours tell Lazarus about Jesus in Jerusalem. He knows. Breathless messenger boys keep running to the village, as if energised by the secret of existence. They are so young. They think they know everything, but all they know is the news.

No, they say, Jesus never mentions Bethany. He is not making arrangements to visit his only friend.

Instead, Jesus is surrounded by rumours of the many miracles not credited by the evangelist John, unexplained events that feature in the other three gospels from which the story of Lazarus is omitted. There are confusing reports that in Galilee Jesus brought the dead back to life. A little girl, people say, though nobody will admit to knowing the details: *'Her parents were astonished, but he ordered them not to tell anyone what had happened'* (Luke 8: 56).

As if they're not going to talk. People talk. Cassius listens. He has no idea what to make of this intelligence.

'Jairus,' his informants tell him. 'That was the man's name. His daughter died and then she was alive again, but the story doesn't smell quite right.'

'Of course it doesn't,' Cassius interrupts. 'Dead people don't come back to life.'

'You'd think he'd want people to know.'

Cassius thinks this through. 'Can anyone prove the girl was dead? You say she wasn't buried, so maybe her revival wasn't all it appeared to be.'

'The father's grief looked authentic.'

'Anyone can fake emotion.'

This story connects with another, about the son of the widow of Nain. He too is supposedly restored to life, which Cassius finds annoying. Cassius wants a messiah he can control, but Jesus is difficult to predict. He hushes up unbelievable powers in which his followers are prepared to believe. He travels to Jerusalem. He

doesn't visit Lazarus. What are the two of them playing at?

In Jerusalem Jesus does nothing in particular, and
therefore does nothing wrong. Cassius watches him from
upstairs windows and from behind solid Temple pillars.
He is reminded of Lazarus. The two men possess a similar self-reliance, which explains why neither has married.
Many men who think too highly of themselves prefer to
stay single.

Cassius listens to his instinct. He has a strong feeling that as long as Jesus and Lazarus are kept apart, the
Romans have nothing to fear.

'Go and see him,' Mary pleads. She is helping Lazarus
back into his sitting position, rearranging the blanket
over his shoulders. 'He's in the city. This is your chance,
before they block the gates again. You have nothing to
lose.'

'He knows where I live.'

'You have to ask him.'

'Ask him what? He's a fraud. Remember what happened to Amos, but then you weren't there that day at
the lake in Galilee. If anything, he should be asking help
from me.'

Mary squeezes his arm, at first to give him comfort and
then to hurt him. She wants to be in Jerusalem embracing
Jesus by the feet, but her brother and sister need her here
in Bethany. She closes her eyes, prays for forgiveness.
Then she sits at the loom and loops in strands of fine white
linen for the betrothal gown. She can't concentrate.

'He is a lamb, he is a shepherd.'

'Well, which?' Lazarus snaps. His head feels like it

could split in half. He pulls the blanket tighter around his shoulders. 'I know about sheep. He knows nothing about sheep. Nothing.'

'He is bread. He is blood.'

'Oh make up your mind.'

Lazarus forbids any further mention of Jesus. He claims he's more concerned about the betrothal, because they haven't resolved the problem of the smell. He stinks of suspended flesh and of innards leaking.

Yanav has done what he can. He gives Lazarus nutmeg to sweeten his breath, boils lemon grass with rose oil and waits for uphill breezes to blow the scent around the house. Not enough. He gives Martha baskets of dried laurel leaves to add to the fire, then pellets of cedar sap, rosemary, incense.

Nothing helps for long. Yanav mixes concoctions of splintered goat horn in warm oil, or willow bark crushed into the fat of a pregnant ewe. Lazarus holds his nose and swallows, because medicine is a question of faith: Lazarus has to believe more strongly in the healing than in the sickness, and elaborate preparations can sway a reluctant believer.

The demon does not come out. The smell remains.

As a small comfort, the betrothal ceremony will at least take place outside, sanctioned beneath the eyes of god. Lazarus is determined to go through with it, because his business is neglected and failing: he needs Isaiah more than ever. He holds Mary's hand. 'You've been so good to me. Isaiah won't let you starve, not when you're family.'

Yanav buys more perfume. Nard is the best, and it comes in oil form in half-litre flasks at three hundred coins apiece. Martha questions the extra expense, but a genuine healer uses only the finest materials. Yanav rubs a handful of the perfumed oil in circles onto Lazarus's chest. He can't understand it: the rash and the pustules stay the same, but the smell is always worse.

Yanav's treatments gradually take effect. True, Lazarus isn't visibly better, but nor is he any worse.

His cough has stabilised, whereas villagers unable to afford a healer would expect, by now, blood to be appearing in the sputum. The blisters on his tongue, a symptom feared throughout the region, have neither swollen nor burst. The pustules harden but stay intact, and astonishingly both Martha and Mary remain untouched. They are models of robust good health.

Lazarus loses weight and his eyesight weakens, but his digestion steadies because Yanav feeds him earth. Every morning he makes a paste with goat's blood and powder from the termites' nest.

Yanav sometimes asks questions about Rome, Romans, and the probability, in Lazarus's opinion, as a respected tradesman in Jerusalem, of a popular uprising that could threaten the rule of the foreign oppressors. But he does this while applying a compress of moss and honey to the scabies rash, and Lazarus usually ignores the questions as he waits for an end to the itching. The end soon comes. Yanav works another miracle when he bleeds Lazarus with a cut beneath the armpit – his body cools, the fever briefly subsides.

He gives Lazarus fish oil to drink, but in a month and a half nothing conquers the smell. The demon is weakening, Yanav is sure of it, but he has yet to cast the enemy out.

Lazarus doesn't always help. He wastes energy on self-pity and regret, because his life feels diminished. Each day holds fewer possibilities than the last, his choices fading as if heroic reunions and legendary adventures might now never happen. Poc. The options disappear, one after another they vanish. Poc.

Lazarus will not have it. Life must not close down. He will stand in Jerusalem for his betrothal, no matter how he gets there. He will assert his will, ride on Yanav's one-eyed donkey, do whatever needs to be done.

4

Yanav chants invocations to every deity he can remember. There are so many gods, and most of them are difficult to please. He exhausts the remedies in his saddle-bags, and makes regular trips to the market to search for fresh ingredients.

It is in the Bethany market, without any warning, that Cassius pulls him aside. Yanav looks sideways at him, at the pale northern sky of his eyes. The Roman is disguised as an out-of-town trader.

'How's Lazarus?'

'This isn't the place or the time.'

'You haven't kept in touch. I hear he's worse since Jesus came to Jerusalem.'

Every healer has a last patient, a heavy defeat. Yanav does not intend his to be Lazarus.

'We know he's running out of money,' Cassius adds. 'Why are you trying so hard?'

'I'm a healer. He's an interesting case. Not what I expected.'

'I only asked you to keep an eye on him.'

'He's dying.'

'Good.'

'Really?'

Cassius is under no obligation to explain himself. He has decided that now is the time for the Romans to influence events. The Sanhedrin priests have mixed intentions, and, although they value the rule of law, they can be impulsive, and act without subtlety. Romans are more experienced in the practice of power, and Cassius prides himself on the delicacy of his judgement — it is better for everyone if Lazarus stays sick. This will neutralise Jesus. He can stage as many miracles as he likes, but his followers will always doubt him if he appears powerless to help his friend.

'I hear you're planning to take Lazarus to Jerusalem.'

'For his betrothal. Have a heart.'

'Be very careful. I don't want him meeting with Jesus.'

The Sanhedrin priests are the next to react. Jesus makes them nervous, especially in Jerusalem, because he knows how to appeal to the dissatisfied. He steals their spiritual attention, and the priests have the most to lose. They have a status to maintain, a living that needs to be earned.

Later, when Lazarus comes back to life, we learn the depth of the Sanhedrin's resentment: *So the chief priests made plans to kill Lazarus too, because on his account many Jews were rejecting them and believing in Jesus* (John 12: 10–11).

Lazarus is not their first encounter with rejection, or the religious competition offered by Jesus. So what would their 'plans' involve? How does a committee of senior priests set about murdering an opponent?

They could hand him over to the occupying forces and intrigue for a crucifixion. But only as a last resort. Alternatively, they can do what they've done for centuries. They call on the Sicarii, the dagger-men.

The Sicarii are a sect of first-century Jewish assassins. Their signature weapon is the dagger, and they are known for their efficiency and discretion. They travel under assumed names, and are expert at living unnoticed among strangers.

In the village of Nain, on the lower slopes of the Hill of Moreh overlooking the Esdraelon Plain, Baruch stalks the widow's boy who claims to have returned from the dead. *'On his account many Jews were rejecting the priests and believing in Jesus.'* Resurrection is as intolerable now as it will be in three months' time with Lazarus. These Jesus charades must stop, and quickly – the Sanhedrin have made their decision.

For three days, mainly from the roof of the synagogue, Baruch watches the widow's house. He changes his position with the sun, so that whatever the time of day he is a shadow within a shadow.

At dusk the widow comes into her yard. She fills a water bowl for her chickens, then throws out handfuls of grain from her apron. She dusts off her hands and looks nervously about, as if she knows. She has felt like this for months, even before the death of her son. She bustles inside and bolts the door.

*

First-century Jews aren't stupid. They're not very different from who we are today, and if they were the events of those times would cease to have any relevance. They're sceptical. They think about Jesus and look for the joke, as in later years comfort will be found in Monty Python's *The Life of Brian* (1979), or Gore Vidal's *Live from Golgotha* (1992).

A gang of jeering young Sadducees, encouraged by the Sanhedrin, follow Lazarus into Jerusalem. They mock his sharp, sick features, the shaven cheeks sunk between bones. He looks like death, but nobody fears contamination because his sisters walk behind him with their heads held high.

'He deserves it. Didn't know his place.'

'Galilean. It was his choice to shave. Can't say he wasn't warned.'

The social acceptance of Lazarus, it seems, is conditional on his success. Either that, or there is relief that his illness disproves the unsettling power of Jesus.

'Looks bad, smells worse.'

They snigger, and laugh at what it means to be friends with the One. They hold their noses and slap their thighs, suck dates and blow out the long dry pips. Whenever the wind changes they shriek and clamp their nostrils shut. Everyone said it was true and it is. He stinks to high heaven.

Lazarus attempts to walk unaided. Yanav and the donkey lead the way, then Lazarus, with Martha and Mary following.

Lazarus trips, and doesn't have the strength to right himself. He falls.

Everyone laughs.

Yanav helps him up, brushes the dust of his clothes.

Lazarus starts coughing, and to keep him moving Yanav lifts him onto the donkey. He weighs hardly anything. The procession moves forward again and Lazarus doubles up with the dysentery. He topples sideways off the donkey.

He is hilarious.

In the city, Isaiah and the Sanhedrin priests are pretending to ignore the presence of Jesus. They have already ordered their extreme response to the rumour that started in Nain. This is their warning to Jesus: don't dare attempt anything spectacular in Jerusalem.

In the meantime, they continue with their ceremonies as usual. The betrothal of Lazarus to Saloma has been arranged for the open square near David's Tomb in the Upper City. The *huppah* is already in place, a silk cloth secured over four poles carried by attendants. The attendants are experienced Temple guards, selected personally by Isaiah. Nobody will be interfering with the betrothal of his only daughter.

This precaution is a gesture towards the unknown powers of Jesus. As is the detachment of Roman soldiers sealing off the street that leads to and from the Temple. That's where Jesus spends most of his time, in and around the Temple, and today he will not be permitted to change his routine.

Lazarus is helped into position beneath the canopy. The silk above his head symbolises the house he will provide for Saloma, the future he has decided is his. He concentrates on standing upright.

Yanav has a large family and many acquaintances,

and a good number of guests have assembled to witness Saloma's betrothal. They have to see it to believe it. Lazarus himself is having difficulty seeing, because common eye diseases have narrowed his field of vision. On both sides he sees black with an edge of grey, but he too wonders whether Jesus has planned a surprise appearance. He squints and scans the guests, turning his head to focus.

Jesus would be jealous. His old friend Lazarus is about to marry. He will father a dynasty, like Abraham, something Jesus himself shows no sign of doing. Jesus can stage as many deceptions as he likes, but family is the centre of every worthwhile life. He, Lazarus, is the better man. It was always him. He could do anything, whatever he wanted to do.

In the crowd, Lazarus makes out a woman he can't place, who immediately from the shape of her he knows he wants. She disappears. He loses her.

Lydia. He didn't recognise her with clothes on. He tries to find her again, and now she is over to his left. With every sway of her hips he realises he's never seen her walk. She keeps disappearing behind family who are strangers. Lazarus wants her to stop, stand still, let him look at her. He wants her captive as she is in her room.

She is over to his right again. She covers half her face with her shawl, moves, slips behind a cluster of cousins.

Sick as Lazarus is, Lydia inflames the embers of his sixteen-year-old self. She fills him with an ache that pulses from his jaw through his heart to his testicles. She is once more on his left, but he can't call out because he's on show under the *huppah* waiting for his virgin bride.

Lydia moves, Lydia appears, Lydia disappears. She will not give him the respite he needs. She is there, and then a procession obscures her.

It is Saloma, heavily concealed beneath robes and veils, surrounded by many aunts. By now, for Lazarus, the ceremony is literally a blur. A matchmaker paid by the day confirms the details of the marriage contract. Instead of a money gift, Lazarus symbolically offers himself as a servant to Isaiah's family, as a provider of sacrificial lambs. Saloma will live in Bethany and be cared for by Mary and Martha.

Lazarus has everything he planned for.

Yet he starts to act strangely, he can't help himself. His head jerks left and right because even with fading eyesight he's desperate for a glimpse of Lydia. He sees her again, now to his right, and suddenly understands what she's doing. She is circling him seven times, and the canopy above his head is a trap with no escape. He wants to lie down. The matchmaker informs him he may now hold his betrothed by the hand.

He is sweating, aching, about to collapse. His eyes flutter upwards in his head and he reaches out his hand, his wrong hand, the one furthest from Saloma.

'Martha, take me home.'

3

The next day Jesus goes looking in Jerusalem for someone who is sick.

Despite suggestions made by the disciples, no one

within the city walls matches his requirements. He therefore leaves Jerusalem by the Sheep Gate, taking the Bethany road. The disciples nod wisely. The Bethesda pool, an impeccable choice. Jesus walks past the Bethesda pool. He looks set for Bethany, like most travellers who leave the city in this direction, and he is halfway there before he stops.

He closes his eyes, and stands quite still in the middle of the road. Time passes. A slight breeze cools his brow, and moves a strand of hair – black, brown, a dirty-blond colour – there are no consistent sources. A bead of sweat defies the breeze, appears on his forehead, rolls between his eyes, down the side of his nose, is channelled forward by his flared nostrils and hangs right at the very tip.

Jesus thumbs the sweat away. He turns round, strides through the gap made by disciples parting, and walks briskly back towards the city. He descends the steps to Bethesda.

He is in a hurry. At the back of the upper pool, a good distance from the water's edge, he approaches a man he's never seen before in his life. Jesus looks down at him, lying on his mat. The man has suffered from paralysis for thirty-eight years, and he has glassy red bedsores and his limbs are wasted through lack of use. Jesus does not weep.

He asks the man if he wants to be well (John 5: 6). It seems a strange question, but malingerers do exist. If this man prefers sickness to health then Jesus can find someone somewhere else whose need may be greater. The paralysed man replies with a complaint. He has no one to help him into the healing pool, and therefore he will never be healed. At which point Jesus loses patience.

He tells the man to pick up his mat and walk.

The paralysed man at the Bethesda pool has been ill for a long time, much longer than Lazarus. He is surrounded by witnesses, many of whom are equally helpless. He picks up his mat and he walks away.

In the killing business there is rarely any sense of novelty. Everyone dies the same, the good and the bad, though the resurrected might be different. They could return from the dead with unimaginable powers.

Baruch has seen the village of Nain curl in on itself. Windows slam and doors are barred, gates get shut and locked.

Nain is staging a funeral, for an agricultural worker with three small children. A month earlier he had grazed his elbow on the olive press. The wound had become infected, causing a fever. The young father died from blood loss after the village potter amputated his arm.

The funeral procession shuffles slowly towards the tombs, passing the house of the widow. The mourners look straight ahead.

Inside the house she's shouting at her son. She doesn't know how she's supposed to act towards him, and her patience has its limits. Baruch waits. Later, after dark, an hour before midnight, the bolt on the door slides back. The boy pokes his head outside. He is fifteen years old and has recently been brought back to life. He is fearless.

Baruch works up some professional distaste. Nobody comes back from the dead. They have no right. He jumps from the roof and lands silently on his feet. The boy does not look round.

91

Three or four boys about the same age converge at the corner of the street. They swear on their hearts they'll follow him to Nazareth and beyond, escaping Nain to live the life of heroes. Their born-again friend nods his head in gracious acceptance of destiny. This, it seems, is what happens to the resurrected. Ordinary life loses its everyday charm.

The leader and his followers and the Sicarii assassin leave the village. They walk in the dark for an hour, then stop in the woods at the foot of Mount Deborah. The boys make a fire beneath the trees and when the son of the widow of Nain lies down, his disciples also lie down to sleep. They do whatever he does, because they too would rather not die.

Baruch waits until the night is calm, and then some more until the fire goes cold. The boy does not glow. There is no protective shield visible around his sleeping body. Baruch is behind a tree, in the clearing, kneeling beside the head of the son of the widow of Nain who is growing his first moustache. On his chin individual hairs are visible.

The wind moves branches in the pines, and Baruch is alert to every nuance of the night. He senses no divine force poised to resist him, not even a providential moon to betray his light-footed presence.

He reaches for his dagger. The night air does not prevent him. A viper slides along the track. The dagger slips in Baruch's hand. The boy wakes. Baruch catches the dagger and kneels on his victim's chest, his free hand clamping tight to the boy's mouth.

Baruch sees it in the eyes — the boy does not want to die, not again, not yet. This is a death like any other.

Baruch jams the dagger in through the stomach and up beneath the ribs, his other hand blocking the boy's airways. He leans close to ensure his voice is the last sound the boy will hear on earth.

'God's wrath is coming,' Baruch whispers. 'Here is god's wrath, today.'

The body convulses. Baruch lies over him until the spasms subside and the body is still. His disappointment is complete. Nothing ever changes.

Baruch retrieves his knife and cleans it on the boy's clothes. Then he scoops a pile of ash from the edge of the firepit and rinses his hands. He smears the blood-dampened ash over his forehead and cheeks, into his beard and over his ears and neck.

The darkness and the shadows reclaim him.

At the Bethesda pool, just outside the city walls, a paralysed man has picked up his mat and walked. Despite the number of witnesses, the city of Jerusalem continues about its business. The Temple is unruffled and Romans patrol their watches; there is no recorded impact on daily life and Jesus goes home to the Galilee.

He has fallen short where it matters, in Jerusalem, where to make an impression he'll need more than a simple healing.

Cassius is satisfied, up to a point. He has kept the two friends apart, forcing Jesus to settle for a smaller event than whatever they'd originally planned. There is no evidence that the Bethesda miracle is followed by any kind of popular acclamation. The Sanhedrin are indignant because the miracle happens on the Sabbath, otherwise nothing.

Nobody is overwhelmed. Jesus hasn't persuaded either the Sanhedrin or the general public to back him, and Cassius is beginning to doubt his qualifications as a client messiah. He needs a messiah who can mobilise support and change attitudes, not a provincial impostor maddened by the desert, beguiled by daydreams and the promise of heavenly reward.

Jesus can't even help his friends.

Everywhere, it seems, Jesus and his believers are in retreat. In Galilee Jairus changes his story: his daughter did not die and come back to life. She was asleep, then she woke. Her father swears that this is so.

In Nain, the son of the widow is found stabbed to death in a wood.

2

During his ministry Jesus makes one public pronounce-ment about Lazarus. The message is encoded, and it con-founds a Roman *speculatore* as completely as scholars down the centuries.

This is Roger Hahn from *The Voice*, an internet source of bible commentary: 'Lazarus is the name applied to the poor beggar in the parable of The Rich Man and Lazarus in Luke 16: 19–31. However, there appears to be no connection between the literary figure in the parable and the brother of Mary and Martha.'

There are many observers, even within the Church, who prefer to deny the reach of Lazarus, and his unique ability to discomfort Jesus. They don't want Lazarus to be fully alive before he dies, because this can distract from what others see as the more important resurrection. Look. It's obvious.

'At his gate was laid a beggar named Lazarus, covered with sores and longing to eat what fell from the rich man's table. Even the dogs came and licked his sores' (Luke 16: 20–21).

Jesus rarely names the characters in his parables. Here he makes an exception, and chooses the name of his only identified friend. This Lazarus, too, the one in the parable, is sick and dying. Coincidence? Remember that a parable is fiction, and Jesus can determine every element in the story.

'Lazarus' is not a name picked at random, the first that enters his head. It is chosen for a reason. Think it through, analyse the coincidence as Cassius does. He is paid to find connections: that's how he understands the world working, and how Rome keeps control of an empire.

In Bethany, at precisely the moment the paralysed man picks up his mat and walks, the smallpox enters its second phase.

There is nothing Lazarus can do. The *Variola* virus in his mouth and throat spreads to small blood vessels inside the skin. A low-level papular rash moves upwards to his forehead, where each pap grows into a raised blister, round, firm to the touch, but also deeply embedded. The blisters move to his upper arms, his upper legs, and proliferate across his trunk, front and back. The pustules begin to leak.

Lazarus is tired, and he swallows a plug of vomit. He plucks at his clothes to ease the itching.

'You should be angry,' Yanav says. 'Furious. Let bad luck fill you with rage. Rage can help.'

No sense of injustice can stall the emerging smallpox, nor the consumptive cough nor the floods of nausea. Lazarus aims at defiance, but is unsettled by sweats and aches and insomnia, and several times comes close to a malarial coma. Yanav pulls him back with large draughts of water, a treatment he'd learned in Babylon.

During the day Lazarus sits slumped inside the house, out of sight of the village, occasionally helped to the latrine. His urine is pink with blood, and he feels as if insects are breeding in his eyes.

When he does sleep, for however short a time, his eyes glue closed.

1

'The time came when the beggar died.'

In the parable, angels carry poor, diseased Lazarus to heaven, while the rich man named Dives dies and goes to hell. The prophet Abraham appears to Dives and explains the balance of the afterlife: *'Lazarus received bad things, but now he is comforted here and you are in agony.'*

While Jesus is telling this parable, Lazarus is in daily agony in Bethany, for reasons no one understands. Jesus is both warning and consoling him: you will suffer and you will die but everything, I promise you, will turn out fine. Trust me. Believe in me.

Jesus in his turn has to trust that his words will reach

Lazarus by the same channels as his miracles, by hear-say and messenger. He can't contact Lazarus directly because the seventh miracle, the raising of Lazarus, has to have maximum impact. Only then will all eyes turn on Jesus when he enters Jerusalem for the final time. To achieve the necessary element of surprise, there can be no suggestion of advance collusion between the two former friends.

Jesus breaks the spirit of this agreement. He can't resist reaching out to reassure his friend, for in the parable the rich man begs Abraham to send the dead Lazarus to his living brothers, as ultimate proof that divine power is real.

'Abraham replied: "They have Moses and the prophets, let them listen to them."

"No, father Abraham," he said, "but if someone from the dead goes to them, they will repent."

He said to him, "If they do not listen to Moses the Prophet, they will not be convinced even if someone rises from the dead"' (Luke 16: 29–31).

Jesus is questioning the Lazarus project. He wouldn't be human if he didn't. He feels the horror of making Lazarus, his friend, suffer. Especially as he knows in advance that resurrection has a limited effect – he wouldn't be divine if he didn't. Are miracles worth it?

This is the question the parable asks. Presumably they are, if the aim is to create stories that last.

4

4

Isaiah brings the news to Bethany in person, not the parable of Lazarus, but something stranger still. It sounds absurd, and Isaiah doesn't expect anyone to believe it, but in Galilee Jesus has supposedly fed five thousand people with some bread and a couple of fish.

By now, for Lazarus, the pattern is established. Jesus performs a miracle, Lazarus moves closer to death.

Malarial sporozoites take advantage of the feeding of the five thousand, the fourth sign as recorded in the Gospel of John. They unclench from their long wait and invade the liver, where they breed into merozoites that rupture their host cells and escape to cause havoc in the bloodstream. Lazarus has a recurrent fever, and each wave of nausea corresponds to a new cycle of parasites breaking free.

The smallpox pustules, after bursting, deflate and dry

up, forming a crust of scabs. Lazarus develops complications. The smallpox becomes haemorrhagic, and in places the internal bleeding makes his skin look charred, as if he's been struck by lightning. This is the black pox. Meanwhile, the scabies mites continue to burrow and reproduce and move. They feel like worms beneath the skin, as if he's already underground.

From the moment of the fourth sign, when the Jesus miracles become spectacular, Lazarus is visibly destined for death. The evidence can be extrapolated from salvaged memories and insights. Thomas Hardy rhymes Lazarus with cadaverous, and the Swedish Nobel prizewinner Pär Lagerkvist, in *Barabbas* (1950), conveys an accurate impression of how Lazarus must have appeared to contemporary observers. His face 'was sallow and seemed as hard as bone. The skin was completely parched. Barabbas had never thought a face could look like that and he had never seen anything so desolate. It was like a desert.'

Lazarus sometimes asks his sisters how he looks.

'Like our brother,' they reply. 'Really, not so bad. Maybe a little better today.'

Isaiah hasn't seen Lazarus since he almost ruined the betrothal, and now the man disgusts him. He pulls out a silk handkerchief and holds it across his nose. He glances at Martha. 'You knew I was coming. You might have cleaned him up.'

'We did.'

Martha keeps a close eye on her brother, taking what she can of him while he's still here, over-alert for any new signs of decline.

There are many new signs of decline.

Isaiah almost sits down, then changes his mind. He hitches up his clothes so they don't touch the floor.

'Of course, this latest miracle never happened,' he says.

He repositions the leather phylactery strapped to his upper arm (*'His kingdom shall never be destroyed, and his dominion has no end'* Daniel 6: 26).

'There are five thousand people who believe it did,' Mary interrupts.

'And thousands who weren't there who don't.'

Isaiah hastily replaces his handkerchief. If Jesus intended to convince the masses, he had missed his opportunity in Jerusalem. In Galilee he could do what he liked, because up in the sticks it hardly mattered.

'I notice Lazarus has stopped sending us sacrifices. Maybe you should start again. For the sake of his health.'

'Money,' Lazarus says, and Isaiah flinches. The fiend can speak. 'Can't afford it.'

'At the Temple we could make you a loan,' Isaiah suggests. He speaks through the forgiving silk of his handkerchief. 'In return you might have a word with Jesus. We're getting tired of his stories. He sets us and the Romans on edge.'

'Jesus means well,' Mary says. She will not cover her nose while Isaiah is in the house, but the smell makes it hard to breathe. 'He has done nothing to hurt you.'

'We are the keepers of the vineyard,' Isaiah reminds her, 'and god doesn't like miracles. Never has. I'm surprised Jesus doesn't know that.'

Miracles are disruptive. When the dust settles there is always damage done – not all the hungry are fed, and not all the sick are healed. Not all the dead can rise, but Jesus doesn't learn. He will know about the killing at Mount Deborah, but still he dupes a large crowd into believing he can change the world.

On behalf of the Sanhedrin, Isaiah has worked out an explanation for this latest miracle, a version of the incident that has circulated ever since. If it is credible now, it would have occurred to the sceptical at the time: the people of Galilee are selfish, which accounts for this recent episode. The Judaeans and Samaritans can agree that the selfish Galileans wouldn't have wanted to share their food. They'd have kept hidden reserves until Jesus gave out the bread and fish he'd been saving for himself and the disciples.

Five thousand Galileans look at each other. As if by magic, their bags and pockets are suddenly full of the bread they'd been hiding and the fish they'd been hoarding for later. They can't let Jesus seem more godly than they are. At heart the Galileans are selfish, but they are also jealous and competitive. They have negative traits to spare.

'Besides,' Isaiah adds, 'in rural areas their eyesight is even worse than here. Who knows what anyone really saw?'

'Couldn't you poison him?'

'If I wanted to.'

Yanav assures Cassius that none of his treatments have any guarantee of success. As a healer he makes estimates, he guesses, but for the fee he demands he has to be seen to be trying. Otherwise no one would believe he could heal.

'Why isn't he dying more quickly? He looks like it should be quick.'

Cassius has decided that for the benefit of Rome Lazarus should already be dead. After this most recent miracle his priority is to restore order, in the sense that what normally happens should happen normally, to remind the Judaeans what's normal. The son of the widow of Nain dies and should consequently remain dead. Cassius sends his spies to report from the village, in case there's a second revival, but this looks unlikely. The villagers have buried the body.

The dead are dead. This is the ending that Judaeans can safely expect, just as Jesus will turn out to be a provincial shaman defeated by the challenge of Jerusalem. His friend Lazarus is a hill farmer in a region with pre-Roman levels of hygiene. He falls ill. He sacrifices sheep. He employs a healer who is ignorant of Greek advances in observational science. Under the circumstances, it is normal that Lazarus's health should fail. All things being equal, he will die.

The death of Lazarus will provide evidence of natural law functioning as usual in the universe. Death is the most predictable of life's events. It is the opposite of a miracle.

'Don't lift a finger to help him.'

'I'm a healer. The sisters will get suspicious.'

'You know what I mean. Do anything you like, as long as it doesn't work. I trust you.'

'I trust you too.'

*

After the fourth miracle, the feeding of the five thousand, Yanav is close to admitting defeat. Everything he knows he has tried, but Jesus outdoes him with a new miracle that sets Lazarus back.

Lazarus can't remember when he last ate a proper meal, but the tack in his mouth tastes like mud and death. The stench around him is ferocious, a hanging presence that mixes nard and incense with necrotic human flesh. The end smell is always there, underneath, however powerful the man-made scents.

Yanav eases his pain. For headaches he applies leeches to the veins behind the ears. The leeches swell like glossy black ringlets — Lazarus as he'd have looked if born as someone else. When Lazarus complains about pressure on his eyeballs, Yanav inserts a leech inside his nostril, on the same side as the eye that hurts.

On other days he sits Lazarus forward in the bleeding position, elbows on knees and fists pressed hard into the sides of his neck. Yanav slices through a bulging vein between the eye and the ear, and catches Lazarus's blood in a bowl.

'Push harder. Hold your breath.'

This doesn't count as healing, Yanav knows. Other healers bleed and leech endlessly, with little or no success. He therefore remains obedient to the wishes of Rome as expressed by Cassius. Even so, he studies the blood for clues. Every day he searches for patterns, solely for his own enlightenment, but sometimes the demon is active and sometimes it is not.

Yanav dresses Lazarus's skin with a paste of crushed lime bark, and when he truly runs out of ideas he consoles Lazarus with stories about heroes. One day they're weak and the next they're strong. Like Samson, they're down then they're up.

This is the basic story everyone likes to hear. Job had his cattle and camels stolen, his servants murdered, his sheep burned alive and his children crushed by a hurricane. He did not despair. He recovered from calamity and lived to be a hundred and forty. Yanav tells tales about characters far worse off than Lazarus is now. And they end up somewhere better.

'Amos,' Lazarus mutters, 'how did it get better for Amos?'

Yanav hasn't heard of a hero called Amos. He blames the fever.

'Gilgamesh,' Yanav says.

He tries out the Mesopotamian demigod Gilgamesh, who is often in trouble and always prevails, his long life describing the great adventure of an active man avoiding death.

After the feeding of the five thousand Lazarus is housebound: his life shrinks to his nest in the corner where he sits on the floor among cushions and blankets. A bowl of soft-boiled walnuts is on a rug beside him, but his wider field of vision has narrowed. He can see clearly, but as if through a tunnel. Sometimes his sisters approach, at others he stares at the bag of dried beans hanging from a nail in the door.

He crushes his cheek against the white hardness of the wall. A spider crawls straight towards his eyes. He grunts, and it changes direction, moving away.

Nothing is preordained. Any second now he will send a message from his brain to his hand. He'll raise his hand above his head. Not yet, but when he chooses to do so. He may not send the message at all — nothing is predetermined because now, he decides, equally, that he will not send the message and he will not raise his hand.

Instead he makes a noise. Unghh. That was unexpected, but he, Lazarus, is the being who made the noise happen. He can decide to do it again. If he chooses, he can make sounds that don't yet exist in the world and will only exist if he, Lazarus of Bethany, consciously decides to make them. Or they will never exist and never have existed if he decides otherwise.

He raises his arm. Unghh. He concentrates so hard on his free will that his eyes lack focus. Unghh. Raises his arm. Unghh. He is acting like a man possessed.

He chooses to stop. There has been some mistake, because he is not this kind of person. Nor is he ready for death, not Lazarus, and personally he can't imagine anyone less suited to dying. He is not the dying type. Too young. Too much ambition.

He has an idea. There is a way to save himself that he hasn't yet tried.

3

However bad Lazarus looks and smells, and whatever Cassius may have decided, Yanav remains convinced that he can feel in Lazarus an indomitable force of survival. He buys an orange-feathered hen.

On the whole, reading the future is more trouble than it's worth, but Yanav has never known anyone resist his cures like Lazarus. He'd like to find out where he's going wrong.

A ribbon of pink light breaks across the hills to the east. A cock crows in the village. Some dogs bark, then go quiet. Yanav squats in a grey pre-dawn corner of the Lazarus courtyard, the hen in the crook of his arm. He strokes its ginger head with one flat finger, makes magical sounds, breath that never quite shapes as words.

The chicken calms in his expert hands, clucks occasionally at remembered courtyard indignities.

Yanav wrings its neck. He sighs, lays the twitching body on the ground. It is warm to the touch. He disembowels it, using the point of his knife to prise out the pulsing guts. He puts aside the heart, which he'll crush together later with some bindweed, then concentrates on the liver. The liver is the origin of blood and therefore the base of animal life. He slices it into the centre of a circular dish, cutting seven sections, each for a specific deity.

The pieces of liver bleed in different ways. He swills them clockwise three times round the edge of the dish, then examines closely the position that each god chooses to take.

At first, he can't make sense of what he's seeing. He must have made a mistake, an apprentice error like swilling the pieces in the wrong direction.

Yanav has never seen an augury like it, and a cold breath passes along his spine. Right is wrong and up is down. The gods are doing something new, he thinks, and the first time round they can make mistakes. That's what they usually do. They make mistakes until they get it right. Many people suffer.

*

Martha fans him when he is hot and Mary wraps him in blankets when he is cold. Yanav sees a frail body holding tight to its soul. Lazarus floats into sleep and out again.

He remembers the Arab traders who used to detour to Nazareth from the Via Maris. He loved to watch them working the marketplace, and he'd sneak glances at their black-eyed daughters. He was sixteen years old. The women found him amusing.

One day in winter, when the seasonal caravanserai moved on, he joined some carpet weavers on the first stage of their journey east. Jesus followed along, and Amos walked closely beside Jesus. Amos had convinced himself that he was Jesus's special friend, even though he was two years younger. To deepen this friendship he'd started acting like Lazarus, only more so. He should bustle ahead, be first at whatever they did.

'You can't come,' Lazarus said. 'No fourteen-year-olds.'

'I'll stop at the lake. Might get some work from the fishermen.'

'You don't know what you're talking about. You can't even swim.'

'I can. Easily as well as you.'

They became part of the Arab convoy, pretending they were adventurers to the heart of Persia.

'Goodbye, Galilee!' Amos shouted. 'I'll be back when I'm rich!'

'Or by sunset,' Lazarus said, 'whichever comes sooner.'

At Capernaum, the weavers rolled out their mats and set up awnings in the marketplace, while the three boys from Nazareth explored the rocky shore of Lake Galilee. They skimmed stones and watched the launch of fishing boats, the sails catching and dragging the men away. Poorer fishermen cast from the beach, wading in as far as their thighs, wrestling with the heavy knots of their nets. Today they were in a hurry. There was a storm coming.

Lazarus had swum in the lake many times, and it was best to find a cove out of sight of the locals. They said swimming was dangerous, and the currents unpredictable.

'Or in other words,' Lazarus said, 'they're old and frightened and have lost their appetite for life.'

'Yes,' Yanav says. 'We can try.'

He gathers scraps of wood from around the village, because Lazarus doesn't have the strength to reach Jerusalem on foot, or sitting astride the donkey. Yanav finds a hammer, and borrows some nails. He cuts rope and devises a solution. Anyone can be a carpenter.

Yanav lashes his home-made stretcher to the donkey. The stretcher is on sleds and has a wooden back-rest so that Lazarus can sit upright, looking home towards Bethany as the donkey drags the stretcher to Jerusalem. Martha and Mary help their brother outside, while Yanav calms the donkey.

Their procession limps away from the village. The dog and the donkey, Yanav and the sisters, Lazarus bumping on the stretcher which scrapes up dust as they go. After an hour they're still in the first valley, and Lazarus insists on trying to walk.

'The strangest figure in the procession, a frightening apparition, was Lazarus,' writes Sholem Asch. 'His yellow-ashen face stood out from among all the others, for it had the aspect of an empty skull above the covered leanness of the skeleton: his legs moved stiffly, like wooden supports, as he followed the ass.'

On the busy track Sadducees and Pharisees point him out. There in that hideous face is evidence of the weakness of Jesus. Not everyone agrees, and for the Jesus believers Lazarus has only himself to blame – he should have made more of an effort, offered himself for baptism in the River Jordan. Only those who demonstrate their faith will be saved.

The three-mile journey to Jerusalem takes all morning, and in his pitiful condition Lazarus is seen by travellers, priests, soldiers, traders, women, children. In Bethany, on the road, near Jerusalem. It is necessary. These are the witnesses who will later swear that Lazarus must have died, that no one living has ever looked so nearly dead.

Lazarus himself has other ideas. He has tried everything else, but not the Bethesda pool.

2

Jesus stood on the shore with their clothes and sandals in his arms. He followed Lazarus in everything else, but never into the water. He couldn't see the point of swimming – it wasn't a skill he wanted to learn.

The brothers raced each other into the lake. Lazarus won, but only just. They dived and sank and sprang back up again, water spuming from their shoulders. Amos did a comic backwards tumble, Goliath in the waves.

'Let's go deeper,' Lazarus said. He didn't like Amos showing off for Jesus. 'If you dare.'

'I like it right here.'

'You can touch the bottom. It doesn't count.'

Lazarus flipped over onto his back, his chin out of the water and also his toes. He checked Jesus was watching. Jesus had always been there, all through his childhood, as faithful as an imaginary friend. With Jesus everything would turn out fine. That was what their friendship had come to mean, and it was this message that Lazarus recognised in his friend's patient eyes.

Amos splashed back towards the shore and was stumbling out of the water. Lazarus taunted him and slapped the waves and laughed out loud until his brother changed his mind.

'No stretchers,' someone says. 'Mats at the back.'

In one of the lower porches they hire a mat at a ridiculous price. Martha hands over the coins because nothing is too good for Lazarus, as long as he doesn't die.

'I'm thirty-three years old,' Lazarus says. 'I'm not going to die.'

Martha adds another coin for luck.

Bethesda is heaving with the sick and dying. The porches and poolside have been packed since Jesus made his visit. Everyone here knows the story. Jesus arrived unannounced, selected a stranger at random, and told him to take up his mat and walk.

Now no one knows where best to set themselves up. Some hang back in the hope that Jesus will come again. Others push to the edge of the pool and wait for the water to tremble. When the reflections shudder, when the sky quakes and the pillars quiver, when the angels pass by, that is the moment to jump.

Lazarus can set up wherever he likes, because of the smell. No one dares come near.

'Next to the water,' Lazarus says. 'As close as we can get.'

He does not believe in miracle visits from Jesus. Even the magic of the Bethesda pool is more reliable. Lazarus wants to live, and there is nothing he will not try.

That afternoon, after the long trip from Bethany, fatigue overcomes him. He fights it, even though he could drop off at any moment. The water laps against the stone edges of the pool, and the glinting light is Galilee, at the lake. He can hear the groaning of the sick, but luckily he can barely see them. He has always been lucky.

In the night he lies awake. It is at night that he becomes a bad sleeper, with a tiredness too important to sleep through. He senses that someone is watching him, and he focuses on individual stars in the sky. Then he wonders if angels pass at night, when no one can see the water tremble.

Quietly, in the dark, he is frightened he's going to die.

The idea is inconceivable. Death is not to be confused with whatever is happening to him. Death is out there, and death happens, but not to him, not to Lazarus, with all his thoughts and memories and feelings.

This is when he has to be vigilant that his fears don't turn into prayers. He must not weaken. He reminds himself that he prefers to plan than to pray, and only he can help himself. He is the one, and he can do anything.

The next day the water is like glass, making clean reflections of the pillars on every side. As he waits, and watches, he discovers that there are sick people at the pool who as part of the mystery of sickness have lost their sense of smell. They recognise Lazarus and are surprised they can get so close.

They approach hesitantly, and pretend to be interested in his health, but Lazarus knows that before too long the question will come. They arrive at it from different directions but the question is always the same. What is Jesus like?

Lazarus looks at the surface of the water. It does not tremble.

'What is Jesus really like? You're his friend.'

'Slow at climbing.'

'No, honestly.'

'Hopeless at swimming. I don't remember.'

Jesus had light flickering around his face, not heavenly light, but sunshine reflected from the trembling surface of the lake.

'Don't keep it to yourself. Tell us how he was as a child.'

Don't ask me, Lazarus thinks. Ask Amos.

1

He waded back out to the same depth as Lazarus, because it was important to keep up, to be as strong as the next boy along.

It happened quickly. Lazarus swam out further and

Amos followed. Lazarus turned back, and Amos had his nose above the water, his hands paddling fast. His neck was strained back at an unnatural angle, and then his head went under. Lazarus thought his brother was play-acting. He got his hands underneath him and pushed him up, gave him a shove towards the shore. He went under again.

'That's not funny!'

Amos came up, paddling furiously, as if panic could keep him afloat. He whined with terror, his lips sucked tight into his mouth.

Lazarus caught him and held him up. He pushed him hard to get him started but his own head went under. He was the taller of the two, and his toe touched gravel on the bed of the lake.

The gravel slipped beneath him. He reached again with his foot but drifted further from the shore, pulled out by the currents of the coming storm. Amos was now closer to the shore than Lazarus but still out of his depth; Lazarus reached down a foot to move closer and found himself further away. His brain wasn't working – he made the mistake several times more before accepting he had to swim.

He splashed hard with his arms, slapping his hands into the water. He aimed himself at Amos but wasn't making progress. He put his foot down searching for solid ground but the gravel dragged him back before he could push himself off.

Now Lazarus, too, felt the strength leave his arms.

Staying alive would take all his effort. Finding his depth. Reaching the shore. He wanted to help Amos, with his whole heart he wanted to save him, but only to the point where he had to save himself. That was as far as his saving would go. Ahead of him Amos went under. Lazarus thrashed with his arms. Amos drifted away from him. Lazarus felt the nearness of death and he knew, with absolute certainty, that above all else he wanted to live.

Jesus stood on the shore, holding their clothes and sandals. He didn't help because he couldn't swim. He patiently watched Amos drown. He watched Lazarus save himself. He did not intervene.

Lazarus remembers every detail — this is not a forgettable experience. On the shore, when he hauled himself out, Jesus had lost that look in his eye that said everything would turn out fine.

The body was never found, or if it was Lazarus was never told. He didn't ask.

He travelled home to Nazareth on the back of a cart, surrounded by veiled women who took turns to press him close to their breasts. He couldn't remember Jesus as a presence in the cart going home, but presumably he was there.

3

3

Innocent people must drown in Lake Galilee. Blameless families are required to grieve. This must be so, otherwise no one would be frightened for the disciples in the storm.

If Jesus is the son of god, then all stories both before and after exist in the service of this one incredible story. Every drowning makes its contribution to the glory.

'When evening came, his disciples went down to the lake, where they got into a boat and set off across the lake for Capernaum. By now it was dark, and Jesus had not yet joined them. A strong wind was blowing and the waters grew rough. When they had rowed three or three and a half miles, they saw Jesus approaching the boat, walking on the water' (John 6: 16–19).

Jesus walks on water. This is the next miracle, the fifth sign of the messiah as recorded in the Gospel of John.

Several explanations are possible. Jesus is standing on an unmapped sandbar. The disciples, confused by threatening weather, experience a moment of collective hysteria. Glaucoma, trachoma, conjunctivitis. In a random sample of twelve first-century Galileans, as many as a third may have suffered from an eye complaint.

Jesus walks on water; the body of Lazarus collapses. His skin retracts and his joints pop with fluid. Veins push outward through his black and yellow flesh. He jolts awake. The whites of his eyes are red.

The fifth miracle sends his body into a dramatic decline. Overnight, at the Bethesda pool, he reaches the invalid stage where on the second morning his sisters talk about him as if he isn't there.

'Now, please,' Mary begs. 'Look at him. We have to send for Jesus.'

'There's nothing anyone can do,' Yanav says. 'It's over.'

Mary looks at Martha.

'We promised,' Martha says. 'Disobeying his wishes could make him worse.'

'How could he be any worse? He doesn't know up from down.'

'We promised him we wouldn't send for Jesus.'

His sisters argue. Lazarus notices a tremor on the surface of the water. He doubts his eyesight but then the reflections break up, clouds in the sky shimmering and cracking. No one else sees it. He could topple himself in, first into the pool as the angels pass by.

He stares at the trembling water. He will hit the surface, sink, probably drown.

'Send for Jesus,' Mary pleads. 'That's all we have to do. Let me send a messenger.'

'Stop,' Lazarus says.

The pool glasses over. It is difficult for Lazarus to speak, as if he's slowly being strangled with the minimum of force. 'Don't send for Jesus. And get me away from the water. It's dangerous.'

Lazarus is going blind.

On the road home to Bethany the darkness at the edge of his vision begins to close in. He sees a migrating crane, sunlight bright on the tips of its wings. He finds it easier to close his eyes than to work out what anything means.

In the final stage of his illness, the various diseases blunder into each other, and the ability of his body's defences to distinguish between self and not-self fades. His immune cells overwhelm some areas and miss the distress signals from others. His B-lymphocites are unable to protect him. His T-lymphocites recognise their doom and surrender.

Death is filthy. Lazarus has no control over his bowels, and is exhausted after retching whatever thin gruel reaches his stomach. He wills his inner workings back into their rightful place, but doesn't know what to imagine or how the unimaginable should properly fit together. The effort of not knowing defeats him.

Poor Lazarus, like in the parable. Perhaps death is for the best, and if there is a heaven he may yet be comforted there.

Mary crouches close to the creaking stretcher, praying into her brother's ear. He beckons her closer still. It hurts him to speak, but if he stays silent the pain does not diminish.

'What?' Mary asks. 'What are you trying to tell me?'

'Stop praying. Send for Lydia.'

'I will not.'

'Send for her. Please.'

Jesus walks on water. Jesus stands on the shore with their clothes in his arms, watching Amos drown. The gap between these two events is the emptiness into which Lazarus subsides.

Were they friends? Not really. Not after Amos died.

Jesus spent weeks afterwards in the synagogue, searching through the holy scrolls. He'd find obscure references to console his friend — *'Come, let us return to the lord. He has torn us to pieces but he will heal us; he has injured us but he will bind up our wounds'* (Hosea 6: 1) — but to Lazarus these were only words.

Amos was gone, and when you're dead you're dead. That's what the Sadducees believed, and their scriptural evidence was easier to find — *'the dead know nothing; they have no further reward, and even the memory of them is forgotten. Their love, their hate and their jealousy have long since vanished; never again will they have a part in anything that happens under the sun'* (Ecclesiastes 9: 5–6).

Lazarus wept. Jesus watched. Lazarus wiped his eyes and walked away.

He grew the first hairs of his beard — again Lazarus was first. He shaved them off. The Rabbi urged the Nazareth villagers to allow for the boy's anger and tolerate his wayward behaviour. This flaunting of the laws was grief, or growing up. All being well, he'd soon return to the fold.

To Lazarus, their tolerance made no difference, because god destroys both the blameless and the wicked. He could be understood or forgiven or ignored, without consequences – their god, if he existed, acted as if he didn't. Amos was dead. There were no divine interventions.

Jesus grew his hair and his beard like everyone else, as if god were not at fault and god was watching and god cared. Jesus kept himself busy. He had sheep troughs to hollow, and advanced classes on the intricate rituals of the Torah. Lazarus sometimes despised him, watching silently as Jesus sanded a nut bowl.

'How special is it just doing what your dad does? We can be more important than this.'

Joseph told Lazarus he was a fool for wanting to leave the village. Lazarus called Joseph a hypocrite. He and Mary had left Bethlehem for a better life, and Lazarus wanted the same.

'Those were exceptional circumstances.'

'Were they?'

'It was ordained.'

'Why should this be different?'

Lazarus and Jesus should have been living in the mountains like lions. Or not in the mountains, but anywhere else but Nazareth.

Their friendship, however strong it had once been, was never destined to last. Quite the opposite. The two boys had to be uncoupled, placing one at either end of the country. Some decisive event had been necessary to prise such friends apart, and that event was Jesus standing inept on the shore as Amos drowned in the lake. Their separation was in the design.

2

Lazarus regrets everything. If this is how life ends he must have made mistakes. He'd planned to live enough life for all three of them.

He remembers the pressure of his early ambition, hot and tight enough to burst. In Nazareth the streets narrowed, the houses shrank to nothing, and he lay awake for long afternoons listening to silence and his echoing solitude. He was dissolving, at one with the dates and figs melting to treacle outside. He has the same feeling now that he's dying.

Joseph said he was too young to leave Nazareth, and anyway none of them were city people. Jerusalem would swallow him whole, while Galilee was safe and his friends were there to help him. Lazarus laughed. He remembered the shore.

Menachem the Rabbi supplied the opportunity. He had always said the two Bethlehem boys were special, but it was Lazarus he took aside. His cousin Absalom near Jerusalem had an opening in the sheep trade. It wasn't much, but a young man with a pragmatic outlook could make a comfortable living. If he worked hard and made connections at the Temple, he could earn himself a fortune.

Martha and Mary would travel with him, to keep him company and help him set up house. Luckily, neither of his sisters was married.

'You are the one I have chosen.' Menachem's milky eyes focused somewhere to Lazarus's left. 'King David, too, left home in his youth. A great future awaits you in Bethany, I'm sure of it. I have prayed for you, Lazarus of Nazareth. God will do the rest.'

Lazarus found Jesus in Joseph's workshop. It was a long time since their last proper conversation.

'I'm going to Jerusalem. Menachem has it all plotted out.'

Jesus was experimenting with fasting, hoping for visions of the heavenly mystery. In real time this meant he was planing the edge of a door in the wrong direction. He could have hurt himself.

'You should come. We'll earn enough for two. Easily.'

It was the final appeal Lazarus would make to their friendship. Despite Amos, he was prepared to make a last effort, because he'd have sworn they still had feelings in common, like not feeling at home in Nazareth.

'Jerusalem,' Lazarus repeated, as if the name of the city spoke for itself. Literally anything was possible in Jerusalem, and he could see that Jesus was tempted.

But it was too late, with too much left unspoken. They were friends, yes, but Jesus would soon be a carpenter, like his father before him. Lazarus had grander schemes in mind; he was leading the way and he could sense that Jesus was jealous. Jesus wished he were Lazarus, but no one gets everything they want.

*

Out in the square the children play sick man tag, keeping one eye open for Jesus, who could appear in Bethany at any time.

There are plenty of visitors who arrive in his place. They drift in from the villages and from Jerusalem. Most are strangers but some are friends, because Lazarus had many friends. They want to pay their respects.

'My brother is not dead.' Martha turns them away. 'You've wasted your journey.'

But Martha can't stop them leaving gifts and offering compliments. They act as if Lazarus is accomplishing a very difficult task, and make it worse by not speaking ill of him, as if there is no hope.

Isaiah makes the trip from Jerusalem.

'I was wondering about the date for the wedding,' he says, but his pretence can't last. He hands Martha a bag of coins, and closes her hands around it. 'Lazarus was a good man. It is the least our family can do. You should take him to see his tomb.'

'He can't see.'

'There is comfort in being well prepared.'

'Our brother is very ill,' Martha says. 'Even small distances are a challenge.'

In this period of terminal decline Cassius visits Bethany several times, and not always in disguise. In battle uniform he rides into the village, accompanied by officers on restless chargers from the garrison. Cassius manoeuvres his immense black horse as far as Lazarus's gate.

Martha comes to the doorway. She squints into the sunlight and dries her hands on a cloth. The Roman horse sniffs in her direction, as if curious to know whether she's edible. Cassius leans forward in the saddle.

'Any signs of improvement?'

Martha turns and goes back inside.

Cassius smiles. Jesus can walk on water but he can't help Lazarus.

Yanav comes out to ask Cassius to leave the family in peace.

'With pleasure,' Cassius says, wheeling his horse away. He calls back over his shoulder. 'And thank you. You've done an excellent job.'

1

Lazarus insists at all times on lamps that are filled and lit.

'Send for Jesus,' Mary says. She can't think it and not say it. 'Send for Jesus. Send for Jesus. Send for Jesus.'

'More oil, more wicks,' Martha says. 'Don't let any go out.'

People can get used to anything, except dying. Lazarus has known for years that Jesus is not coming to Bethany and he will not come. In the day as at night he tells the passing of time in the guttering of flames in oil. He is terrified when a wick starts to flicker and smoke.

More lamps! More! Don't let the light go out.

Lazarus rarely speaks. When he makes the effort, it is to curse the winter of his birth. He should have been killed in the Bethlehem slaughter, as good as dead from the moment he left the womb.

'Fight,' Mary says. 'Stay alive long enough for him to come.'

'Mary, Jesus has had his chance. He was in Jerusalem. He didn't want to see us.' Martha has no patience for false comforts. She asks Yanav if there's anything else they can do.

He shakes his head. Yanav tends to Lazarus's hair, cropping it so short the ridges of his skull are visible. Every other day he shaves him. The smallpox scabs have dried and Yanav smoothes oil over the pocked skin of Lazarus's face, consoling him with long strokes of the Syrian copper blade.

Martha takes her brother's hand, and Lazarus grips on hard. If he holds on tight enough she'll lift him to his feet. If she lifts him gently he can walk.

'Where do you want to go, Lazarus?'

He pulls, but he does not rise up. His wasted arms tremble.

'Lazarus, where?'

He falls back.

He tries to speak, tries to say. His thoughts and memories and feelings have come to nothing. It doesn't matter how much anyone learns. Poc. The knowledge disappears. One thing after another, and Lazarus plucks imaginary objects from the air. The opportunity to marry. Poc. The decision to be good, or the chance once more to see Lydia naked. Poc poc. To have children of his own and to show them the glory of the Temple. Poc.

Months ago, work had slipped from his power. Then Jerusalem, then Bethany, then his own yard. He has this room. He has Yanav the healer and his sisters.

Martha takes Mary in her arms. They are both exhausted.

'Don't cry, Mary. Don't cry, my baby girl.'

They break apart, and holding hands they need only a brief second of eye contact. They turn to face their brother and Martha takes an audible breath.

'We're sending for Jesus,' she says. 'Whether you like it or not.'

_2_

2

Yanav volunteers to deliver the message.

'I know the road.'

'The Romans will stop you,' Mary says.

'Maybe they won't. I have a good reason for travelling as far from Bethany as I can. I'm the healer who couldn't heal Lazarus. I'm escaping my failure.'

Neither the Romans nor the Sanhedrin will want Jesus near Jerusalem at the time of Passover. Pilgrims are arriving in their thousands, and at big annual festivals the potential for civic unrest is greater – they definitely don't want Jesus in neighbouring Bethany intent on working a miracle. That's why Yanav has to take the message. He has been the main source of Roman intelligence about Lazarus, and is therefore above suspicion.

Yanav knows that Lazarus has very little time. Even as he prepares his donkey, news arrives of another miracle, the last before the raising of Lazarus. This one is less striking, but Lazarus's body couldn't have coped with a third consecutive Jesus spectacular.

Jesus meets a man who has been blind from birth. The disciples ask whether his blindness is a punishment from above. '*"Neither this man nor his parents sinned," said Jesus, "but this happened so that the work of God might be displayed in his life"'* (John 9: 3).

'It is a sign,' Mary says. No setback yet has lessened her faith, and she welcomes news of this latest miracle. 'Lazarus is nearly blind. Jesus healed a blind man. How much more direct do you want him to be?'

'Mary, I love you very much,' Martha says, 'and I hope Jesus can help, but maybe he's forgotten about Lazarus. They were friends a long time ago.'

After feeding a crowd of thousands and walking across water, this healing of a blind man is difficult to interpret. Jesus seems to be going backwards, because healing is something he's already done: the nobleman's son, the paralytic at the Bethesda pool.

His powers may be dwindling. Yanav will have to hurry.

'Jesus went back across the Jordan to the place where John had been baptising in the early days. Here he stayed and many people came to him' (John 10: 40–41).

It will take two days for Yanav to travel from Bethany to Jesus at the river. Two days, and then in Bethany they will find out whether Jesus remembers, and if he cares. The son of god will have the power to heal Lazarus immediately he hears the news. Two days, if Lazarus can last that long.

The sixth miracle, where Jesus mixes mud and spit into the eyes of a man blind from birth, is weighty enough to fulfil its purpose. With the lightest touch, so close to the end, this gentle miracle breaches the final defences of Lazarus's body. As the mystic poet Khalil Gibran records in *Lazarus and His Beloved* (1933), 'He himself will never return. All that you may see is a breath struggling in a body.'

It is his mind that coerces his heart's demand for breath, the resilient tumult of thoughts, the insistent pulse of memory. Lazarus remembers Amos, and wishes the truth or falsehood of miracles weren't so vitally important. Miracles provide evidence of a god active in human affairs, and an attentive god could have saved his brother from drowning, could have helped Lazarus in his agony long before now.

'Rest,' Mary says. 'It is done.'

'Keep breathing,' Martha urges. 'Think ahead to your wedding. Are we allowing Absalom to speak?'

In Jerusalem Yanav is approaching the Roman check-point at the Damascus Gate. There are ten or twelve armed soldiers and, standing ahead of them, leaning against a pillar, Cassius picking at his fingernails with a brass pin.

'The healer is fleeing,' he says. He stands up straight and tosses the pin aside. Yanav hears it drop. 'This can only be good news.'

'Lazarus is dying. Today, tomorrow at the latest.'

'If you're leaving, I believe it. Unless you're headed for the Galilee?'

Yanav's face remains blank. He reminds himself

that Cassius suspects everyone, all the time, but Yanav is confident that the gods are at work. Miracles, if true, are more intimidating than Rome. He needs to see for himself.

'Further away,' he says. 'Somewhere I can repair my reputation.'

'I'm sorry. An unfortunate consequence. But you've been well rewarded.'

'I have. I'm not complaining. Send your report to Rome. Tell the consuls this is the end of the story.'

'Glad to hear it. Is there anything else you think I should know?'

'Don't be friends with Jesus.'

1

A day goes by. Lazarus needs to stay alive for one more day, but his closeness to death is a glimpse of hell. Visions of hell are brought back to the living by the dying who are later spared. They remember how death feels – night pierces the bones, is inside the bones, and then the suffocation.

Lazarus struggles to breathe. Dragons squat round his neck and squeeze. His lips are sliced off and his tongue wrenched out. Flames scorch his nose and mouth, burning down his throat and splitting his innards.

He is stuck, always stuck, plunged so deep in a stinking pit of slime that even his clothes detest him. In a pit of slurry, of fire, in a pit of vomit or shit but always a pit

because, come the end, the living look down from above.
Mary and Martha look down at him, and he is below and
he can't reach up.

We all have to go through it. Hell is life in the instant
before death. It is before, not after. This is how we know
in such detail the logistics, transmitted from generation
to generation. Survivors come back with the horror.

Lazarus prefers to suffer than to die: hell is preferable
to death. When his soul threatens to drift, Lazarus heaves
it back. After a year of sickness he needs one more day.
One day, is all. He breaks it up hour by hour, determined
to keep breath in his body.

His soul sometimes escapes, rising high above the
specific wreckage of his body, and he knows when this
is happening because his soul has perfect vision. It
appraises the loose yellow-black skin of his body, but his
disembodied self feels nothing, smells nothing. There is
no smell in the afterlife.

At least, no sense of smell has featured in the many
documented instances of near death experience. There
is a pattern. An out-of-body sensation is followed by the
tunnel, and finally the bright white light. Lazarus has a
soul and it rises up. His soul enters the tunnel, and at the
end of the tunnel is a light.

He had not expected it to be like this.

Lazarus refuses the light, turns and slides down the
tunnel and drops with a clout into his rotten body.

In his hellish pinhole vision he sees individual tears
on Mary's cheeks. She is wringing her hands, as if she
wants to pray but can't find the place to start. Something
new is wrong, something worse than when she was last
looking down. Yanav will have reached Jesus by the river,

and Mary believes Jesus can heal at a distance, like he did with the nobleman's son. Jesus knows, and Lazarus is not improving.

The bible has more precise information. The New Testament remains the first place to look for remembered news about Jesus, and in Bethany there is little that Mary can add:

When he heard that Lazarus was sick, he stayed where he was for two more days (John 11: 6).

1

1

For Lazarus, in the last hour before his death, there is no miracle, no seventh sign. The story as told by John abandons him, and a sequence he doesn't understand is left, for him, unfinished: this is how death feels, and not just for Lazarus. Too soon; incomplete.

He cries fat salt tears. They stall on his cheeks. In the lion's den or swallowed whole by a whale. Taken up in a chariot to heaven, but not like this, not fending at death but failing to keep it at a distance.

Death is horrible and stupid and it can't be and it is. He curses creation to its face, because god is cruel and god does not exist.

Lazarus lies down on his side, and he knows he is down. He curls up into the shape of his beginning, clutches his skull with his fingers and squeezes. What comes next is the end.

Mary kneels and reaches for his hand. Martha takes the other and he clings on so rigidly they think he's dead, but it is only panic at a vision of death. He makes one last effort, always more effort.

'Is there a light?' Mary asks. 'Can you see a light?'

Lazarus contorts his lips, struggles to voice a sound. He fails.

His scarred, shaven face flattens against the mat. His reddened eyes are huge in his gleaming skull, and objects directly in front of him present themselves as if for inspection, demanding look at me now for the very last time.

There is a dish of shelled walnuts. They had a walnut tree at the house in Nazareth – but at the end even memories vanish. Poc. Concentrate, look. The flesh of the walnut is the origin of life. Look at its little arms, its foreshortened legs and muscular thighs. It has such telling skin.

How great and varied is the world of things. They too disappear. The bag of dried beans behind the door, poc, and the low table, poc, and the walnuts. Poc. Death is destroying all things on its way to claim him. He stares into the white heat of a flame that sends out halos in every direction.

Poc.

Blackness. Too soon. He releases his sisters' hands; they hold on tight.

His body has gone, his brain has gone, that's all he can think, even though he knows the brain lives on if he can think like this. His eyes spring open, see nothing.

Martha sobs bluntly.

Lazarus gives up the fight. He rises above the pit,

133

ignores pain's message about the importance of staying alive. It doesn't matter. Millions have come before him, and millions more will follow.

Go on, then. Come on. He finds the courage to move towards the light, towards the darkness. What does it matter.

Lazarus now is dead.

O

He sold blemished lambs at the Temple. He cheated shepherds and made compulsive visits to a prostitute. He was insensitive and self-important, he was beloved and he was dead.

There should be exceptions, Martha thinks, individuals with a god-given second chance. Death is unfair.

She and Mary kneel over the corpse of their brother. It is laid out on the newest straw mat they could find, but Lazarus dead is not Lazarus. His face was never that still. Several hours later his beard is growing, like a recrimination.

'Jesus brought two people back to life,' Mary says. She is useless at helping with the body. 'He can't just leave us like this.'

'Don't, Mary. You're making it worse.'

'*You're* making it worse. Try harder to believe.'

'In what?'

'In something, anything. Believe in Jesus.' Mary sits

back on her heels, eyes and fists squeezed shut. 'I won't accept he's dead until he's buried.'

Through the first night, Martha watches the body. Lazarus doesn't change. His fingers and lips are chill to the touch, and there is no exhalation of a departing soul. Lazarus her brother is grey and dead.

More accurately, considering the events of four days from now, he has detached himself from his body. There are conflicting ideas about where he goes next.

The Jewish tradition would have him in Sheol. According to the Book of Enoch (160 BCE), Sheol is guarded by six hundred and sixty-six angels who separate the righteous from the wicked. The wicked are drowned in lakes of fire. *'You have put me in the depths of the Pit, in the regions dark and deep./ Your wrath lies heavy upon me, and you overwhelm with all your waves ...'* (Psalm 88).

The pit. The blazing pain and suffocation. Sheol is recognisable as a version of hell, or the universal experience of the last gasp of life. Lazarus has been through Sheol. He is now somewhere else.

Khalil Gibran (*Lazarus and His Beloved*) pictures him in a better place: 'there is no weight there, and there is no measure'. Lazarus is in a 'green pasture', and by comparison the world we know is a desert.

Others, like the philosopher-novelist Pär Lagerkvist, tell a different story. According to Lagerkvist, Lazarus will later say: '"I have experienced nothing. I have merely been dead. And death is nothing."'

Lagerkvist presses for a more satisfactory answer.
'"Nothing?"'
'"No. What should it be?"'

The answer, for those we love, is green pastures and a land without weights and measures. Although 'nothing' is also a popular choice, a next-best bet, since second-best is what most of us recognise from life. Death is nothing (which may be better than hell), and therefore nothing to fear.

However, it seems unlikely that Lazarus could have survived nothing. Nothing can come out of nothing, whereas his and other stories have come back about death. After death there is something, and this is where Lazarus is now. It is not the life we know but also it is not nothing.

Which is of little immediate consolation to Martha.

On the second day the growing smell of corpse over-takes the fading smell of sickness.

'The time may not be right,' Mary says. 'Jesus must have a reason.'

Martha slaps her face. Mary puts her hand to her cheek. Outside, the wailers wail.

O

On the second evening is the funeral procession. Lazarus is lifted onto a litter called a *dargash*, and his body is carried head-high as far as the tomb. He is placed carefully in the upper chamber, and left with his sisters who will prepare him for burial.

It is a Thursday.

Eight days from now, the burial of Jesus will follow a similar basic procedure, and will require the same extravagance of spices: *'a mixture of myrrh and aloes, about seventy-five pounds. Taking Jesus's body, the two of them wrapped it, with the spices, in strips of linen. This was in accordance with Jewish burial customs'* (John 19: 39–40).

Martha first washes the body. Her brother has lost his soul. He is soulless, stiffened meat and cold bones, and Martha bites her lips as she completes the ritual practices not reported in the later burial of Jesus. She binds shut her brother's jaw, tying it closed with a strip of linen wrapped several times round his head. She binds his bloodless lips, the texture of overboiled fish.

'Mary, do something useful. Mix the spices, prepare the linen, anything.'

Mary kneels and prays. There is no money for burial clothes, so Martha is using the betrothal gown. She rips it into strips, one long tear after another. She has spent the last of their savings on the wailers and the *dargash* and the spices, more myrrh than aloe because myrrh is slightly cheaper.

'We have a flask of nard left over,' Mary says. 'We could add that to the bandages.'

'It's worth three hundred shekels.'

Mary's lip quivers. Martha looks up from wrapping her brother's fingers.

'I'm sorry. I shouldn't have hit you. I'm sorry.'

They work together, soaking strips of linen in the spices mixed with oil. Then they pack the remaining myrrh and aloe against the body and between each new strip of cloth. Seventy-five pounds is a huge amount of spice. Lazarus's body will not smell, except of myrrh and aloes, for a very long time.

They arrange his arms down the sides of his body, and bind them tightly. Mary shies away from strapping his knees, his ankles: it is too final a gesture, too utterly hopeless. Besides, they've run out of linen.

When they can do no more, the sisters lift the body between them. Lazarus is almost weightless, hollowed out by disease. They carry him down to the lower tomb; fetch lamps, surround their brother with light. Their fingers touch. They leave while the flames are bright.

Outside, in the flat shock of daylight, they turn and

shield their eyes for the end. Absalom and Faruq seal the tomb, rolling a huge fitted rock across the entrance.

Lazarus is buried.

1

1

He could be trapped inside his body. In the search for Lazarus there are those who follow him into the earth, attentive for signs of life.

For Norman Mailer in *The Gospel According to the Son* (1997), death is a place where maggots speak: '"Oh Yeshua," said Lazarus, "small creatures speak to me, and they say, 'You are not our master, Lazarus, but our wiping-cloth.' Thus speak the maggots."'

The authors of the medieval Mystery plays seize on this same information. They too have Lazarus buried alive, and he is eloquent about his ordeal when he returns: 'Wormes shall in you brede / As bees do in the byke, / And ees out of youre hede / Thusgate shall paddokys pyke.'

Martha catches a sob in her throat, grabs her skirts and hurries back to the house. Something of Lazarus the man will always remain with the body.

At the house she throws the blanket and the new straw mat outside, and burns them both. She puts the rugs and low brass tables back into position, but then can't leave the room without making tiny adjustments. The tables aren't quite right; nor are the rugs. She can never get the room precisely as she wants it.

That night she sleeps a little in the darkest hours, but is woken for the third morning in a row by wailers who aren't that good at wailing. Not enough feeling. Not even close.

Mary does what she can. She boils water and makes dough for bread, but forgets she has to cover it. Their father is dead and their mother is dead and now both their brothers are dead. Experience counts for nothing – her heart is unhardened to grief.

The sisters spend the day after the burial blaming themselves.

Mary should have prayed harder, believed more sincerely.

Martha should have called for the healer as soon as Lazarus fell ill. They should have tried Bethesda while he could still reach the water.

During the third night, in the silence, Martha accepts that she'll have to cope. Her desolation is complete.

In the morning, Mary is beside herself with excitement. 'Martha, wake up! Jesus is coming! They say he's on the road. He's almost here in Bethany.'

Martha dresses quickly. She ties her apron and runs to the gate, her hands clenched into fists by her sides. *'If you had been here, my brother would not have died'* (John 11: 21). Mary comes out of the house. She runs and falls down. *'Lord, if you had been here, my brother would not have died'* (John 11: 32).

Lazarus is dead and this is the truth in Bethany: Jesus has forsaken his friend.

2

1

'*Jesus wept.*

Then the Jews said, "See how he loved him!" ' (John 11: 35–6).

Jesus is weeping when he finds the tomb, weeps at the stone across the entrance.

'*Take away the stone*' (John 11: 39).

Which is when Martha, out of confusion or spite, mentions the smell: '*by this time there is a bad odour, for he has been there four days*'. She knows this is nonsense – she prepared the body herself – but she can't allow Jesus to go unchallenged. He has arrived too late, and there is nothing he can usefully do.

Jesus wept.

Is that all?

Martha wants more, and in this episode the Gospel of John has lost shape in the move between languages.

Translation scrapes off an edge of intensity, until modern English texts have Jesus *'deeply moved in spirit and troubled'* (John 11: 33, New International Version).

In the Greek original he is *embrimomenos*, he is *angry*. He weeps, yes, but Martha is right: weeping is not enough. He is utterly furious:

> All the blood went to his [Jesus's] head, his eyes rolled and disappeared, only the whites remained. He brought forth such a bellow you'd have thought there was a bull inside him, and we all got scared. Then suddenly while he stood there, trembling all over, he uttered a wild cry, a strange cry, something from another world. The archangels must shout in the same way when they're angry ...'Lazarus!' he cried. 'Come out!'
>
> (Nikos Kazantzakis, *The Last Temptation*, p. 127)

The Greek tradition, as represented by the novelist Kazantzakis, preserves the emotional truth of the scene. Jesus had learned this tearful anger many years earlier from Lazarus, on the shore of the lake in Galilee. Lazarus, too, had been enraged by the harshness of the hand of god.

At the tomb of Lazarus, Jesus weeps for his friend as his friend had wept for his brother Amos, with anger as well as pity. Jesus weeps for then and for now, for himself and for Lazarus, and for the worst which is yet to come.

2

Most of the surviving evidence about Lazarus originates in this instant. The paintings and etchings, poems and plays, sculptures, operas and symphonies all unfailingly centre on the raising of Lazarus from his tomb. Unfortunately, these varied testimonies lack consistency in the detail.

The squabbling starts with his physical condition.

The stone slides back and Lazarus emerges into the light. His linen grave clothes are stained with aloe juice, and fluids the body releases in death. He can barely move. He falls flat on his bandaged face.

Martha and Mary rush to unwrap him, their hands trembling against joints and muscles miraculously warm and intact. They roll him over to see his face, and Lazarus stares at the sun, his mouth unbound and agape.

Descriptions of his decomposed body are simply wrong – Lazarus as a skeleton, with a green head, or his body riddled with worms, he 'stynke as dog in dyke'. Before his death, yes – afterwards, no. Lazarus does not return half dead in an advanced state of decay, a golem in the shadow of Jesus.

If he did, the bible might have said so.

The other extreme is equally unlikely. In *An Epistle* (1888), Robert Browning reports that Lazarus was 'As much, indeed, beyond the common health / As he were made and put aside to show'. Yet Lazarus cannot come back as an impeccable human specimen. He is a man like any other, at least as far as this is possible for someone who has suffered, died, been entombed for four days, and now finds himself blinded by the Bethany sunshine.

Nevertheless, the covered noses need explaining. In many of the surviving records there are witnesses to the raised Lazarus who immediately hold their noses. He doesn't smell — Martha has made sure of that. The covered nose is therefore less a reaction to an odour, more to a resurrection. This action, faithfully noted across the centuries, is a judgement.

Look again at that painting by the three Limbourg brothers from the fifteenth century, a contribution to the *Très Riches Heures* entitled *The Raising of Lazarus*. One of the onlookers pulls his tunic across his nose while holding out his other hand palm forward. He is resisting the evidence that Lazarus is back from the dead. When bystanders cover their noses, they're saying that Lazarus is not true. He should smell like the dead. He cannot be believed.

There is another consistent oddity in these illustrations. In the Limbourg image, the two men nearest to Lazarus bow down before him. From Rembrandt through Julius Schnorr von Carolsfeld to Gustave Doré, there are immediate eye witnesses who prostrate themselves at the sight of Lazarus raised.

At a rough count, from the artistic evidence of the centuries, about half kneel down before Jesus. The other half bow low to Lazarus.

The raising of Lazarus is the seventh and decisive miracle in the Book of John. Immediately, something new is seen to begin.

'A large crowd of Jews found out that Jesus was there [in Bethany] *and came, not only because of him but also to see Lazarus'* (John 12: 9).

They see Lazarus carried aloft, half conscious, man-handled from the tombs to the village. Alongside the weeping there is cheering and applause.

Lazarus raises a limp hand to acknowledge the acclaim. He suffered and was buried and on the fourth day he rose again with glory to ... to what? The questions can wait. He is receiving, finally, the attention he deserves.

'Leave him be!' Absalom shouts, shoving people away, taking charge. They carry Lazarus across the square and down to the village *mikveh*. 'He must cleanse himself after contact with the dead!'

'Ask him!'

'Afterwards! Ask him when he's clean!'

Lazarus is suddenly alone in the cave of the *mikveh*. In the half-dark he tumbles into the water, floats, makes himself sit. The silence beneath the rocks feels like a space between life and death.

He watches the strips of linen soak from his body. He swivels his eyes left, then right. They are working; he can see without pain. He cautiously pushes the middle finger of his right hand against his upper front incisor. The tooth is solid in his head. He scrapes the length of his tongue along the sharpness of his fingernail.

The oil from the myrrh and aloes separates as glob-ules of fat on the water. Lazarus peels himself free and, sitting naked in the water, he examines his body. He checks the tops of his shoulders, the backs of his hands. There is no visible scarring from the rashes or the pox, and when he breathes deeply with relief, no sharp ache in his lungs.

His fingernails need cutting. He inspects the groins between his toes. He is thinner, but then he's been ill — checking his hips and behind his knees he sees no other evidence that dying has aged him.

He washes vigorously, beaks his nose into his armpits. He sniffs at his chest, the crook of his elbow, then cups his hand in front of his mouth. Not even his breath smells. He is confident that this is so.

An echo. He looks towards the entrance. Nobody there.

Lazarus lies back and sinks his mouth beneath the water line. He blows out bubbles of air. Only his eyes and nose break the surface, and above him on the roof of the cave blisters of water threaten but do not fall.

He is hungry.

The shuffle of a footstep. Lazarus cocks his head, his ears out of the water. A single drip from the stone ceiling, then silence. No one would dare, he thinks, no one would dare intrude on the untouchable friend of Jesus.

His beating heart slows. He lies back and relaxes his neck, lets his head slip under, his mouth, his nose. He stays like this for several seconds, testing himself for special underwater powers retrieved from the life hereafter. His face slips out and he takes a breath, then he shuts his eyes and submerges again.

A hand closes over his nose and forces his head to the bottom.

3

1

What do we know?

In the twenty-first century after the events described, the bible can be seen as unreliable, even fictional. In any quest for the historical Lazarus, however, the Christian New Testament remains an invaluable resource.

'So the chief priests made plans to kill Lazarus as well, for on account of him many of the Jews were going over to Jesus and putting their faith in him' (John 12: 10–11).

Not everyone is ready to bow down before Lazarus, whatever he may have experienced.

The Sanhedrin want him dead, and this information has endured for two thousand years. The chief priests 'made plans', but they couldn't know that the time and place were not in favour of plan makers.

The possible death of Lazarus, so soon after his

resurrection, offends our notion of what a god would allow. This accounts for the imaginative difficulty of trying to recreate a convincing murder.

'Lazarus started to scream,' Kazantzakis writes in *The Last Temptation*. He has decided that Barabbas, a well-known criminal, will be the murderer. 'Barabbas seized him by the Adam's apple, but was immediately overcome with fright. He had caught hold of something exceedingly soft, like cotton. No – softer, like air. His fingernails went in and came out again without drawing a single drop of blood.'

Kazantzakis is mystified. He has Barabbas, an amateur assassin, grab Lazarus by the arm: the arm comes off in his hand. Barabbas can't get his knife through Lazarus's throat, which resists him like a 'tuft of wool'. Finally, 'he seized him [Lazarus] at both ends and twisted him and gave him a snap. His vertebrae uncoupled and he separated at the middle into two pieces.'

This is not a realist portrayal grounded in contemporary fact. The implausibility in the detail suggests that the Sanhedrin-planned murder of Lazarus must have failed. The story doesn't ring true. The slaying of Lazarus, so soon after he returned from the dead, is incompatible with our instinct for what should happen next.

No, Lazarus wasn't killed in obedience to orders issued by the Sanhedrin. Not straight away.

2

He releases the rising silver of his final wasted breath. His eyes widen, his cheeks swell. This time Lazarus will die.

The hand snatches his hair and yanks him upwards. Lazarus bursts from the water and gulps a tremendous draught of life.

The hand pushes him under again.

But think of his two poor sisters, who have suffered enough. God is making an effort to communicate his presence on earth at this time, and not exclusively through anguish and affliction.

The hand pulls him out again. Lazarus heaves in air and blinks, flails, gains his footing in the pool.

'That's the second time I've saved you,' Yanav says. He is up to his waist in the water, and holds Lazarus away from him by the hair. 'Don't do anything stupid.'

Lazarus lashes out towards Yanav's face. Yanav snaps his head back and lets Lazarus go. The water surges against the edge of the pool and rebounds against them.

'I wanted to see if you'd fight for it. You like being alive, don't you?'

Lazarus shakes drops of water from the ends of his fingertips. He raises his fist. 'You're lucky I don't kill you.'

'I wanted to know if you'd scare. Come on, I brought you some clothes.'

As Lazarus dresses, Yanav wrings out his hems. He has seen Lazarus weaken and die, but the privileges of a healer rarely last long. The intimacy fades as soon as his patients are well.

'I'm all ears. Tell me how the two of you did it.'

Lazarus cinches his belt and looks up. 'That's a very good question.'

'What's the answer?'

'You just tried to drown me. You won't be the first to know.'

Immediately outside the cave about two hundred people are jostling for position. Isaiah is at the front, standing slightly ahead of Absalom. There is no way past them. Yanav has followed Lazarus into the light.

'Incredible,' Isaiah says. The crowd allows him to speak – he is a member of the Sanhedrin council. 'Such a wonderful surprise. Congratulations. This is extraordinary.'

Isaiah narrows his eyes as if to see through Lazarus to the other side. Lazarus bangs his heart with his fist.

'Solid as the day I was born. Yanav inspected me thoroughly. I'm all in one piece.'

'He's a lucky man,' Yanav says. 'Alive and healthy.'

'Thank you. I am. I think.'

Lazarus looks over Isaiah's head towards the village. Passover sunlight makes the flat white houses float and tremble, and that's where he wants to be, reunited with his friend. Separating the two of them, a shimmering mass of people, examining every movement Lazarus makes. He kneels and picks up a stone. It is smooth, warmed by the sun, and he lifts it and lowers it. Lazarus

153

weighs the warm stone in his hand. He drops the stone
and it lands in the sand with a thump. He has control
over objects, and he feels alive. Possibilities open up
again, destinations are within his range. He feels he
wants to run.

Isaiah coughs into his hand, and the hand stays close
to his face, fingers hovering near his cheek.

'Contact with the dead carries a strict tariff,' he says.
'Full ritual washing and seven days' absence from the
Temple. The Sanhedrin will want to speak with you.
There's no obvious precedent.'

'What was it like?' Absalom asks. He cuts across Isaiah
but his voice remains gentle, full of hope. The ends of his
long eyebrows quiver. 'Did you see anyone we know?'

There is too much that Lazarus doesn't understand.
He looks around for evidence of the presence of god. On
a nearby rock a lizard lifts one leg, then another, uncon-
vinced of the solidity beneath its feet. Jesus will be able
to explain. Jesus is in Bethany and all Lazarus need do is
ask.

3

'Jesus is sleeping,' Peter says. He takes this opportunity
to show Lazarus that no one is as close to Jesus as he is.
'What he did today wasn't easy. For anybody.'

'This time yesterday I was dead. I have some questions.'

In the Book of John, Lazarus has a non-speaking role.

His questions remain unasked, but that doesn't mean he didn't try.

After the miracle, Jesus and his disciples are invited into the house of Lazarus, Martha and Mary. Jesus withdraws to the upper room, and Peter keeps Lazarus away from the stairs. In his own house, which is full of strange men with tics and nervous twitches. Life has repeatedly surprised the disciples, and they haven't fully recovered.

Lazarus wonders if he smells. It's the way they look at him, their hands fluttering close to their noses. The disciples have abandoned their families and walked from the Galilee, so how is it that Lazarus receives special attention without even leaving home?

'Tell us what it was like.'

'Let me speak with Jesus.'

Peter does not move from the foot of the stairs, big hands loose by his sides. Unlike the others he doesn't twitch, which is why they call him the rock. He is a stone, this man, and his large impassive face is stone, but he wishes that Jesus, just once, had called him friend.

'Please,' Lazarus says. 'We have some catching up to do.'

'Do you want to thank him?'

'I don't know. What counts as good behaviour after a resurrection?'

Lazarus is already impatient with their limited outlook. Perhaps he'll thank Jesus warmly for all he's done. But, now he thinks about it, he might also suggest that Jesus could have come earlier, or stopped him from falling sick in the first place. It seems churlish to complain, but every first word he imagines saying is 'but'.

The bible is therefore accurate, up to a point, about the initial silence of Lazarus. On this particular subject, and for a while there will be no other, he isn't sure where to start.

Four days is too long. A piece of Martha's heart stays buried with Lazarus in the tomb. Maybe Jesus thought she'd be good at death, that after her mother and father and Amos she'd learned how to cope. He was wrong.

She mashes chickpeas with oil in a bowl, bunches her skirts to move to the fire, kneels and fusses with embers. Out of habit she tosses on sprigs of rosemary, for the smell. It is better to keep active, and not to look too closely at Lazarus.

He takes a scoop from the cooking bowl with his finger. Martha slaps his hand. At a practical level, they can't afford to feed thirteen strangers. Or they can, but they'll have to sell the only remaining flask of nard. And Mary will need to help. She's at the top of the stairs, sitting, waiting, doing absolutely nothing. Jesus might wake up, she thinks, and choose her for a vital errand.

Martha sweeps, straightens, reorders the universe while keeping an eye on her pots. Her response to miracles is to stay firmly in the world she knows.

'Slow down,' Lazarus says. 'Stop working. Talk to me.'

He balances on one leg and pulls the other knee towards his chest. He loves what his muscles can do. Peter crosses his arms. Lazarus wobbles and sniffs his armpit. 'Was I really dead?'

'You were dead. We all cried. Jesus arrived in the village. He cried too.'

'But you're sure I was dead?'

'It was horrible.' At last Martha stands still, hands bunched around the handle of her broom. 'He hasn't even said sorry.'

'I don't think he has to apologise.'

'There are so many of them. We can afford one more meal, and then that's it. Tell him.'

'Martha. I'm a rich man. Let them stay, if that's what they want. I can feed Jesus and his disciples for weeks.'

'You don't understand anything, do you?' Martha reaches out her hand and touches his cheek, her mind adding up the cost of the mourners, Yanav, the herbs, the perfume. 'Nothing was too good for you, Lazarus, as long as you didn't die.'

Lazarus presses her hand to his cheek. He wants to reassure her, to remind her of the miracle.

'I died and came back to life.'

'Yes,' Martha says. 'But what for?'

Resurrection builds an appetite. However little we know about the resurrected, they are uniformly hungry. The daughter of Jairus is twelve years old. She is brought back to life and Jesus completes his miracle with two clear instructions: *'He gave strict orders not to let anyone know about this, and told them to give her something to eat'* (Mark 5: 43).

Jesus himself, when the moment comes, is constantly eating after his return from the dead. In the Gospel of Luke he eats with the travellers he meets on the road to Emmaus — *'he was at the table with them'* (Luke 24: 30) — and in the painting *Christ at Emmaus* (1598), Caravaggio spreads this table with roast chicken, bread,

157

apples, pears, grapes and a pomegranate.

After the Emmaus meal, Jesus returns to Jerusalem and appears to the disciples. *'"Do you have anything to eat?" They gave him a piece of broiled fish, and he took it and ate it'* (Luke 24: 41–43). In John he appears to the disciples on the shore of Lake Galilee. *'Come and have breakfast'* (John 21: 12) and no one speaks until the fish and bread are finished.

Lazarus too is hungry. In the bible his only recorded act after leaving the tomb is to eat dinner in the Bethany house. *'Martha served, while Lazarus was among those reclining at the table with* [Jesus]*'* (John 12: 2).

This is his opportunity to talk, but first he has to eat. He is famished, and as he chews and swallows he organises the questions in his mind: why did you leave me so long? Will I ever remember what happened? What now is the plan?

Lazarus tries not to anticipate the answers, but with Jesus the old habits return, and he is used to leaping ahead. He and Jesus, best of childhood friends from Nazareth, will pick up where they left off, arm-in-arm, invincible. Lazarus had been with Jesus in Bethlehem at the beginning, he was there in Egypt and in Nazareth, and now in Bethany near Jerusalem he is the final and conclusive sign: he and Jesus are destined for glory.

Lazarus asks Peter, with all due respect, if he'll give up his place next to Jesus. Peter hesitates, but makes way.

Jesus turns towards Lazarus. His eyes smile sadly. He puts his hand on his old friend's shoulder. Lazarus blinks. He wonders if his questions are stupid. He blinks twice.

He opens his mouth to speak and Mary comes in with the nard.

What happens next is known widely. Mary interrupts the dinner, at last finding her role in the story. Everyone has to move and furniture must be shifted so that she can kneel at the feet of Jesus. She uncorks the flask of nard, pours out the perfumed oil and washes his feet with her hair.

Sometimes, Mary wants to say, words are not enough.

4

1

Lazarus spends the night after his resurrection on the roof, under the stars. His house is full, and he is acting on a strong craving for open spaces.

He does not immediately sleep. He regrets not speaking with Jesus, to confirm his conviction of being brought back for a purpose. Now Peter has reclaimed him, at least until the morning, and Lazarus lies awake wondering if a resurrection can wear out, wear off. He gazes at the stars and breathes the clean night air slowly in, slowly out.

In the simplest terms, after he returns from the dead, is Lazarus happy or is he sad?

Saint Epiphanios, Bishop of Constantia in Cyprus (367–403 CE) claims that Lazarus will live on for another thirty years. In the next three decades, according to ecclesiastical tradition, he will only smile once.

This is a possibility.

On the other hand, the American playwright Eugene O'Neill (*Lazarus Laughed*, 1925) depicts a Lazarus brimming with joy at his second chance among the living. 'Laugh! Laugh with me! Death is dead! Fear is no more! There is only life! There is only laughter!'

Lazarus wouldn't have been human if he hadn't experienced a little new-world optimism, like Ishmael in *Moby-Dick* (1851): 'all the days I should now live would be as good as the days that Lazarus lived after his resurrection; supplementary clear gain of so many months or weeks as the case may be'.

All the same, the documentary evidence weighs in the other direction. In front of the tomb of Lazarus, Jesus weeps, and weeping is a stubborn feature of the earliest salvaged memories about Lazarus. Johan Huizinga in *The Waning of the Middle Ages* (1924) describes 'the popular belief, then widely spread, according to which Lazarus, after his resurrection, lived in a continual misery and horror at the thought that he should have again to pass through the gate of death'.

On the night before the day known in the Christian calendar as Palm Sunday, Lazarus turns onto his stomach on the roof of his house. Chin on hands, he stares over the moonlit hills of scrub and rock, and a Bedouin fire burns brightly in the distance, like an answering star to the heavens.

Lazarus has the feeling he's being watched. He listens for a command, like those received by the prophets, then hugs himself and rolls from side to side. He chants 'here I am, here I am, here I am'. God does not respond with the consoling near-echo of I am here.

Lazarus plans ahead for tomorrow, his second day

back on earth. He won't make the same mistakes twice. This time around he'll keep Jesus close, and value their friendship as he did when they were young. He'll trust that instinct, once so strong and now rekindled, that he and Jesus will live as heroes. Tomorrow is the first day of the rest of his life: Jesus will explain about Amos, and clear up the differences between life and death.

'Here I am,' Lazarus whispers. 'Here I am.'

His chant loses meaning, becomes a sequence of the sounds of nothingness, until eventually beneath the stars on the roof in Bethany, Lazarus falls asleep.

2

He shakes himself awake. Already the sun is halfway towards noon. He jumps up, makes a fresh start, bundles down the outside steps, shouts at Martha for his breakfast.

A disciple is sitting beside the door. Nathaniel? Matthew? Lazarus can never remember their names. This one like the others is bearded and dark-skinned, and smells of sweat and fish. His left eyelid is trembling.

'Jesus asked me to thank you. Your hospitality was most welcome.'

'Where is he?'

'They left for Jerusalem, everyone except me.'

Balthazar or Andrew stands up and sniffs, testing the air. He raises his hand but instead of covering his nose he holds his eyelid still.

'Can you tell me what death was like?'

'He can't have left. Not without letting me know.'

'Was it very glorious?'

'We haven't had a chance to talk.'

Lazarus runs into the village square, as if to catch stragglers before it's too late. Jesus is long gone, and in the village the mood has changed.

Bethany is exhausted. The mid-morning sunlight makes sharp edges along abandoned crutches, while bandages brown with tidemarks of blood curl and crack in the dust. There are charred stones around cold fires. This is what the absence of Jesus looks like.

'Peter asks that you stay in Bethany.' The disciple has followed Lazarus into the square. 'We'll send the doubters out from Jerusalem. When they see how alive you are, they'll believe that Jesus is the one.'

It is the morning of Palm Sunday and Jesus has left Bethany leading a triumphal procession into Jerusalem. The true believers have escorted him, laying down palm leaves beneath the hooves of his donkey. The one remaining disciple is even now waving goodbye to Lazarus as he turns the corner of the Jerusalem road. He too has gone.

In Bethany, it follows that anyone left behind is an unbeliever. Three women drawing water at the well complain about a stolen donkey. Lazarus walks towards them. They turn their backs and call in their children.

He takes another step. The women raise their chins and pinch their noses.

Lazarus runs back to the house.

'Mary went with him,' Martha says.

She is on her knees scrubbing the spillage of last

night's perfume from the floor. Lazarus squeezes her shoulder, and she pushes her cheek against his knuckles to be sure he's there.

'I'll make you some breakfast,' Martha says. She aches to her feet, holding her back. 'How are you feeling?'

Lazarus finds some bread in a jar, bites, chews, swallows. Takes another bite, more thoughtfully. He is waiting for a surge of strength, a sense of unstoppable euphoria.

'Everything's wonderful,' he says. 'Impeccable. I was dead and now I'm alive.'

'Is it the money? Is that what's worrying you?'

'I'm not going to worry about money.'

'Look on the bright side,' Martha says. She uncorks one jar after another to see how much the disciples have left behind them. 'At least we've got the house to ourselves.'

The gate creaks.

It is Isaiah, who is not in Jerusalem with the believers. He walks into the house unannounced.

'I'm here to fetch you,' Isaiah says. He has recovered his priestly composure since yesterday, but Martha won't give up her brother so easily, not again.

'Let the man breathe. His head's still spinning.'

'We need him to answer some questions.'

If Lazarus is true, then Isaiah and the priests of Jerusalem have wasted their lives. None of their prayers or devoutly observed rituals can save them, not if the saviour is a man who barely respects the Sabbath. Jesus and Lazarus, together, make fools out of every virtuous Jew, and out of the hypocrites too.

'Lazarus, you have to tell us the truth. Jesus did not

bring you back from the dead.'

'Didn't he?'

'Seriously. You followed the rules in Leviticus, and like any sensible man you paid for sacrifices at the Temple. God was appeased and eventually he ensured your recovery.'

'No one will believe that.'

'You weren't as sick as you looked. Lazarus, you did not come back from the dead. I will not allow it. You'll bring shame on me and my family.'

For the first time Lazarus remembers Saloma, and what a good idea that had seemed, before he died.

'Leave him alone,' Martha says, 'he hasn't done anything wrong.'

'He came back to life. Deny it was Jesus and after a decent period all will be forgotten. You can trade again, like before. You can earn some money, marry my daughter.'

'Can I? I was dead.'

'Stop it, Lazarus. The Sanhedrin want everything returned to normal. And quickly. You've been summoned to reassure them that this will be so.'

'In Jerusalem?'

'In Bethany.'

'As if the high priests would come to Bethany.'

'They're already here.'

3

The Bethany synagogue is a single-storey whitewashed building.

Among the seventy-one members of the Sanhedrin are priests who consider the three-mile journey from Jerusalem, most of it uphill, a scandal beyond repair. They console themselves with scriptures, *'Dust you are, and to dust you shall return'* (Genesis 3: 19), and some have rolled extra verses into their tightly strapped phylacteries: *'As waters fall from a lake, and a river wastes away and dries up, so mortals lie down and do not rise again'* (Job 14: 11–12).

If only that were so. Isaiah leads Lazarus into the middle of the synagogue and the priests draw back, making space. The status of the man has yet to be decided. An accidental touch might make them unclean – seven days' absence from the Temple, and at Passover, too.

Lazarus has the peculiar impression of being unwanted, an intruder at his own trial. Light floods through windows high in the walls. He has an itch on the inside of his knee.

A younger priest, who has come prepared for the smell of the dead, covers his nose with a handkerchief. Others are eager for revelation, and they start shouting all at once:

'Is there a judgement day?'

'Are you the messiah?'

'How did you get food and water into the tomb?'

Their eyes pin Lazarus from every direction, searching for whatever knowledge or power they suppose he has, or for physical scars from his dying.

'Have you witnessed the kingdom of heaven?'

'Is it overcrowded?'

'Are there any animals?'

The priests would like Lazarus to confirm what they already believe.

Lazarus scratches the itch on his knee. Stops. Scratches again. He has been bitten by a mosquito during the night, which seems unnecessary.

'How wide is the lake of fire that divides the righteous from the wicked?'

'Are the six hundred and sixty-six angels armed with chains of fire?'

'Are the angels *all the same size?*'

Caiaphas calls for quiet. He is the high priest of Jerusalem and he prefers to avoid theology. The junior priests quieten down. They acknowledge the supremacy of Caiaphas, and his responsibility for making a judgement.

Henry Wadsworth Longfellow, in his verse play *Christus: A Mystery* (1872), shows Caiaphas deciding the fate of Lazarus: *'This Lazarus should be taken, and put to death / As an impostor.'*

Caiaphas misses Palm Sunday in Jerusalem because he is examining Lazarus at the synagogue in Bethany. As are Joseph of Arimathea and Nicodemus, both of them Jesus sympathisers who are also members of the Sanhedrin. Jesus enters Jerusalem unopposed because the ruling priests are absent. This explains why on that particular day Jesus, surprisingly, has the freedom of the city.

Thanks to Lazarus. Lazarus is the seventh and greatest miracle, a flagrant breach of natural law that has consequences throughout the week that follows.

'Lazarus came back to life,' Nicodemus says, pre-empting Caiaphas and appealing for tolerance. 'Nowhere in the scriptures is resurrection condemned as unlawful.'

'We have reliable witnesses to Lazarus emerging from his tomb,' Caiaphas agrees. His voice is measured, almost tired. 'I don't wish to dispute this incident. However, I believe it is true that no one saw him die.'

Sadly, it would seem that Lazarus returned from the dead without any easy information. If he had described to the Sanhedrin what death was like, then that would be knowledge we have. We would have had it since the time of Lazarus, and news this important we would not have forgotten.

We do not have that knowledge. We have no idea what to expect from death.

Many recollections of Lazarus express frustration at his failure to communicate. The British laureate Alfred, Lord Tennyson (*In Memoriam*, 1849) confronts Lazarus directly: 'Where went thou, brother, those four days? / There lives no record of reply, / Which telling what it is to die / Had surely added praise to praise.'

Lazarus doesn't know, or he can't say. This doesn't stop the question being asked, and in O'Neill's *Lazarus Laughed* a chorus embodies the clamour of competing voices demanding that Lazarus should speak: 'What is Beyond?'

On Palm Sunday a sceptical crowd reassembles in Bethany hoping for a glimpse of Lazarus. Lazarus, tell us if you can, what is beyond?

And how bad is it for sinners?

Around the edges of the Bethany square, Baruch the assassin slips between shadows. He watches, he waits. The crowd grows with waverers sent by the disciples from Jerusalem — if you don't believe in Jesus then go and see for yourselves.

Resurrection is the best of miracles. Every single person in Bethany that day can think of someone dead they sincerely wish were alive. Life after death is everything, but of all the dead, they want to ask, why Lazarus? What about us, and our dead?

Baruch remembers the strangers he has killed. What would they say if they came back now? He shakes the thought from his head, and replaces it with practical calculations about when and where. Overnight, Lazarus has become as famous as Jesus. Unless he makes an elementary mistake, he will rarely be alone and vulncrable.

The Sanhedrin Council send Lazarus, escorted by guards, under orders back to his house. The priests are now free to argue amongst themselves.

'Other than his sisters,' Caiaphas repeats. 'Is there anyone credible who can vouch that he died?'

'The healer left before the end.'

'There is nothing for us to discuss,' someone says, in the tone of knowing best. 'Messiahs do not come from the Galilee. And Lazarus can't have done what they say.'

'Why should he be different from anyone else?'

Caiaphas tilts his head one way, holds it a second, then tilts it the other. He wants them to appreciate that he has considered this problem from every side, and although judgements other than his are possible, and he respects disparate views, his own opinion, on balance, is probably correct.

'Yesterday, the Roman governor arrived in Jerusalem from Caesar Maritima. This level of excitement is not what he was hoping to find. However, we can't dispose of both Jesus and Lazarus. That would be too much.'

'You're getting ahead of yourself,' Nicodemus says. 'We don't have power over life and death. Only Rome has that.'

'I know,' Caiaphas says. 'But apparently Lazarus has already died. This is what is being said.'

The Jewish god promises salvation through proper conduct and respect for the priesthood. After thousands of years god is unlikely to change his mind and offer salvation through a man.

'So which one?' he asks. With great care he pulls from inside his clothing a large silk handkerchief. 'The raiser or the raised?'

Caiaphas looks left and right. Nicodemus knows his law. The Sanhedrin can't sentence anyone to death, but the priests seem slow in understanding his suggestion about Lazarus. Killing a dead man is hardly a crime. He shakes out his handkerchief, and places it elaborately over his nose. He holds it in place, moving only his eyes.

Slowly at first, as if at any moment they might change their minds, the Sanhedrin priests begin to cover their noses. Not all of them, but nearly enough. Caiaphas looks at Isaiah, who returns his gaze. Caiaphas does not look away until, with obvious reluctance, Isaiah gathers up the front of his tunic, and presses it over his nose.

'Kill him?' someone asks.

The priests with covered noses nod their heads.

'Kill him.'

'Kill Lazarus.'

4

The Bethany tombs blacken the afternoon brightness like broken teeth. Every stone door has been rolled back or smashed, leaving dark arched gaps the length of the sunny escarpment.

Resurrection is a wonderful idea. Everyone agrees on that, but only Lazarus has risen up. The stench of rotting bodies settles beneath the breeze from the desert. No wonder so many people in Bethany are covering their noses.

Lazarus flattens his back against a rock. Caiaphas had explained that the Temple guards were a precaution, for his own protection. They are stationed outside his door, so they missed his escape when he jumped from the roof. He is now alone, but feels someone is watching. Lizards skit like quick beige sticks. He should turn back. He can run to the village whenever he wants.

He jogs over to his tomb, hesitates at the open entrance, peers inside.

The rear wall is dark. A hand reaches out and Lazarus leaps backwards. A beggar with no teeth hustles towards him on one knee, smiling the red of his gums, but stops at Lazarus's footprints. He wipes up the dust and sucks his fingers.

'Get out! Go away!'

The man bows low. He touches his forehead to the ground. Lazarus is confused, but then it comes, the edge of euphoria he'd been expecting earlier. This man is a beggar, but he knows. Lazarus is the one.

Lazarus waves his arms and shouts out loud. He aims a kick that makes the beggar scuttle out of range. He picks up a stone and throws it, because he can.

'And don't come back!'

Then he plunges into the coolness of the tomb, where he listens to his living heart. Even here, where no one can see him, he feels he is being watched.

The tomb is part of the Bethany tour.

Follow the signs from the bus stop, walk past the gift shops and the house that is most likely not *The Home of Lazarus Martha and Mary*. Keep going. Further up the hill, in the lower half of a wall on the left-hand side of the road, is the narrow entrance to the tomb. There is no wheelchair access.

In Lazarus's time, this would have been a natural escarpment, but efforts over the centuries to keep his story alive have contributed the road and the al-Uzair mosque, built directly over the tomb. On either side of the mosque stand two churches, one Roman Catholic and the other Greek Orthodox. These additions are not relevant to the central experience.

The tomb remains a cave cut into the rock, a man-made underground space. It is one of the better tombs, with two levels, and when Mark Twain visited in 1869 he said, 'I had rather live in it than in any house of the town.'

Lazarus paid for an upper and a lower chamber. Seven steps descend steeply to the lower section, which is grey-black with the limited light that filters down. Lazarus steadies himself with a hand against the rough-cut wall. There is a strong smell of spices, of excess aloe and myrrh.

He waits for his eyes to adjust, tries to remember the events enacted in this place. He is searching for clues. Where did he go? How did he get back?

It is the smell that tugs at his heart. He closes his eyes to capture a memory as faint as the memory of a dream, but thinking doesn't feel as if it's going to work. Logic isn't the mechanism to grasp the truth of whatever happened here.

He sits on the lowest step, squeezing the bridge of his nose between his fingertips. No. Nothing.

He pinches some dirt from the floor, granulates it between his fingers. A noise. Someone has entered the upper chamber.

'Go away! I told you not to come back!'

Lazarus fixes his eyes on the entrance above. A shadow on the step, then the shape of a man. It dips at the waist and dives straight at him.

In Bethany, the tourist trade was founded in 33 CE, on the day visitors arrived in search of Lazarus.

Yanav organises the daytrippers into an eager bustle

of customers. 'Don't push at the back!'

This explains why Lazarus is alone and vulnerable at the tombs. Visitors to Bethany already have secondary attractions in the square, like the thrill of bartering for Lazarus's blood.

'Drink it as it is!' Yanav suggests. He makes his pitch while holding a clear vial of blood to the light. 'Or make a compress to wrap an injury. Drip it onto salt or sugar and feed it to your children! I promise you, the blood of Lazarus will keep them safe.'

Or if they can't be tempted by blood, Yanav has a stock of recent fingernails. He can vouch that he was personally responsible for cutting a supply of hair from the head of Lazarus himself.

'Burn it in the rooms of the dying. Bring solace and some extra days to those who you do love.'

Lydia has enough memories without buying offcuts from his body. She is desperate to see how Lazarus has changed. An experience like this will have changed him, and she is prepared for the worst, for the Sholem Asch expectation of a contented Lazarus with 'the wise, gentle smile of one who had penetrated all secrets and had come through to peace, the smile of one who had looked into the face of Death, and conquered him' (*The Nazarene*).

If Lazarus has solved the ultimate mysteries then Lydia doubts that she'll be needed. They will never be together, she has already accepted that, but one last time she wants to see him for herself.

Baruch pins Lazarus face-down to the ground like an animal for branding. He presses the cold blade of his knife flat behind Lazarus's ear.

'Not again,' Lazarus grunts. He struggles but makes no progress. 'Yanav, get off me. You know I want to live.'

Baruch makes a fighter's calculation. Lazarus has lightweight bones, and not enough muscle to surprise him.

'What is beyond?' he hisses.

Lazarus stops moving. He doesn't recognise the voice.

'Lazarus, my friend, tell me what is beyond. If you do, I'll make the killing quick.'

'I don't know.' His voice is muffled by the inside flesh of his cheek crushed between his teeth. Baruch pulls his head up by the hair. 'If I knew I'd tell you.'

'Tell me, or you'll wish you stayed dead.'

'Wait! There is something!'

'What? What is there?'

'I don't know what. I can't remember. But there must be something, or I wouldn't be here.'

'You're a liar.'

'I'm not a liar.'

'You're a well-known liar. You say you came back from the dead.'

'I never said that.'

'And now what? You think you're going to live forever?'

Lazarus suddenly decides he's had enough. Sickness couldn't kill him. Yanav didn't drown him. The beggar bowed down before him. Whoever his attacker is, he is outrageously ignorant of destiny.

'What are you waiting for?' Lazarus says. 'Kill me. Find out how long I have to live.'

With the boy in the forest Baruch had fumbled his

knife, a basic error he wouldn't usually make. This time he's allowing Lazarus to speak. Nothing is as it was.

'How did you keep your scheme a secret?'

'Kill me.'

'Where did you hide the food?'

'You can't do it, can you? I frighten you.'

'I can do it. If you don't like it, just come back.' Baruch leans forward so that his lips are close to the heat of Lazarus's ear. 'God's wrath is coming. Here is god's wrath, today.'

The dagger jars loose from Baruch's hand, skitters across the floor. Lazarus twists himself free and scrambles away. He turns and sees his attacker flee up the stairs, then leaps towards the dagger, seizes it and jumps into a crouch. He points the blade at the new arrival on the far side of the tomb.

Cassius has his hands on his knees and is breathing hard. He puts up one hand.

'Lazarus, lay down the weapon. I'm arresting you in the name of the empire.'

5

1

In the Russian tradition, above all others, there is a yearning to know more about Lazarus. He is the patron saint of second chances, and his example ought to be instructive. There are times when everyone would like to start again.

In the novel *Crime and Punishment* (1866), by Fyodor Dostoyevsky, the student Raskolnikov kills an elderly woman with an axe. He is not instantly struck down by an avenging god, and is further disconcerted by his lack of remorse. He decides to visit his girlfriend Sonya, who is a prostitute, and on her chest of drawers he finds a bible ('an old one, second-hand, in a leather binding').

'"Where's the bit about Lazarus?" he asked suddenly... "Go, read it!"'

Sonya then reads to Raskolnikov from John 11, verses

1–44, finishing at *'Jesus said to them, "Take off the grave clothes and let him go."*

'"That's all there is about the raising of Lazarus," she whispered sternly and abruptly, and stood unmoving, turned away to one side, not daring to raise her eyes to him, as though she were embarrassed.'

That's all there is.

Sonya closes the book, but they both know there should be more. In the aftermath of his crime, Raskolnikov has turned to Lazarus, not to Jesus, because for Dostoyevsky the resurrection of Lazarus is 'the great and unprecedented miracle'. It promises hope to a true unbeliever, or would do if only more of the story survived. Yes, Lazarus came back to life, but what then, what happened to him next?

The biblical Lazarus fails to provide the guidance that Raskolnikov needs. 'All she [Sonya] could see was that he was horribly, infinitely unhappy.'

Raskolnikov is Lazarus, disconsolate and unsmiling, 'infinitely unhappy', surprised to be alive but uncertain what this life is for.

2

They tie his hands, loop a rope around the binding, then fix the rope to the saddle of a Roman horse. This is the second procession of the day from Bethany into Jerusalem, and the less well known of the two because the believers who tell the story of Holy Week are active in the city with Jesus.

'*Where I am, my servant also will be,*' Jesus is saying in the Temple at this precise moment. '*My father will honour the one who serves me*' (John 12: 26).

By the end of the week Jesus will have been arrested, imprisoned, beaten and executed. Even so, on this day in Jerusalem he is at liberty to travel and speak as he wishes. Both the Sanhedrin and now the Romans are preoccupied with Lazarus, who stumbles over trampled palm leaves littering the Jerusalem road. Every time he falters, the rope tugs him onward.

Lazarus, too, is followed by a crowd. The believers are with Jesus, so those who walk with Lazarus do not believe.

'If that's him, he's hardly worth it.'

'Jesus saved *one man* in the Jerusalem region.'

'And calls himself messiah.'

'Lazarus was his friend.'

'Isn't that always the way?'

'They cooked it up years ago.'

'And no one saw Lazarus die.'

They toss his name about like an unwanted gift: the malingerer Lazarus, the charlatan, the liar Lazarus of Nazareth. Inside the city walls, women lean out of windows. Men leave their work to catch a glimpse of him.

'They're taking him to the fortress.'

'The Romans have chosen Lazarus. They think he's the one.'

Children cower behind adult legs, and teenagers compete to look a dead man in the eye. Many hold their hands over their noses.

Lazarus and Jesus have overreached themselves. Nobody with any sense believes in resurrection. Dead is dead. They're Galileans too far from home, fake messiahs counterfeiting a special relationship with the Jewish god.

'They're the same as the rest of us.'

'No one escapes death.' On this point everyone can agree. 'And especially not Lazarus the overseer. He was always a bit strange. I never liked him.'

'Fear would be the wrong response,' Cassius says. 'Though to look at, you don't seem very frightened.'

Cassius polishes an apple, checks his reflected face in the skin. 'The Antonia Fortress is the safest place in Jerusalem. That's what we built it to be.'

Lazarus nods. Beside the door, he notices, is a small shrine to Minerva, goddess of victory. Beyond the door, for more pragmatic interventions, two Roman soldiers stand guard. 'You're going to kill me.'

Cassius replaces his apple in the fruit bowl which is the centrepiece of a low rectangular table. 'Help yourself,' he says. 'If you're hungry.'

Lazarus bumps his toes over the tiles in the mosaic floor. If he were dead, how would he know? He imagines he is dead, and it turns out the Romans have conquered everywhere, even the afterlife.

'If I'm dead you can't kill me. Therefore I have nothing to fear.'

'First things first.'

'So what comes first?'

Cassius clicks his fingers. One of the guards unties Lazarus's hands. The soldier tries not to touch him, treating Lazarus with the same caution as foreign novelties from previous campaigns. Lazarus is as unlikely as a crocodile, and possibly as treacherous.

'Stay by the door,' Cassius tells him.

No one wants to be alone with Lazarus, not even Cassius. Even without the alleged death, the rapid healing is against nature. If he can do this, they all think, what else can he do?

'I brought you here for your own protection.'

'I knew it. You're going to kill me.'

'That may not solve the problem. For example if you come back again. I've called for the garrison doctor. He will be with us shortly.'

Lazarus glances at the doorway. There wouldn't be soldiers guarding the doors of heaven, not even a Roman heaven, unless heaven wasn't safe for Romans. And then it wouldn't be heaven. He can't sustain this bravado. He is not dead, nor is he fearless. He is alive on earth in the Antonia Fortress, and he is frightened.

'If we do kill you we'll do it properly,' Cassius adds, sensing that at last his words are having an effect. He pushes on. 'Death the Roman way means crucifixion, and no one comes back from that.'

'Please. I haven't broken any laws. Not that I know of.'

'I was there at the tomb. I saw what happened.'

'So what did you see? Did I come back from the dead?'

'In some ways, for your sake, I hope so. If you're lying then the penalty for false witness is death.'

'The penalty for everything is death.'

'That's justice for you. We're going to check your physical condition. Take off all your clothes.'

3

The Lazarus resurrection, like other supernatural events in the Christian story, can enrage the scholastic mind. 'Higher Criticism' emerged in Germany in the eighteenth century, and the higher critics subjected the bible to the same objective analysis as other historical documents. Their aim was to establish the truth of biblical narratives.

David Friedrich Strauss (1808–74), who extended the work of Friedrich Schleiermacher (1768–1834) concluded that the Lazarus story was a 'myth'. In his highly influential *Life of Jesus* (1863), Ernest Renan considers it a fraud perpetrated by the disciples to grow the Christian community.

Cassius resists such intuitive umbrage, the equivalent of assuming that Lazarus smells. True and false are such primitive categories. He prefers to ask whether the raising of Lazarus can be useful.

In Bethany, a blue-eyed Bedouin lost in the crowd, Cassius had watched Jesus weep. Angry, uncomfortable, Jesus had called Lazarus out from his tomb. The incident had been compellingly staged.

Cassius will admit that Lazarus emerging from the darkness of the tomb, flapping and falling in his funeral rags, had been an unsettling spectacle. Not what he or anyone else had expected. It was unbelievable. He had flung his gourd of water to the ground, put his hands on his hips. This should not be allowed, not after he'd sent his briefing to Rome. He'd confirmed in writing that

Lazarus was dead, and claimed this as convincing proof of the weakness of Jesus. In Judaea, he reported, there was currently no identifiable threat.

He has now had a day and a half to subdue his indignation, to rationalise what he's seen and not to believe his eyes.

Cassius is no stranger to the divine. As a junior officer he'd once stood within twenty paces of the Emperor Tiberius in Rome. He will never come closer to a god on earth, but with the emperor it is easy to tell. He shines. He gives off light.

On this occasion Cassius has decided to be philosophical, in the manner of Cicero: 'For nothing can happen without cause; nothing happens that cannot happen, and when what was capable of happening has happened, it may not be interpreted as a miracle ... We therefore draw the conclusion: what was incapable of happening never happened, and what was capable of happening is not a miracle' (*De Divinatione* 2:28, 44 BCE).

Cassius is culturally in sympathy with Cicero's Roman approach: Lazarus may well have come back from the dead. Fine. Absorbed. One day Rome will discover how and why, even if in every time and place until that day the event will remain a mystery.

To kill him as the Sanhedrin wish to do is a wasted opportunity.

'I asked you to take off your clothes. I suggest you cooperate.'

What is worse than death?

Lazarus being sent to Rome as a trophy. This is the standard imperial response to awkward religious figures.

Humiliate the shaman. Lock him in a travelling cage, and parade him naked to Rome.

In the Forum the senators will titter behind their hands at the Jew back from the dead. They will keep him in reserve for an afternoon of applied theology at the Circus — god's chosen cadet against god's unblessed beasts. A dilemma to intrigue Caesar himself, if Lazarus is lucky.

But first the senators will ask him what is beyond.

If he fails to answer they will tire of him. Then they will torture him, to ensure he tells the truth. Reason permits deceit, and pain suppresses reason. Lazarus will not lie if his rational faculties are inhibited.

It is a simple question, Lazarus — tell us what is beyond.

They start with the flogging whip, or *flagellum*, made with straps of leather embedded with glass or nails. If this doesn't kill him, the torture can progress to more intricate equipment like the *equuleus*, the 'young horse'. Iron weights are involved, and a narrow customised bench.

In his *Lives of the Twelve Caesars* (119 CE) the historian Suetonius describes a first-century torture invented by Tiberius (14–37 CE), the emperor at this time. Tiberius would force his victims 'to drink a great quantity of wine, and presently tie their members with a lute string, that he might rack them at once with the girding of the string, and with the pressure of urine'.

Tiberius will be succeeded by Caligula, notorious for his use of flames and saws. It is at this stage that prisoners call for their mothers, then after that for their god.

If Lazarus insists on remaining silent, refusing even

under torture to share his experience of the beyond, the Romans will wash their hands and crucify him.

The agony will be worse than any illness. It may be worse than death.

Nothing can surprise Lazarus, not now. This is how he keeps himself calm. He reminds himself that anything can happen, good or bad. In which case, has he learned more than anyone else?

He is lying face-down on the floor, naked, his arms and legs spread in a star. Mosaic squares stipple his belly when he breathes. The doctor, a Greek with a long face, is examining the skin behind his ears.

'Turn over. Lie on your back.'

The doctor inspects Lazarus's gums, then thumbs up his eyelids.

'There's no smell, is there?' Cassius is leaning against a wall with his arms crossed.

'Mosquito bite. Inside of the left knee.'

'Is that significant?'

'He's not invulnerable. And look at his breathing. Like you and me he has to get air to his stomach. His liver has to move blood around the body.'

'Can he feel pain?'

The doctor pinches his ear, hard. Lazarus jerks away, covering his head. Cassius kicks him his clothes.

'The worst is over,' he says. He dismisses the doctor but not the guards at the door. 'Sit down, Lazarus. Eat an apple.'

While Lazarus dresses, Cassius taps the pads of his fingers against his lower lip, fleshing it out. 'I have one more question.'

185

They sit opposite each other. Lazarus takes an apple
and bites into it. His gums aren't perfect — he leaves an
imprint of blood on the exposed white flesh.

'You want to ask what is beyond, don't you?'

'No. I want to ask if your god makes mistakes. Roman
gods get it wrong all the time.'

The gods Cassius has known since childhood are
imperfect, omniscient but not all powerful — they give
fire to the titans and the titans are tricked by men. Jupiter
shrugs his shoulders. Life goes on.

'Earlier today Jesus arrived in Jerusalem on a donkey,
as prophesied in the Book of Zechariah. I'm a foreigner
and even I know that. There are other scriptures predict-
ing a messiah from the line of David who comes from
Nazareth. A star will shine brightly above his birthplace
in Bethlehem.'

Lazarus reaches for a second apple. They'd studied
the verses about the donkey back in Nazareth, and Jesus
knows his scriptures.

'Was there or was there not a star over Bethlehem
when you were born?'

'There was a star over every baby born in the village
at that time.'

'Yes,' Cassius says. 'But all of them except you and
Jesus are dead. You too came into Jerusalem on a donkey,
when you went to the Bethesda pool.'

Lazarus swallows his mouthful of apple. 'I'm the son
of a mason from Galilee. I was born in Bethlehem and
fled with my family into Egypt.'

'Exactly. You're everything the scriptures said you
would be.' Cassius scratches the skin at the side of his eye.
'And doesn't the messiah come back from the dead?'

4

Everything is about Jesus these days, and has been for two thousand years.

It is Sunday night, one day after the resurrection of Lazarus, at the start of what has come to be known as Holy Week. During the next seven days Jesus will preach and make promises. He will eventually get himself arrested, tried, crucified and buried, and on the third day he will rise again to judge the quick and the dead.

Lazarus is a precondition for all these events, because the raising of Lazarus inspires the believers who accompany the triumphal entry into Jerusalem. This in turn explains why neither the Sanhedrin nor the Romans can take immediate action against Jesus – *'yet they could not find any way to do it, because all the people hung on his words'* (Luke 19: 48). Without Lazarus, Jesus would never have lasted until Friday.

As it is, his exact movements between now and then are disputed. For several days Jesus circulates freely while nothing is heard of his friend. The dramatic events towards the end of the week, starting with Thursday night's arrest in the Garden of Gethsemane, tend to eclipse the days that come before.

At some point, probably on the Monday, Jesus *'entered the temple area and began driving out those who were buying and selling there. He overturned the tables of the moneychangers and the benches of those selling doves'* (Mark 11: 15).

Otherwise, across the four canonical gospels, events

remain vague until Thursday. Jesus spends Monday to Wednesday *'teaching in the Temple'* (Luke 21: 37). He is sighted at Bethany (Mark 11: 11) and on the Mount of Olives (Luke 21: 37), which suggests he can move in and out of Jerusalem as he pleases. This is consistent in all four gospels, and his freedom of movement is not entirely explained by the safety-in-numbers aspect of a supportive crowd (Luke 19: 48).

Lazarus is the answer. Two thousand years of Jesus has obscured the renown of Lazarus. The Romans have one of the friends safe, so they are less concerned about the other. Jesus is at large in the city because Lazarus is imprisoned in the fortress.

'Are you the king of the Jews?'

'I'm an overseer of Temple livestock.'

'Good,' Cassius says. 'I don't think we have a problem with that.'

'I cast a shadow,' Lazarus adds. 'When I get sick I die.'

The great fear in Jerusalem at this time is that any claimant king of the Jews will disrupt the peace between Rome and occupied Judaea. Cassius has a plan, based on the accepted principle that a messiah should aim to do some good. Instead of adding to the tension, a messiah should start by easing political relationships.

'You're betrothed to marry the daughter of a senior Sanhedrin priest.'

'How would you know that?'

'Imagine how stable this country could be if a provincial messiah married into the Sanhedrin with the blessing of the Romans. Every angle is covered — all would be sweetness and light. You and I should make a visit to Isaiah, your prospective father-in-law.'

'I don't think messiahs get married.'

'Messiahs can do whatever god ordains.'

Cassius is thinking ahead, already composing his report to Rome, but Lazarus is wilfully slow. 'You don't have a choice,' Cassius says. 'Look where you are now. This is your destiny.'

'Because you say so?'

'Or god does. One or the other. Whichever you prefer – both at the same time.'

'That doesn't sound right.'

The consuls in Rome are waiting for positive news, and for Cassius to explain his mistakes. 'No? Then perhaps you should experience the alternative.'

The next confirmed sighting of Lazarus is at the crucifixion of Jesus.

Karel Čapek, who earlier enjoyed his joke about Lazarus dying from a chill, is equally flippant about the crucifixion. Lazarus is resting in Bethany (after the stress of recent events) when he and his sisters hear news of the imprisonment of Jesus. Martha and Mary are confident that Jesus in his turn will be saved by a miracle.

The intervention, they imagine, will come in human form. Jesus will be rescued by those who owe him a debt – the nobleman from Capernaum, the man who picked up his mat and walked, the blind man who now can see. An army of five thousand fed when hungry will descend on Jerusalem to deliver Jesus from harm. Lazarus will be their leader.

Yes, he'd like that very much, only he hasn't been

well: 'I don't feel up to all this — the journey, the excitement ... I should so much have liked to go.'

Čapek's story is funny because absurd. Lazarus has to be present at the crucifixion. Where else would he be? The idea of his absence is laughable.

There are thousands of figurative representations of the passion and death of Jesus, and in most of the classic images a clean-shaven witness can be found in the keening crowd. From Fra Angelico in 1420 to Max Ernst in 1913, Lazarus is there. Look at a Tintoretto or a Rubens, or any of the masters of the Dutch school. Lazarus attends the crucifixion of Jesus, often in a favoured position at the front left portion of the canvas.

On Friday at midday, Lazarus will be with Jesus on the hill at Golgotha. By that time Lazarus, too, like his sisters in the story by Karel Čapek, will believe he can save his friend.

Between the Sunday and Thursday of Holy Week, like the bible itself, Lazarus loses track of time.

His cell in the Antonia Fortress is a narrow room three floors above the level of the street. Lazarus stands on the end of his bed to look through the window high in the wall. A half-starved man might squirm his way through, but the outside walls offer no obvious handholds.

In the street below a cart rolls by. It is filled with straw, heading for the Temple stockyards. The street is very far down. Lazarus would have to be incredibly lucky not to kill himself. Another hay cart passes, and stops directly beneath the window. Lazarus looks down on the driver's head, and the driver has no idea he's there.

Lazarus sits on the bed, which is as long as the cell and half as wide. At regular intervals faces peer through the barred opening in the door. He sits on his hands. At least he has his health.

He sleeps.

Cassius bangs on the door. Lazarus wakes up.

'I thought you were dead.'

'I was sleeping.'

It is dark. Cassius goes away. Lazarus sits and watches a shiny black cockroach take its chances across the floor. It wants to eat and reproduce and be king of all the cockroaches. Lazarus steps on it.

He lifts his foot, and waits for the cockroach to come back to life. It does so. Several times. As long as he doesn't step on it too hard.

He flops back on the bed, one arm trailing off the side. He counts the times Jesus has ruined his life.

5

Depression is one way in which death shows its strength. Some of the blackness of the tomb remains, and it is the darkness Lazarus can't endure. The darkness and enclosed spaces and time going by.

Does Jesus know where he is? And had he always known it would come to this, even as a child, when they ran free in the hills above Nazareth?

Lazarus is increasingly sure he's alive, truly alive, and with every hour that passes it is harder to believe he died. If he'd died, genuinely, then he'd still be dead. He wouldn't be sighing at the sorrow of life in a cramped Roman cell.

He bites his lip until it bleeds. Later, he plucks out a clutch of eyelashes. He doesn't believe in resurrection. It wasn't death that he'd experienced, but some unnatural state of suspension, which Jesus has inflicted upon him.

If he knows. If Jesus has always known.

When Amos drowned he knew, and when Lazarus left Nazareth for Bethany. He knew that selling sheep to the Temple was an ill-omened business, and that Lazarus would never marry or return to the Galilee, would fall sick and die and come back to life and be imprisoned in the Antonia Fortress. This was always the shape his life was going to take.

The white days of their Nazareth childhood tilt and catch a different light. They have a dark underside and make unwelcome shadows: there is no coincidence and there is no luck. The story of Lazarus is a device in the life of Jesus.

Lazarus is overcome with self-pity. That's right, Lazarus, it isn't fair. Fall on your knees and blub. Whine and cry. Wish that you were dead.

He crawls across the cell and plants his forehead flush against the rough plastered wall. It is a long time since he prayed, and in the past he was always relieved when no one answered. It was a solace to know that he was on his own, and that whatever happened was up to him.

Now he genuinely hopes to be heard, but has forgotten how to do it. Lazarus has mislaid his certainty about what he wants, or what is worth having.

He curls up on the floor and puts his hands flat between his thighs. The mosquito bite on his knee is healing, life's miracle at work. His body is renewing itself for no obvious reason, and he grieves for his over-laid childhood. He grieves for his vanished future and his poor, deserted sisters. He grieves his own ugly death, and his plans that have come to nothing.

Lazarus weeps.

Inside Isaiah's house, the tables and chairs are so neatly arranged it is clear that visitors are barely welcome. There is a background hush of shuffling, of women taking up position to eavesdrop.

'Lazarus would have liked to be here,' Cassius says, 'but he is temporarily indisposed. He wanted to apologise for his unseemly behaviour at the betrothal. I know it's no excuse, but at the time he wasn't feeling well.'

'I'm honoured that a Roman official should take an interest.'

Isaiah has an urgent meeting with the Sanhedrin. He is in full priest's regalia but he bows nevertheless. Not so deeply that his eyes leave Cassius. 'If you've come about Jesus, we priests in Jerusalem know where he's hiding. The situation is under control.'

Cassius nods. Religion doesn't have to cause trouble, not when managed correctly.

'We'll take care of Jesus, I promise,' Isaiah says. 'We don't approve of civic disturbances of any kind.'

'That's why I'm here. I want to persuade you to look ahead, take a broader view. Lazarus too has his follow-ers. He doesn't make promises he can't keep – no pulling down the Temple and rebuilding it in three days. Give Lazarus a second chance.'

'Too late. We already have plans for Lazarus.'

'Let him marry Saloma, for the good of everyone involved.'

'Lazarus died. That normally annuls any betrothal.'

'Is that why you voted for the Sicarii to intervene? Or was it just to free Saloma from a marriage contract?'

'That wasn't my decision. Every member of the Sanhedrin was there.'

'As well as some Roman spies. Call off the assassin. Let Lazarus live.'

'I can't do that.'

'Then Lazarus can't heal your daughter.'

Isaiah takes a step forward, eyes narrowed. 'Of course he can't. Nobody can. She's beyond help.'

'Lazarus came back from the dead,' Cassius says, meeting Isaiah's gaze. 'What more does a messiah have to do?'

'Heal the innocent. Yes. We all know that. Me, you, Jesus and every Judaean from here to kingdom come. Healing should be any messiah's first and most important task '

For twenty-five years Isaiah has accepted god's gift of a daughter who can't keep food in her mouth. She can be treated for months at a time with no visible improvement to her leg, and healers have proved worse than useless. Yanav gave her a drink of leaves and seawater while three miles away the dead came back to life. Why is his love and devotion unrewarded?

'Agree to the marriage,' Cassius says. 'You'll see what Lazarus can do.'

*

194

On Thursday morning, after four days and nights in a Roman cell, Lazarus wakes up with the hard weight of his head on one ear, and hears the march of approaching soldiers. He startles upright, and the footsteps go quiet. He lies down again and listens, crunch, crunch, but the sandals are not coming closer. It is the sound of the pulse in his neck, a stomping at the back of his jaw.

He decides to kill himself, as an act of revenge.

He sits upright, rubs his fingers over his cheeks and chin, but his deadly razor is back in the house in Bethany. He hasn't shaved for eight days, including being dead, and he'll soon look like a believer in god. The lie is too much to bear.

He stands on the end of the bed. His shoulders are level with the sill of the window. If he can get his head through, and then his shoulders, he knows the rest of him will follow. He has been ill. The muscles in his upper body are not what they were. Everything is ordained.

He pulls himself up, turns his head sideways and hauls his shoulders through. His body scrapes halfway out before his hands confirm no holds on either side of the outside wall. Directly below him a cart full of straw rolls by. It does not stop beneath the window.

He is stuck head-first out of a window on the third floor of the Antonia Fortress. His lower legs are braced against the ceiling to keep him in, and there is a fatal drop to the cobbles of the street below. He is not a favoured son of god. That would be a terrible misjudgement to make.

Now is the time. He angles his body downwards and straightens his legs. He slips through the window, turns in the air, his legs coming over behind him. The last thing he sees, looking above, is the empty sky over Israel.

It is cloudless, a clear blue eye.

The crucifixion of Jesus is designed to attract attention. It says Look at Me, in direct competition with the resurrection of Lazarus. Jesus needs to outshine the great and unprecedented miracle, the raising of Lazarus from the dead. If he fails to do so, there may be uncertainty about which is the main event.

Lazarus is the latest in a series of resurrections that viewed together look like experiments: Lazarus, the son of the widow of Nain, and before that the daughter of Jairus in Capernaum. All three are trial resurrections, prototypes. Jesus is testing the limits of the form.

Years earlier, on the shore of the lake in Galilee, Jesus had learned that siblings should be spared. No one should have to suffer, like Lazarus, the death of a brother or sister. The daughter of Jairus, who will die, is therefore an only child. Jesus then discovers, because she is a daughter, that grief is equally unbearable for a father.

For his next attempt, in the village of Nain, he picks an only child whose mother is a widow. No brothers, no fathers. The widow has experience of death, but her suffering too is astonishing. The outright grief of the parent confuses the value of the resurrection, because if Jesus can bring children back to life, it would be kinder to save them before they die.

Jesus lacks the human instinct. He tries again.

Lazarus is next, and as Jesus learns compassion he improves the basic set-up. Lazarus is not a child. His

196

parents will not suffer. Resurrection is going to damage the fewest number of people if it involves an unmarried adult who has lost his parents and has no children.

Martha and Mary can't be helped. No one is entirely alone, and like the widow of Nain the sisters have experience of death. They already know what it's like to lose a brother. Also, they have each other. God can't think of everything.

By this stage Jesus has understood that Lazarus needs to be buried. In the two previous resurrections, life had returned too soon, and witnesses will take every opportunity to disbelieve. If the bodies aren't buried, a faked death or deep trance lingers as a possibility. Jesus corrects this flaw with Lazarus. His friend is dead four days, buried for two. Martha mentions the smell.

Lazarus is by far the best designed of the three trial resurrections, though room for improvement remains. He is called from the tomb in public, but the hardened cynics and Sadducees still insist doggedly that nobody saw him die.

Jesus registers this objection. He intends to stage an undeniably public death.

Lazarus lands on his back in a cart of straw.

Immediately he lands, the cart jolts and starts moving forward.

His body is unscathed. He wipes the straw out of his eyes and mouth. The cart, carrying feed for the sacrificial animals, will be heading for the Temple. Jesus spends his days at the Temple, and the two men are yet to sit and talk, but Lazarus refuses to be pushed around like this. If he can't kill himself he'll save himself, he alone, without the help of Jesus. He can be his own saviour, correct his own mistakes.

Saloma first. He'll apologise for the charade of their betrothal, and set her free. Then Lydia.

He climbs out of the moving cart, and takes shelter in the shadow of a wall. No one has seen him. He walks, then runs, in the opposite direction to the Temple entrance and Jesus.

At Isaiah's house, they are expecting him.

'How can that be? How did you know I was coming?'

'A Roman called Cassius claims you can help us.'

'Cassius didn't send me. I wanted to talk about Saloma.'

'We know.'

In an upper room, with lamps alight, Isaiah's women have attempted to soften the atmosphere — they don't have Lydia's experience. Saloma is overdressed and areas of the uncovered wall make harsh reflections from the flames. She is lying in a nest of cushions. Her bare feet twitch in terror. She whimpers, turns to the wall and buries her face in her arms.

Isaiah and his wife accompany Lazarus to the room. After four days in a Roman cell he stinks of sweat but neither of them cover their noses.

'Signs and wonders,' Isaiah says, gesturing towards Saloma in the corner. 'Now is your chance to make me believe.'

'That isn't why I came. I wanted to tell you we can't get married.'

'You are betrothed,' her mother says.

Isaiah nods. 'By law you can touch my daughter.'

Lazarus feels the strength of their longing. They

want so much to believe that Lazarus, even against their instincts, is true. He kneels beside Saloma and she bangs her head against the wall. Then she covers her ears with a blanket. He reaches out towards her, stops, feels the heat from her hunched shoulders on his hand.

'Heal her!' Isaiah desperately wants Cassius to be right. Lazarus has died and is now alive and he will touch Saloma and through this miraculous contact Saloma will be healed. 'You or Jesus, I don't care which. Come on, Lazarus. Do some work.'

Lazarus rocks back and stands up. He has not touched Saloma. He realises, possibly for the first time, that he is not the equal of Jesus.

'I'm not a healer.'

'You didn't even try.'

'You'd have to ask Jesus,' Lazarus says. 'And probably believe in him too.'

Isaiah flares his nostrils. 'That's very convenient, because Jesus has gone into hiding. Somewhere in the Lower City, with the thieves and prostitutes. How can he help if we don't know where he is?'

'I'll find him for you. I used to know my way around.'

6

1

Have you found Jesus?

This is what they ask when they come to the door. Christ on earth is elusive. If he had never gone missing, we'd know where he was.

The hide-and-seek of the Christian Jesus has its origins in Holy Week, because the bible never commits to his exact whereabouts. In the Gospel of Mark, Jesus spends Sunday night in Bethany. There is no mention of Lazarus, because Lazarus is imprisoned in the Antonia Fortress. Jesus uses Bethany as his base until Wednesday morning, and then he stays in Jerusalem.

His movements are kept secret intentionally, and the theologian Marcus Borg cites Judas Iscariot as the reason: 'By reporting that Jesus sent two disciples to make clandestine arrangements for the Passover meal, Mark has Jesus withhold from Judas its precise location, so that Judas cannot tell the authorities where to find Jesus during the meal.'

The instructions given by Jesus suggest a network of contacts attuned to preconceived signals and coded phrases: *'Go into the city, and a man carrying a jar of water will meet you; follow him, and wherever he enters, say to the owner of the house, "The Teacher asks, Where is my guest room where I may eat the Passover with my disciples?" He will show you a large room upstairs, furnished and ready. Make preparations for us there'* (Mark 14: 13–15).

Lazarus has been separated from Jesus for many years, living far away in Bethany. He has been sick, and he died. On the Thursday, after his escape from the Antonia, Lazarus can know none of the prearranged signals. He like everyone else has to search for the son of god, and for the same reason: if he finds Jesus, Jesus may have the answers. Why should Lazarus be alive? What is the purpose of his existence? He wants a second chance at asking what his second chance is for.

His first task is to infiltrate the Jesus network in the Lower City. He knows someone who should be able to help.

2

Lazarus launches himself up the ladder two rungs at a time, and bursts into Lydia's attic. The lamps are flickering but Lydia is not at home.

Baruch slams the trapdoor shut.

'Make yourself comfortable. No charge.'

For the first time Lazarus gets a clear view of the assassin sent to kill him. He is dark, heavy, an offence against Lydia's careful version of heaven.

Lazarus recoils and trips over a cushion. He has a soft landing. He looks desperately for a weapon, grabs a rounded flask of perfume and holds it ready. 'What have you done with Lydia?'

'She hasn't been here since Saturday. Remember Saturday? You came back from the dead.'

Baruch feints one way but moves the other, easily deflects the bottle that Lazarus throws at him. He catches Lazarus by the arm and tumbles him into the cushions, jamming his elbow into his side. He reaches round Lazarus's neck, and grips him by the jaw. He could break him like a chicken.

'If I wanted to kill you you'd be dead, several times over. The Sanhedrin priests have changed their plan. I've been ordered to leave you be.'

Lazarus tastes the salt sweat from Baruch's palm. He can feel the creak of his bones about to break.

'They're aiming for Jesus instead. He shouldn't have upset the tables of the moneychangers. By doing that, he saved your life.'

Baruch pats Lazarus twice on the cheek, then releases him. 'I should say he saved your life again. Twice in a week. Some friend.'

Lazarus rubs blood back into his arms. 'If you're not going to kill me, what do you want?'

'Very little. Hardly anything. Just one thing. It's about last week, and where you went. I want to know if there's anyone waiting.'

In the tomb Baruch had been nervous, uncertain. Now that he's had time to think, he is terrified. He has always sincerely believed that when his victims died they were dead.

'Remember I could have killed you. So tell me. Are they waiting? It's not as though I make the decisions. I just do the killing.'

Lazarus says: 'I'm looking for Jesus. Do you know where he is?'

'Maybe they'll forgive me. In the Sicarii our training starts at seven years old. I never had any choice.'

'Help me find Jesus. I know you can do that.'

Baruch looks up sharply. 'Are you after the money?'

'What money?'

'The priests have set money aside, as a reward for whoever brings him in. Someone will claim it sooner or later.'

'But not you?'

'I'm a killer. That's what I do. I'm not an informer.'

'So you do know where he is?'

'I know where he was last seen. Tell me what I can expect on the other side.'

Lazarus stares into the assassin's frightened, unblinking eyes. In return for news about Jesus, he gives Baruch what he wants.

Cassius needs five or six men, no more, but he is out of the habit of asking permission.

'You were wrong about Jesus,' the governor says. He is a balding, middle-aged administrator. Every inconvenience is a direct assault on the authorised idleness he'd been promised. 'You reported in writing both to me and to Rome that Jesus couldn't gather a following in Jerusalem. You captured Lazarus but you let him escape.'

The governor is not impressed. He has cancelled all leave, and Cassius will not be allocated even one soldier to develop his hunches about Lazarus. Passover is a volatile festival. It reminds the Judaeans that they're expecting a messiah and the end of the world, but there will be no end of the world, not with Romans in charge.

'Why have we lost sight of Jesus? What do your spies think they're doing?'

The spies have been keeping Cassius informed about the movements of Lazarus. After his escape from the fortress Lazarus had been seen leaving Isaiah's house, and then later he was spotted in the Lower City. The spies will not, however, lay a hand on him. They know where he's been.

'I can pick up Lazarus, but I need those legionnaires.'

'Why didn't you flog him? The soldiers stay here in barracks. Jesus is the one we want.'

Cassius goes to the marketplace below the west wall, where Yanav is continuing his brisk business in genuine Lazarus relics.

'Where is he?'

'Which one?'

'Either. Both.'

'Maybe in the same place,' Yanav says. 'Lazarus is searching, like everyone else.'

'And where exactly is he looking? Take an educated guess.'

'If I were him, I'd start where Jesus was last seen. Bethany. Anywhere else is speculation.'

Cassius thinks: what would Lazarus do? He'd be smart, and travel at dusk, to attract the least attention. Cassius decides to get ahead of him. He crosses the Kidron stream, alone, and settles down behind a shrivelled fig tree. He is hidden from the road and he waits. Birds return to their nests, and night falls heavily on the last of the day, squeezing out a final grey layer of light.

Lazarus turns the corner. He walks briskly, like someone who knows he's being watched.

Cassius follows him, up the gravelled tracks through the uneven groves of the Mount of Olives. Silver leaves twitch green and grey in the twilight. Lazarus can make this journey in his sleep, but as the night blackens, dark as the inside of a sack, Cassius becomes confused. He trips over a tree root and skins his hands. He scrambles upright, but the incline is against him and he bangs his knee. It feels as if the whole world is against him.

He can't keep up, nor see where he's going. He sits down, and breathes deeply, because regular breathing is good for logical thought.

'Yaaaah!'

Shouting aloud also helps. He rubs the heels of his hands into his eyes, then pushes the skin of his forehead towards his hairline. He lets go and becomes himself again. Organise, he thinks. Fetch a horse, wait for some moonlight to ride by.

He turns back towards the city – saving people is harder than he'd expected, but he isn't giving up. If Lazarus can be persuaded to cooperate, then nobody will have to die.

3

At first, Martha doesn't recognise him. The last time she saw her brother he was tied to a rope being dragged away by Romans. She spent hours grieving him a second time, and then Jesus returned from Jerusalem. He calmed her, and almost convinced her that everything could turn out well.

His beard has grown. She mistakes him for Jesus, but then the moon comes out and there he is, Lazarus her brother, alive yet again.

Before his death, Martha hadn't cried in thirty years. Now she cries every day. Tears come as she rushes towards him, as she pulls at him and holds him close. She slaps her wet cheek against his neck, his shoulder, then holds him at arm's length to check his face.

'What about the Romans? Where are they?'

'Where they always are. What are you doing outside?'

The house, the *Home of Lazarus Martha and Mary*, is pale in the moonlight. Beside the bay tree in the courtyard a fire is snapping, and Martha had been sweeping embers back towards the flames. Lazarus wants a closer look, and with his first step he kicks a chip of crockery across the yard.

'We're burning everything,' Martha says. 'Every object you ever touched. The priests ruled the house was unclean, defiled by contact with the dead. One of the younger ones made me collect the kindling.'

'I heard Jesus was here. After I was taken by the Romans.'

'He said it didn't matter, that we'd soon forget. They're only possessions.'

Lazarus sees the remains of his razor near the base of the fire, the copper blade twisted and blackened.

'The rugs,' Martha says. 'Gone. The blankets we carried from Galilee.'

Martha has saved what she can for everyday use. Otherwise their life is in ashes: clothes, bedding, the bolt of silk that Mary and Martha were keeping for weddings never destined to happen. 'Jesus is probably right. You can't take it with you.'

'Is he here now?'

'Not since yesterday.'

'So you've had to do this on your own?'

'Not quite,' Martha says. 'I've had help.'

'Mary came back? I'm glad.'

'Not Mary. Jesus sent someone from the city.'

A woman backs out of the house carrying a tray with an engraved brass teapot and matching goblets. She turns, and Lydia recognises him immediately, despite his beard, his fatigue, the darkness and his surprise at seeing her in the doorway.

'Look who's back from the dead.' She smiles. 'Not too bad, considering. I heard you had a green head.'

Cassius can predict the future. He decides what Rome needs and then makes it happen.

Lazarus will be the Roman client messiah. Not Jesus. Lazarus will neutralise the threat posed by Jesus, or any other impostor, and consolidate peace in the region for decades to come. Cassius has it all mapped out. Judaeans are infected with too much hope for god, and Lazarus can be the next affliction, a messiah who is not the king of the Jews and who doesn't act provocatively during major religious festivals.

The Church of Lazarus Christ will not change the way things are, not too much. It favours law and order, naturally, and is tolerant of gods and religions from elsewhere. Lazarus himself will reward the ambitious and punish the lazy, but no one should give up everything they own to follow him. Stay at home. Respect property and stability, relax. The world is not approaching an end and these are not the last days before a decisive battle between light and darkness.

In fact, life tomorrow will be much the same as it is today. This is one of Rome's most important unstated objectives. Tomorrow will be the same as today, if not slightly better.

Cassius reaches the Fortress to find that the Antonia horses have been transferred to the stables at the Praetorium. He curses and changes direction. The governor is wrong to be anxious: religion has to be managed, not repressed. It can distract the people from thoughts of rebellion, keep the children out of trouble and men in bed with their wives.

Lazarus will be the son of god, and Lazarus will belong to Rome.

They eat with Absalom's family in Absalom's house. Lazarus is impatient to get back to Jerusalem, to continue his search for Jesus.

'What about the Romans?' Martha asks.

'They're more likely to find me here than in the city.'

'Sit down,' Absalom says. 'You don't need to run. Jesus brought you back and he knows what he's doing.'

Lazarus is also hungry, and this is the Passover meal of roasted lamb and matzoh to celebrate the deliverance from Egypt. He'll eat quickly, he says, and then he'll go. He sits cross-legged on the floor between Lydia and Martha, and eats as he has eaten every day this week: each meal could be his last.

Absalom is describing the Passover meals prepared by his mother, and Lazarus sees him for what he is, a kindly old man with expressive eyebrows who talks to the dead at night.

'I asked her if she noticed your visit. She didn't reply. Perhaps you saw her and she didn't see you?'

'Yes,' Lazarus replies. 'That must be it. Don't worry. Your mother is there like everyone else. They are waiting for us.'

He had said the same to Baruch. What Baruch now does with that knowledge is up to him, but on balance as he eats Lazarus decides that life after death, specifically his own, has been revealed for the greater good. Absalom, for example, wants to hear that his mother exists. He can resist asking whether she has been judged, or if the afterlife is overcrowded or up or down or dark or light. His mother still is, which is all he needed to know.

Absolom calls for wine. 'To absent friends,' he says, and they drink.

Lazarus is amazed by the changes since he was last in Bethany. Absalom's serenity extends to sharing his table with Lydia, because Jesus suggested he should. Jesus, it seems, is a calming influence: Martha is resigned to the destruction of their home.

209

'Life is short,' she shrugs. 'We worked hard. We saved money. Jesus has a different idea of what's important.'

'Which he hasn't yet shared with me.'

Lydia laughs. 'Same old Lazarus. Thinner, especially in the face, but still a little jealous.'

There is something radiant about the others that Lazarus envies. It is like the reverse of death. A light has been ignited in them, or like flowers in springtime first one then another of them blooms. They have opened up to belief, poc, to new possibilities.

Lazarus feels excluded from this unexpected optimism. They have changed in his absence, as if they know more about Jesus than he does. Even now, he wants to defend the uniqueness of his childhood friendship.

'I came to find Jesus,' he reminds them.

'You should definitely talk to him,' Lydia agrees. 'It would help.'

'That depends,' Martha says. 'Jesus doesn't want to hear him complaining.'

'It's not for me. It's for Isaiah. He thinks Jesus can heal Saloma.'

'Oh Lazarus, you can do better than that. Start by being honest with yourself.'

'Jesus is in danger. The assassin told me the priests have offered money to anyone who betrays him.'

'Yes.' Lydia says. 'We know.' She looks at him evenly. 'The Romans are chasing you. The Sicarii may decide to kill you. You're trapped in a rotten betrothal and you're oblivious to the people who love you. We understand why you're looking for Jesus.'

Hooves clatter in the square. A single rider dismounts,

and they listen to footsteps heading away from them, in the direction of Lazarus's house.

'Quick. Find me somewhere to hide.'

4

On the Jesus side of the story, Thursday is also an eventful evening. While Lazarus is eating in Bethany, the disciples and Jesus are preparing themselves for what will turn out to be the last supper they share together. The meal will be eaten in the upstairs room of a Jerusalem inn. The location is secret, but archaeologists suggest a site close to the Siloam pool in the poorer Lower City.

In first-century Palestine the last supper would not have been prepared or served by men. The lamb and the bowls of bitter herbs would have been sent up from the inn below. Mary arranges them on the table. She places the bread and pours the wine.

When the meal finishes, Jesus will leave the inn. He and the disciples will walk to the Mount of Olives. No one knows exactly why. It may be, only hours before his arrest, that Jesus suddenly craves the open air, among olive trees, and a hillside where he can see and hear what the ancients saw and heard before him. He was brought up in Nazareth. He prefers outdoor spaces where simple truths remain true: fire and food, shelter and sleep, man and beast.

Or he may decide to leave Jerusalem at the suggestion of Judas Iscariot, after a discussion about the security of the upstairs room. Judas is wary of making accusations, but he suspects Mary of a loose tongue. He'd followed her to the market earlier that day, and when out buying bread she spoke with her sister Martha.

Or the reason Jesus leaves the inn is simpler still: no one can sleep through the noise of Passover celebrations rising from the room below.

There is another possibility. Jesus knows that Lazarus will set out from Bethany and make his way to the inn. Jesus always knows, and Lazarus must not become involved until the time is right. He is needed tomorrow, in the fading light, on the inevitable Hill of Skulls.

Cassius throws back the curtain covering the doorway.

'I know he's here.'

Absalom feels strong, less afraid of death. One week has changed everything. 'He went back to Jerusalem.'

'Lazarus, not Jesus. I don't mean either of them any harm, I promise.' Cassius holds out his arms. 'I'm alone. I came to find Lazarus. He's an extraordinary person who's had an exceptional experience.'

'You've got the wrong man.'

'I don't think I have.'

'I think you have,' Lazarus says. He steps into the room from the storage area where he'd tried to hide. With one foot in a wooden bucket, he'd felt absurd. Besides, Cassius was alone.

Lazarus sits down. He makes a point of looking into his bowl, pushes some bones over in search of meat.

'Look at me sitting quietly here among friends. No thunderbolts, no lightning. Let's not pretend. I am not the one.'

'Humility is exactly what I'd expect. You came back from the dead.'

'We're glad Lazarus is with us,' Martha says. 'Of course we are. But we give our thanks and praise to Jesus. When you meet him, you'll see why.'

'I've met Lazarus.'

'Yes,' Lazarus says. 'In the Antonia Fortress. What's changed?'

'I've changed. Your escape from the Antonia was miraculous.'

'I'm just lucky. And you're outnumbered. Apart from you and me everyone in this room believes in Jesus.'

'Jesus is finished. One of the disciples betrayed him. I heard it from an informer in the Temple guards.'

He has their full attention.

'Is that true? How can we warn him of the danger?'

'You can't. Not unless you know where he's hiding.'

There is no time to lose. They leave Bethany as Jesus in Jerusalem says: *'Take and eat; this is my body'* (Matthew 26: 26).

Cassius ties up the horse. He wants to blend in, like the *speculatore* he is, a pedestrian like Absalom and Lydia interested only in following Martha towards Jerusalem. They're going to save the friend of Lazarus, and Martha knows from Mary where to find him.

'Drink from it, all of you' (Matthew 26: 27).

Lazarus keeps an eye on Cassius, and on the facts. He does seem to be acting alone but Romans can't be trusted. Lazarus does not let Cassius out of his sight.

Martha leads them across the Kidron stream and takes the most direct route to the inn, through the

213

Siloam Gate. As Lazarus enters the south of the city Jesus leaves it to the east, taking the Sheep Gate for a short walk to the Garden of Gethsemane.

In the narrow alleys of the Lower City, cats fight and midnight washwater is launched from upstairs windows. Martha stops outside a popular inn, at the foot of a wooden staircase.

'Cassius goes first,' Lazarus says. He is learning from his mistakes – sometimes it is wiser to hang back, and to be the one who follows.

Cassius climbs the stairs, tries the handle of the door. It is locked. He puts his ear against the wood, knocks. 'It's Lazarus. We've come from Bethany. Let us in.'

A key turns in the lock. Mary opens the door.

The room itself is *furnished and ready* (Mark 14: 15), as famously depicted by Leonardo da Vinci in *The Last Supper* (1497). There are three rectangular windows in the far wall, looking out now on festive Passover lamps, and open to snatches of traditional song spilling through the night. Rectangular drapes hang from the side walls, and the ceiling is a boxed shape of beams.

'They didn't tell me where,' Mary says. 'But it's late. I don't expect they'll be long.'

Mary has witnessed the covenant of the bread and wine, and it hasn't surprised her to open the door to Martha and Lazarus. Their lives have been determined by Jesus since the day Lazarus first had a headache.

'Are you hungry?'

'We've eaten.'

Lazarus studies the long trestle table covered in a white cloth. He sticks breadcrumbs to the pads of his

214

fingers, brushes them off and picks up a cup from the centre of the table. He peers inside. It is empty, apart from an intact fly wing in a dreg of wine. He puts the cup back down. He could be happy, if he knew what he was hoping to find.

'What now?' Lydia asks.

'We wait,' Lazarus says. 'We have to trust, if he's the man you think he is, that our warning will reach him in time.'

They sit down at the table, and unusually all of them are on the same side. No one feels comfortable. They stand up. Cassius hopes Lazarus is taking in the banality of the surroundings. Nothing special. Martha stacks plates.

Some time later Lazarus is sitting on the floor, his back against the wall between two of the hanging drapes. Lydia is beside him, sitting close because the space is narrow. He assumes he knows what she wants.

'There is something,' he says, is the most he feels he can offer. 'There is not nothing.'

The outside of her thigh touches his.

Lazarus starts again. 'If I could explain it, I would. It's like you can see everything, but it isn't seeing. Everything that has happened and everything that will happen is utterly there, but there's no there or then and nothing is happening. I think it's shapeless and colourless, because no shapes or colours fit what I remember about death. Although death isn't the right word. If I try to define it I end up describing here.'

He gestures around the upstairs room at the inn. 'It's not like here at all.'

Dying is easy. Anyone can do it. Living is the problem

– Lazarus has been brought back to life and he can't explain himself. Luigi Pirandello (*Lazarus*, 1927) therefore concludes that he has nothing to say:

> Dead!...And he doesn't know a thing about it! Where's he been? He ought to know... And he doesn't! If he doesn't know he's been dead, that's a sure sign that when we die, there's nothing on the other side... Nothing at all.

Khalil Gibran reaches a different conclusion. True nothing, by its very nature, would annihilate everything inside it. He admits that Lazarus is 'silent, silent as if the seal of death is yet upon his lips', but the man has been dead and is now alive and Gibran can only suppose, in all honesty, 'there is something else'. Or as Eugene O'Neill exults in *Lazarus Laughed*: 'there is no death'.

What else can Lazarus say, after dying and coming back? This is what he knows as a certainty: 'There is something beyond.'

Lydia looks at him blankly. 'That's not what I was going to ask.'

5

Lazarus falls asleep, despite the imminence of significant theological events. He is not alone. That same night, the apostle John has slept at the table in *The Last Supper* (1447) by Andrea del Castagno, whose image predates that of da Vinci. In Gethsemane, the disciples

Peter and James will fall asleep three times while Jesus is *'deeply grieved, even to death'* (Matthew 26: 38).

Sleep is a gift offered to anyone involved with Jesus at this time. Lazarus and the disciples sleep while they can, because the season of miracles is about to end.

Meanwhile, there is no evidence of a single person dying in Jerusalem between the resurrection of Lazarus and the death of Jesus. For one week the city holds its breath, and the gateway between this world and the next goes unfrequented.

By the early hours of Friday morning, however, the influence of the raising of Lazarus is fading. The gateway is about to open again, and the signal for this to happen is a betrayal in Gethsemane by a disciple for money. There will be a kiss, an ear sliced off in anger, an arrest. An unjust trial, a death. Life on earth resumes.

Lazarus startles awake. He senses a change, but Jesus is not back and he settles beside Lydia and sleeps again, dreaming of escapes across the desert. Sleep is gifted most powerfully to Lazarus; he is a friend and he has suffered and he still has much to do.

We have to imagine, given the context, an immense organisational project. Everything is connected.

In the desert, many years earlier as Joseph's cart creaked uneasily towards Egypt, the future was written. The return from Egypt, the childhood in Nazareth, the death of Amos, the break with Jesus, the resettlement with his sisters in Bethany.

At a nothing wedding in Cana, Jesus turns water into wine. Half a lifetime away, Lazarus develops a headache.

The son of god has to learn his mortality. This is the purpose of Jesus's childhood, which introduces him through Lazarus to risk and ambition. Jesus unravels from perfection as Lazarus his friend teaches him everything he needs to know. Lazarus leads the retreat from omniscience, always going first, demonstrating the ignorance of the human condition.

Eliakim the father of Lazarus falls from the roof of the theatre in Sephoris. Lazarus doesn't learn. He climbs an even higher building, in the rain.

Lazarus teaches Jesus how to grieve, when Amos dies. Lazarus weeps and hacks away his hair and shaves, while Jesus learns from him fear and unhappiness, vanity and denial, anger and self-pity and every mortal folly.

From Lazarus Jesus learns how to weep, and at the tomb of Lazarus he weeps.

If Lazarus doubts the existence of god, it is because someone has to show Jesus how. Jesus tries it too, during his forty days alone in the desert, and finds doubt to be a horribly authentic human experience. He doesn't want anyone else to feel that way – it is the doubt that he has been sent to eradicate.

Jesus brings Lazarus back to life and people see and should now believe and thus the end of the story. But not even Lazarus believes, not completely. With hindsight a resurrection is so obviously not the end, just as Jesus foretells in the parable of 'Lazarus' and the rich man refused his entry into heaven.

Not that the experience of Lazarus is ever wasted – he has taught his friend how to die.

Human death involves resistance. Jesus must suffer. He must want not to perish.

*

Jesus is arrested by Temple guards and taken to the house of Caiaphas, where he is tried by the Sanhedrin priests for blasphemy, and found guilty. He is bound and transferred to the Praetorium, in the former palace of Herod the Great. This is life on earth reactivating after the miracle of Lazarus, as Jesus wishes to experience it.

In Mel Gibson's *The Passion of the Christ* (2004), his face is already bleeding when he stands accused before Caiaphas. He has a deep cut on his cheek in the shape of a fingernail, and his right eye is swollen and closed from a welt administered somewhere along the path from Gethsemane. A thick lower lip smudges his voice as he speaks through mouthfuls of blood.

Priests knock him down. He gets back up. They spit between his eyes, into his nose. Temple guards beat him with short sticks, taking slices out of his forehead, and they hang him from a roof-beam by chains.

Then they hand him over to the Romans, who punish him for alleged sedition. In an outside courtyard, Jesus is chained to the base of a column. Two soldiers select canes with the correct amount of bend, as they would for anyone who threatened a popular uprising. They each in turn take a two-step run-up and lash Jesus forehand, backhand, forehand. They start with his back and buttocks, then move on to the backs of his thighs. Then his face. They open up wounds and then cane the open wounds.

The *flagellum*. In *The Passion of the Christ* the strands of leather have scraps of iron tied to the ends. The iron clutches into the muscle, and at each lash the whip has to be ripped clear of the body, pulling with it a scatter of flesh. The soldiers strike crossways and lengthways. They exhaust themselves and flail at his head.

Jesus collapses at the base of the pillar, and slides in his own fresh blood. This is no place for the son of god, or for not the son of god.

The soldiers reach down for him. He is below them, in the pit of a personal hell. Jesus has started to die.

'Lazarus, wake up!'

Mary is shaking him by the shoulder. Friday morning has dawned and he shades his eyes with his hand.

'What? What is it?'

Mary tells him everything she knows. The trial in the house of Caiaphas, the transfer to the Praetorium, the Romans, the death sentence.

'No,' Cassius says. He too is blinking sleep from his eyes. 'This is wrong. I did not recommend this.'

'We came here to save him,' Lazarus says. He recognises instantly that his task of great importance has arrived.

'Wait,' Martha says. 'Stay here. We don't have all the facts.'

For Martha there is always danger, and Lazarus has heard and ignored her from his earliest childhood. Everything is dangerous because of death. If it weren't for death, nothing would be frightening, or not unbearably so. Don't go there, because you might die there. Don't do that because you might die doing it. As if he can stay where he is and do nothing and never die.

'You're too late,' Cassius says. 'Resurrection was a step too far. Bread and loaves, yes. Walking on water, maybe. When he brought you back to life that was the blasphemy. Nobody wants to believe it, not your priests, not my superiors.'

'So we'll deny the resurrection,' Lazarus says. 'We'll buy him some time.'

Lazarus will swear on his mother's life they'd been planning it together for years, a plot between friends with each of them fully prepared. But that isn't true. Poc. The truth flickers and threatens to light up. He came back to life. Jesus has divine powers.

'There is another way,' Cassius says. 'Announce that you're the messiah. You, not him. Then they might set him free.'

'Because I came back to life? You said resurrection was unbelievable.'

'Not necessarily. Not if you're sensitive to the authorities. You have to trust me. That's the only way you're going to save him.'

'Jesus is the messiah,' Mary says. 'Anything else is a lie.'

'Where are you going? Come back,' Cassius says. 'Are you going to follow my plan?'

'I'm going to save the saviour.'

The Irish poet W. B. Yeats, in his short play *Calvary* (1920), has Lazarus confront Jesus on the route to his execution at Golgotha. Yeats decides that this moment, of all moments, is when Lazarus should call Jesus to account.

The likelihood of this possibility depends on how close Lazarus can get to his friend. In Jerusalem, the crucifixion is Friday's major event, a blunt demonstration of life's talent for letting Judaea down. Miracles are followed by death. Healings and the resurrection of

Lazarus and the hope of the life to come are all ended by death.

Jerusalem is livid with disappointment. People shout 'King of the Jews' and 'Messiah' and 'Lazarus'. They mock every mistake that Jesus has made.

'A death for a death! Jesus for Lazarus!'

To restore the order of the universe, one of the two has to die. Lazarus has understood the nature of the exchange, but his impact on what happens next will depend on his position in the crowd.

Look again at the pictures. There he is in the lower left corner of a Tintoretto, or a triptych of the Delft school. The truth survives in these records of inspiration, with a poorly shaven man conspicuous amongst the witnesses. He is trapped four or five deep in the mob, unable to approach any closer.

But Yeats is essentially correct, despite his poetic embellishment. Lazarus is involved. With a surge of self-importance, he believes that he, Lazarus of Nazareth, can justify his friendship with Jesus by saving him from crucifixion.

6

The execution of Jesus, which takes place in Jerusalem at some point between 30 and 33 CE, is an accepted historical fact. It is described by Josephus (37–100 CE) in his *Jewish Antiquities* (18: 63–4), and confirmed by the Roman writer Tacitus (56–117 CE) in the *Annals* (15: 44). The crucifixion is mentioned by Lucian of Samosata

(125–180 CE) and by the Syrian philosopher Mara Bar-Serapion (dates unknown).

It also features as a key event in the gospels of the New Testament (65–100 CE) and in every record of early Christianity. Despite this extensive coverage, however, none of the sources provide a fixed procedure for Roman crucifixions in Jerusalem. There is no precision about the exact manner in which Jesus was attached to the cross, or the shape of the cross, or whether ropes were used in addition to nails.

Archaeologically, only one relevant artefact has been recovered from crucifixions in early Palestine. In 1968 the physical anthropologist Nicu Haas recovered the remains of a crucified man from a first-century burial cave in north Jerusalem. If these remains are representative, then the evidence worth noting is a right heel bone split by a four-and-a-half inch iron spike. Nothing comparable has been found before or since.

The spike, or nail, remains in the bone because no one could pull it out. The practice at the time, or so it is widely believed, was to reuse nails, but this one has twisted at the point into a fishhook barb. The spike has gone through the bone and blunted itself against a knot in the vertical piece of wood used for the crucifixion.

The wood remnants on the point of the nail are identified as olive. It seems unlikely, given the logistical demands and the expense, that hardwood beams would have been imported to Palestine solely for crucifixion. In the absence of suitable wood for crosses, easier and cheaper to nail offenders into the native olive trees.

One last point, to ensure the picture is clear. The nail goes into the rounded heel bone at right angles to the foot, and not into the bones at the front. This suggests the feet were placed either side of a thinnish piece of wood, with a separate nail for each heel. Mature olive trees have trunks of a suitable width. As for the hands, the dig produced no evidence of bones from the arm or wrist pierced with similar spikes.

In first-century Judaea, outside the city of Jerusalem, the olive trees on Golgotha are stripped of leaves. Many are gouged in the trunk a short distance above the ground, the bark encrusted with blood turned brown. The Romans reuse their nails, and they reuse the trees.

There are smaller stains in the side branches above head height, because a mature olive tree can be re-used for a crucifixion three or four times. If the branches are kindly placed.

A soldier steps between Lazarus and Jesus.

He is wearing full military uniform in the late morning heat. The dented metal, the leather kilt, the sweat, everything about him says he'd prefer to be in Syria for a straight fight against Parthians. He holds his lance diagonally across his chest, and shoves Lazarus back.

Jesus is surrounded by a knot of soldiers, his hands bound, his head bleeding. He is learning his lesson from Lazarus, dying in the open in front of witnesses, a verifiable public death.

Out of the Gennath Gate, up the hill. It is the sick who most stubbornly insist on hurting him. The unhealed and the unbelievers spit on him, and with palm leaves they slice at his upper arms, at his thighs and his face. The Roman soldiers kick him when he stumbles.

Lazarus catches glimpses of his friend's face, plainly

terrified as he tries to protect himself. His disciples, among so many others, have abandoned him. Only his friend Lazarus can help him now.

Cassius had seen his first crucifixion at the Flavian amphitheatre in Rome. The victim had been an adult male lion. He remembers the skin tight over the white belly, and the hideously stretched tendons in the legs. It was somehow worse than watching a man on the cross, although lions, he noted at the time, did not last as long as men.

According to Paul in one of his letters, the crucifixion of Jesus *'disarmed the rulers and authorities and made a public example of them, triumphing over them in it'* (Colossians 2: 15).

There may be some truth in this.

Cassius, for example, regrets that crucifixion is considered any kind of solution. His own proposal of a client messiah would be more effective at keeping the peace. But the crucifixion, like the resurrection of Lazarus, is happening nevertheless, and the death of Jesus may have its uses. A messiah does not get executed like a common criminal, nailed into the nearest olive tree. Messiahs escape death, and they escape the Antonia Fortress. They are protected by god from the lethal Sicarii.

Crucifixion is ugly and deplorable, but in this instance the fault lies with the regional god. All religions should be true, so claiming to be the one true god is as aggressive a manoeuvre as a divinity can make. Look down now on Jesus. Look at the results. Divine arrogance will not be tolerated, not by other gods, not by the Roman empire.

*

It is midday. The sky darkens to the colour of bad meat, silver and purple.

Jesus is hoisted off the ground, and his arms sized against branches. This tree has been used before. One of his arms is angled backwards and lashed to a branch so that his shoulder has to twist, the other is crooked and slightly higher. Two other condemned men go on either side, one in front and the other about level.

The Romans have no interest in aesthetics, or symmetry, as long as the arms are above the head to maximise the pain. The feet, too, must be clear of the ground. Jesus will die with his blackened toes inches from the earth and salvation.

Only the heels are nailed. One four-and-a-half inch spike on either side. The scratch of splintered bone is audible above the heavy thud of the mallet. A woman shrieks, and can't stop herself. She goes on and on.

Lazarus feels no particular compassion.

Death is a big episode, but it is not the end. It is, after all, only death, however spectacular. Death is not the climax it used to be, not for Lazarus.

The clouds close in — *'When it was noon, darkness came over the whole land'* (Mark 15: 33), and this is when Lazarus is certain. There is a god and he is watching, providing the ideal weather for two boys from Nazareth, clouds blocking the sun that otherwise would blind them to handholds as they climb.

Lazarus watches Jesus. He observes the strain on his body, toes flexing for solid ground, head dropped low on his chest.

Look at me. Look up and look at me. He wills Jesus to

obey. Believe in me, and take strength from me.

Jesus looks up.

In the absence of compassion Lazarus is calm, confident about what he needs to do. He projects his thoughts through and beyond the eyes of Jesus, and there inside his friend's skull he recognises his own death, a brain crying out for an instant and then another instant more of life.

I cannot die, Jesus thinks, with my thoughts and memories and feelings. I have seen things and done things that other people will never see and do.

So has everyone else, Lazarus reminds him. We all die.

Look at me. Lazarus is not giving up. Look, here I am, standing on the shore. I will not intervene, but everything will turn out fine. Every time Jesus raises his chin from his chest his eyes search out Lazarus.

You're nearly there, Lazarus thinks. Come on, it's easy.

Death is nothing and there is nothing to fear.

This is what Lazarus is for.

The hours that follow are described in the gospels. Jesus suffers. At some point a sponge soaked in sour wine is lifted to his lips on a stick. This is cruel or kind, designed to mock him or to give him strength: no one can remember.

Many in the crowd would have been hoping for better entertainment. *'Let the messiah, the king of Israel, come down from the cross now, so that we may see and believe'* (Mark 15: 32). They note the sudden storm-clouds, the reputation of Jesus, and the presence of Lazarus. They

227

assume there's a good chance of seeing a spectacular reversal, and with luck even a miracle.

Jesus takes three hours to die, which for a crucifixion is neither mercifully short nor proof of abnormal endurance. It is an average, ordinary life expectancy when a body is mistreated in this way.

The influence of Lazarus is evident to the end and beyond. When Jesus stops breathing, the soldiers have orders to confirm his death. *'But when they came to Jesus and found that he was already dead, they did not break his legs. Instead, one of the soldiers pierced Jesus's side with a spear, bringing a sudden flow of blood and water'* (John 19: 33–34).

Jesus continues to improve on the death of Lazarus. Crucifixion, then the spear to make sure. No one will ever doubt that he died.

'Jesus said, "It is finished." With that, he bowed his head and gave up the spirit' (John 19: 30).

It is finished. For Jesus it is finished, but not yet for Lazarus.

7

1

In churches observing the Byzantine Rite, Lazarus Saturday is a leading religious festival. Bright colours are used for vestments and the Holy Table, and, uniquely in the Christian year, the standard order of service for a Sunday can be celebrated on a different day of the week.

For one Saturday every year, a week and a day before Easter, Lazarus is the equal of Jesus. In the Apolytikion for St Lazarus they sing *We cry out to you, O Vanquisher of Death!* On Lazarus Saturday the Russians bring out the caviar. The Greeks make a spiced bread called *Lazarakia*, shaping the dough into a man bound for burial.

Catholics and Protestants are less enthusiastic: perhaps they're inhibited by the three out of four gospel writers who ignore Lazarus completely. In some ways they'd prefer him to disappear, but Lazarus keeps coming back. The memory of Lazarus is stubborn, and insists on his survival.

In Jerusalem on the Saturday after the execution of Jesus, one week after the resurrection of Lazarus, it is feasible that Lazarus Saturday will become the central day of a newly forged religion. Jesus will be secondary, because Lazarus has vanquished death. He is the survivor, and the only living pathway to god.

2

The evangelist Mark provides the fullest record of Holy Week. He reports on every day between Palm Sunday and Friday's crucifixion, but he has nothing to relate about the Saturday. For Jesus, at that point, the story is finished. He said so himself.

From Friday afternoon at about three p.m., when Jesus dies, Lazarus becomes god's representative on earth. Something extraordinary would need to happen to displace him.

Lazarus watches strangers haul his friend down from the olive tree. They fumble the body, a heavy object thumping hard to the ground. The corpse is gathered up again, gently, as if the dead care.

The crowd breaks up, falling away from Lazarus. He doesn't notice them go, nor, at first, does he realise that someone has come to stand very close beside him.

'You're still alive,' Cassius says. 'You're a very lucky man.'

Luck has nothing to do with it, because Lazarus could have foretold this moment, like a prophet. As a child he'd felt special, and without him Jesus was always likely to come to harm. He remembers the amphitheatre in Sephoris, when he'd saved Jesus from falling. He'd never understood how he'd managed to do that.

From inside the city comes the single note of a trumpet, announcing the start of the Sabbath. Stragglers turn away from the manhandling of the body of Jesus: there is a rush to bury him before the sun goes down.

'You have the rest of your life in front of you,' Cassius says. 'The man who came back from the dead.'

No one but Cassius acknowledges the presence of Lazarus. The last witnesses give up their wait for a miracle. Jesus is not the messiah, and therefore none of the stories were true. Lazarus is not true. He can safely be ignored.

'Only you have vanquished death,' Cassius says. 'It must feel like being chosen.'

Lazarus questions his purpose on earth, as he has done every day since he emerged from the tomb. Usefully, he has acted as a distraction to the authorities, allowing Jesus an extra week to preach in Jerusalem. He has consoled Jesus in his last living hours, and that is a wonderful thing to have done. But what is he for next, what is he for now?

'Someone will have to take up his work,' Cassius says. 'Jesus is dead. It is finished.'

'For him, yes. One messiah at a time is enough.'

Lazarus spends Friday night on the hill, outside the city walls. Golgotha is an area of tombs and quarries, with

access routes and steps joining the various levels. The
bare olive trees make twisted silhouettes on the ridge
line.

He sits with his arms round his knees, and in the
night-time the tiniest incidents are possible visits from
god. Every breath of wind is a sign, as is the sand chasing its tail over a moonlit rock. He listens for restless
demons, for strays sweeping across the empty spaces,
and for jackals, wolves, lions. He imagines himself in
the wilderness like a lost prophet, waiting for the word
of god.

Yanav sits down beside him. He has instructions
from Cassius to encourage the notion that only a messiah can come back to life. It is written in the scriptures.
He should suggest that a messiah with a genuine commitment to the Judaean people would listen carefully to
Rome.

'Jesus was an interesting man,' Yanav says. 'I liked
him. What he did for you was miraculous.'

'I know.'

The two men sit side by side, not speaking. Yanav
hates getting involved with religion. He heals the devout
and they tell him that god is working through a healer.
Which may be true, but the faithful should appreciate that Yanav is an important part of the process. If it
weren't for him, Lazarus would have died months earlier. He'd have muddled the timings of god.

Until today's crucifixion, Yanav had preferred the
coherent thinking of the Romans. He admires them
for their trust in observable cause and effect. He has
believed, on balance, that the Roman version of progress
is preferable to any other. Now he's not so sure.

The heavy clouds of earlier in the day have cleared. The moon is out, and on its surface is the familiar blurred image of Cain slaying Abel.

'What does it all mean?' Lazarus asks.

Yanav picks out the stars in their fixed, impenetrable patterns. He has his instructions from Cassius, but he chooses to disobey them.

'Lazarus, let me help you. Demons are trickier than anyone can imagine. They've possessed you once and they'll want you again. You'll need my expertise.'

'I don't think so. I came back to life. I don't feel at risk.'

A shooting star grazes the night sky. The gods are up to something. Yanav saw the signs in Jesus when he heard that Lazarus was sick, and again when Lazarus stumbled from the tomb. Whatever the gods have in mind, Yanav doesn't trust them to do it without consequences. He does trust them, being gods, to get it done.

'Don't stay in Jerusalem, not after this. I'm travelling south. You can be my assistant.'

'I should stay.'

'My partner, then. We'll split whatever we earn.'

'I can't. What about Mary and Martha? And Lydia. I have too many reasons to stay.'

'And one big reason to leave. Cassius has plans for you. He'll expect you to teach.'

'He thinks people will want to follow me.'

'And prophesy. That's a basic requirement of the job he has in mind. Can you read the future?'

'As well as Jesus could.' Lazarus looks towards the knuckled olives on the brow of the hill.

'The healing, the signs, the wonders,' Yanav goes on. 'He wants more from you than you can give.'

'You could stay and help me. Especially with the healing. We could work it out together.'

'Did you hear about the boy from Nain? Yes, the dead one. Resurrection doesn't have to end happily.'

'He didn't have the support of the Romans.'

'Leave while you can. Tonight. Be gone by the morning. That's my honest advice.'

3

Saturday is the Jewish Sabbath. Lazarus is woken by sunshine over the walls of Jerusalem, and the sun rising day after day is astonishing. Yanav is nowhere to be seen.

Sabbath restrictions mean that not many Judaeans will venture from the city to the tombs on a Saturday, and for an executed criminal like Jesus there is neither mourning nor wailing. Instead, Lazarus hears a noise that reminds him of his father in Nazareth: mallet on chisel on stone. A steady, determined tap.

He goes to investigate the sound out of curiosity, but with no clearer ideas than that. He wishes he and Jesus had talked more. Like everyone left behind, he regrets not asking more explicitly for guidance while Jesus was alive.

The Romans ignore the Sabbath. Conscripted soldiers chisel at the edges of the stone that closes the tomb of Jesus. They widen the join so that mortar can be plugged into the gap, to seal the entrance. Jesus is buried in a small, single-chamber tomb, and their work will soon be done.

'We're making certain,' Cassius says. 'No tricks this time, no pre-planned miracles.'

'So you're back on duty?'

'No one else knew what to do.'

Rome's defeated enemies will stay dead. There are few truths more essential to the sustainability of the empire. 'It won't happen twice.'

'Is that what you're expecting?'

'Everyone saw Jesus die. He's not coming back.'

'You have Roman soldiers tending a corpse.'

'I know,' Cassius says. 'A complete waste of time and a perfect job for the military. How did you sleep?'

'How do you think?'

Mary is approaching from the direction of the tented pilgrim encampment to the north of the city. Her eyes are red from weeping, and when she sees Lazarus she bursts into tears and runs headlong towards him. She throws herself at his feet.

'I knew you'd be here.' She hugs his legs and crushes her cheek against his knees. 'Do what you have to do.'

Christians usually interpret Lazarus as a prefiguring of Jesus, who is Christ. This is the purpose of Lazarus's life, for those who believe in his literal existence, and his narrative function in the bible for those who don't. The death and resurrection of Lazarus foreshadow those of Jesus, and of all the dead to come.

Yet Jesus Christians (those who believe that Jesus is Christ) rarely appreciate the full extent of the advance work performed by Lazarus. In the history of their friendship, Lazarus always goes first. He suffers and dies first. He grieves first and disbelieves in god and leaves home first.

Jesus watches and learns. He will not be leaving his tomb after only one day. Too soon. He knows this from Jairus's daughter, and even after the violence of a crucifixion he will want to avert suspicion that he simply fell unconscious. At the other extreme, Lazarus was dead for four days. Too long. Four days invites awkward side issues, like the smell. Lazarus is the trial and Lazarus is the error. He enables Jesus to identify the ideal period to be dead before coming back.

Mary can't be expected to know this. Like anybody aggrieved by the death of a loved one, she wants him back immediately.

Mary takes her brother by the hand. 'You know what you have to do.'

I could be happy as a favoured son of god, Lazarus thinks. He alone has survived death and burial, and returned fresh from the dead: his childhood passion for the scripture heroes was in fact an education. God was watching, and god has plans for him.

Lazarus faces the sealed tomb door. The soldiers are clearing away their tools.

'Jesus,' Lazarus says. He clears his throat and starts again. 'Jesus, come out.'

There is a crack in his voice, which sounds timid even to him.

'Again,' Mary says. 'Face the tomb as if you mean it. He's only been buried one night.'

'They've mortared the door. I saw them do it.'

Mary tilts her head to one side. 'Lazarus, say it properly, before it's too late.'

Lazarus searches the cloudless sky. Nothing. 'I can't. I'm sorry. I don't believe I can call him out.'

'You've got this the wrong way round,' Cassius says. He looks from Lazarus to Mary as if settling a dispute. 'Lazarus isn't at fault. It's Jesus who can't come back.'

'Jesus is the son of god.' Mary prepares to turn away. 'I shall pray for you. I'll pray for you both.'

'Let her go,' Cassius says. He takes Lazarus by the elbow. 'There's something I want you to see.'

4

Inside the city walls, despite the Sabbath, Lazarus attracts attention. People shout his name, which soon adds to the numbers who follow him.

Lazarus is a lodestone for the recently bereaved, and today Jerusalem aches with unexplained grief, the feeling that those we have loved should not die. Lazarus is hope – no one is more alive than he is, and recent events have encouraged this year's Passover pilgrims to expect a messiah. Unpredictable weather patterns, disturbances at the Temple, a nervous Roman governor: this is how the final revelation will begin.

As a religious idea, Jesus has failed. He is dead. He is therefore not the son of god and will not save Israel for god's chosen people. He needs to be replaced.

Lazarus is soon walking at the head of a substantial crowd. In the cramped streets of Jerusalem strangers reach out to touch him. He is solid flesh. He has not abandoned them, and as faithful pilgrims all they need do is follow.

The procession continues to grow, and Cassius tells Lazarus what to say.

'I am the way,' Lazarus repeats what he hears whispered in his ear. 'I am the way and the life.'

The words travel back and forth in a rapid murmur.

'And anyone who believes in Lazarus,' he adds, 'shall never die.'

This is the living messiah they expect.

'What is beyond?' someone shouts, and without any prompting Lazarus provides the answer. Why shouldn't he? He has lived this experience. He is the only person alive who might know.

'There is not nothing,' he says, or how could he be here now? 'Believe me, I have been there, and beyond this world we know there is something without end.'

The Church of Lazarus Christ shines across the future.

The people of Judaea have a talent for belief. The feeding of a crowd of thousands with two loaves of bread and five small fish. A carpenter who can walk on water, in a storm. Why not Lazarus?

Lazarus will offer himself as a leader with experience of the mysteries of existence. He will be like Jesus, but less irresponsible. He will hesitate to recommend a diet of locusts and honey, and is unlikely to require periods of fasting in the desert. He'll get married and live in the city, the messiah of second chances, the hope of regretted lives.

Try again. Rise up and start afresh.

Believers in Lazarus Christ may shave or not shave, circumcise their children or not. Lazarus doesn't mind. They may choose to work or seek entertainment on the Sabbath. Veils will not be required for women, who can enter the Lazaran synagogue by the front door and learn their scriptures with the men.

As long as Lazarans respect the authority of Rome they may believe whatever they like. Let the Romans take care of today, and with the right spiritual guidance, carefully administered, Palestine can become a new Gaul, full of prosperous Roman citizens living in religiously free cities.

One of which might be named after Lazarus, or after Cassius.

Lazaran Christianity will save Jerusalem from the certain doom of failing to assimilate with Rome. It concerns itself with the next world, not this one, which belongs to the wealthy and powerful and always will.

Lazarus offers peace and stability, an invitation to embrace material comforts, and evidence for thinking most positively about death.

Everyone will be happy.

Saturday's Lazarus procession ends not at the Temple but at the Bethesda pool. At Passover, the numbers in and around the water increase with those seeking solace after exclusion from the Temple. The ill and imperfect, the diseased and disabled gather to wash themselves clean. Lazarus recognises his earlier symptoms many times over. He sees the work of Jesus left undone.

'Go out and do good among the people,' Cassius says.

'There are so many of them. Where do I start?'

Lazarus is the victim of a miracle. He has no privileged explanation, nor secret indication of what to do next. Like anyone else, he wonders what to expect of himself. He looks at his hands, his forearms. He is sadly lacking in luminosity, and this confusion is one of the reasons that the era of miracles is about to end. In future, the faithful will be asked to believe without spectacular interventions, and most believers can do this: it is part of what makes them faithful.

At the Bethesda pool, Isaiah bundles his way through the sick and lethargic towards Lazarus. He has important news about Saloma.

'Is she worse?'

'No. That's just it. We think she's getting better.'

Yanav watches from the road above the Bethesda pool. His half-blind donkey chews on roadside weeds, bags and jars sagging across its back. The dog leaps on ahead.

Yanav plans to stop for a night or two in Jericho, and then turn south along the Dead Sea to Idumea. The Idumeans are great believers in the powers of peacock feathers and astronomy.

He takes a last look at the pool below him. From a distance, Cassius has the trick of blending in, but Isaiah is easy to spot with his extravagant arm gestures, pulling in his memories, throwing out his hopes.

Yanav has done what he can for Saloma. Last night he left a new concoction with her mother, thinking it might help with the spasms. One day, demons will be as easy to cast out as stones from a shoe, but not yet.

He regrets not learning more from Jesus, but envy

240

had made him stupid and he'd missed the public healings. At least he'd been there in Bethany for the miracle
of Lazarus, and he'd memorised the words of the spell:
Lazarus, come out.

He tries the three words in a different order, alters the
stress and intonation. These words have power, and if he
can find and control it then at some stage that knowledge will come in useful elsewhere.

'Isn't that right?' Yanav says, clicking his donkey back
to the road. He pulls her head round and whistles to the
dog.

They'll be all right, the three of them, because Yanav's
fame goes ahead of him. He is the healer of Lazarus, the
man who came back from the dead.

5

'We think she's getting better,' Isaiah says. 'She smiled
at me.'

Lazarus spreads his arms to take in the sick and poor
at the Bethesda pool. 'One among so many.'

'Don't stop at Saloma,' Cassius says. 'Of course not.
You're needed here.'

Isaiah is planning ahead. Saloma is sitting up with
bright eyes and her mouth closed. She is changing almost
by the hour. To be fair, Lazarus has also changed. He
squandered his money making sure he didn't die, and is
no longer the catch he was.

'You were very sick when you made certain decisions,'

Isaiah says. 'You came to my house to apologise, and I wouldn't begrudge you a change of mind.'

His daughter is healing, but Isaiah has already identified more to want: a messiah will never make everyone happy, as Jesus discovered. 'Release Saloma from her betrothal. Give her some time to concentrate on getting well.' Also, Isaiah has seen what happens to messiahs. He doesn't want to rush into an alliance with Lazarus, not now.

'They should marry,' Cassius interrupts. 'Set a good example.'

'In a perfect world,' Isaiah says, 'I agree. But none of the priests are going to buy lambs from a dead man, not for some time to come. That's the reality.'

'He has the gift of healing,' Cassius says. 'Saloma is recovering. What more do you want?'

Isaiah wouldn't mind knowing the future, if Cassius is asking, and also how to measure happiness. An explanation of luck and the nature of god would be useful, and a guide to what awaits us after death. Lazarus can't even remember whether the afterlife is good or bad, which would be valuable information to have.

'We're very grateful,' Isaiah says, 'but we also have to be careful. Look at Jesus. Healing is fine, but there are limits.'

'Help us to organise a gathering,' Cassius says. 'Lazarus, what do you think?'

He thinks it is never too late to start again and he should try to do some good. Lazarus knows he didn't heal Saloma. He didn't even touch her, but so much depends on belief.

'We should so something here, at the pool,' Lazarus

says. 'I know what it means to be sick, and people will come.'

'Excellent idea,' Cassius says. 'Remind people you're alive. Unlike some others.'

'I wish I could help,' Isaiah says, 'but I can't. Not on the Sabbath.'

'Then we'll do it tomorrow, Sunday morning. We'll make this a Sunday Jerusalem never forgets.'

'Can you show me the way?'

A man with an eye infection is trying to find the edge of the pool. His trachoma is so advanced that his eyelids have swollen and turned inward, the eyelashes scratching the cornea.

'I can tomorrow,' Lazarus says.

'Will you tell me when the angels pass by?'

'Tomorrow morning. We'll bring good news, something for everyone.'

Isaiah is impatient to get home. He wants to monitor Saloma's recovery.

'Lazarus has the support of Rome,' Cassius reminds him. 'We will look favourably on any assistance you can offer.'

'I'll send out Arab messengers. They're not constrained by the Sabbath, and they'll let everyone know.'

This is enough, and Lazarus and Cassius watch Isaiah leave. They have until tomorrow to organise a memorable event.

'I think Jesus would have wanted this.' Lazarus says. 'Every time he looked up, when he was dying, his eyes searched for mine. Every time.'

Cassius nods, even though Lazarus exaggerates. Every

time Jesus raised his head his eyes searched for Cassius. It was distinctly unnerving.

'Yes. He knew you were the one. He was making you accountable, handing on the role.'

They exchange some ideas, feeling for the shape of the future.

'It will have to be spectacular,' Cassius says. 'Did you ever feel you could do what he did?'

'He was the follower, not me. We're different, but in Nazareth I was never second-best. We need something exceptional, completely convincing.'

The Romans control the water supply to the city, and have done since they built the high-level aqueduct. By opening sluice gates elsewhere in the watercourse they control the levels in the Bethesda pool.

'You control the water in and out?'

'Of course we do. Jerusalem wouldn't have clean water if it weren't for us.'

'So you can make the surface of the water tremble?'

'Whenever we like, just by regulating the system.'

Lazarus laughs. He now understands why the water moves, but the precise moment can still be ordained by god, and angels may still pass by. 'You've given me an idea for tomorrow,' Lazarus says. 'Let's plan the biggest miracle since the day I walked from my tomb.'

They agree on the timing and the general principle. Cassius will arrange the details while Lazarus stays out of sight. The effect will be more dramatic if everyone wonders where he's gone, and whether he's coming back.

Cassius puts his hand on Lazarus's arm. 'Don't worry about the betrothal. We can change Isaiah's mind.'

*

In most fictional accounts biblical prostitutes are unhappy. They are women who have made wrong choices, or against whom circumstances have conspired. In Philip Pullman's *The Good Man Jesus and the Scoundrel Christ* (2010) his scoundrel Christ pays for sex with a woman who has an ulcerating cancer of the breast. Christ fails to heal her.

After listening to Jesus preach, Lydia knows that life doesn't have to be like this. There are other possibilities. It is Saturday and Jesus is dead, but from her own experience she is not appalled or especially surprised by an unhappy ending. His teachings still apply, and life will improve for those who live it well.

In Bethany, Lydia borrows the loom that belonged to Absalom's mother. She assembles it in the empty upstairs room of the abandoned Lazarus house, and hums to herself as she slides the yarn back and forth, finishing a blanket that Mary once promised to Absalom. Mary stays in Jerusalem, because the city is where she feels she should be.

Lydia waits in Bethany.

When Lazarus was dying — and Lydia heard this from Martha, so it must be true — Lazarus had asked for her. He has a second chance, and he wouldn't come back to life to make the same mistakes.

At some stage, and this is equally true for the historical Jesus, we must avoid a preoccupation with attempts to establish factual propositions.

The evidence about Lazarus is fragmentary, and may have been misinterpreted in the two thousand years between then and now. Textual and pictorial records can be transmitted inaccurately, or contain errors inserted by copyists.

At best, the Synoptic gospels (Mark, Matthew and Luke) can be regarded as conveying an oral tradition both embroidered and embellished. John, as I've already mentioned, is demonstrably creative in his structuring of events. So where else is there to look? How can we ever be sure?

A point of stagnation has been reached in scholarly and theological studies. A new approach is needed, and imaginative representations are an undervalued source of data. Evidence can be extrapolated through careful research, making a significant contribution to the sum of our knowledge.

With Lazarus, but also in many other fields, innovative discoveries can be made by trusting the historical human imagination. Admittedly, reconstructions have to be revised as new imaginative records become available, but biographers should stay faithful to the patterns that consistently emerge.

Jesus will soon be resurrected. Lazarus will stop smiling for the foreseeable future. These improbabilities have been documented at length, and cannot now be ignored.

It is Saturday night. Lydia is naked.

Lazarus looks ahead, feels for the shape of his destiny because any life he can imagine may be the life that comes true.

'Will you marry me?'

Lydia detaches the half-finished blanket from the loom and lays it on the floor in the upstairs room. They have a sack of flour as a pillow. Lazarus too undresses, lies beside her, and from the darkness outside crickets provide a pulse to the warm-blooded night.

'This house,' Lazarus says, 'is as empty as death.'

'And that's not all bad, is it?'

The information that Lazarus has struggled to communicate is now familiar, but at the time, when Lazarus brought back his lack of knowledge, it was radical and new: god is everywhere and nowhere, before and after, real and fictional, in any given case a concept that words will never capture.

'Not the scriptures?'

'Not even the Jewish scriptures.'

Lydia brushes the back of her hand over his growing beard, dark with specks of grey on the chin. She is close to him but distant, and T. S. Eliot salvages her attitude in *The Love Song of J. Alfred Prufrock* (1917): 'Would it have been worthwhile', he asks, 'To say: "I am Lazarus, come from the dead, / Come back to tell you all, I shall tell you all" — / If one settling a pillow by her head, / Should say: "That is not what I meant at all. / That is not it, at all."'

They stare at each other, justifying to themselves the decisions of past lives. Lazarus reaches out and they hold each other close.

A messiah should marry, Lazarus thinks, for no better reason than the greed of human love. He wants Lydia near him, all the time. 'We'll announce the betrothal tomorrow, at Bethesda. I'll walk around you seven times in front of a thousand witnesses. Our lives can change.'

'Yes,' Lydia says, 'they can. But you shouldn't look too far ahead.'

She presses against him, her belly against his hip, flesh against bone. He presses back, flesh against flesh. With Lydia he is a man not a god – a consolation to them both.

'This is not the last time,' Lazarus says. 'I promise.'

'That's all I wanted to hear.'

'We'll start again. Wait until tomorrow. You won't believe your eyes.'

6

On Sunday morning, reality asserts itself. Jesus is resurrected, and nothing is the same again.

As always, Jesus has learned from Lazarus: three days is the ideal period to stay buried. No one mentions the smell or speculates about the colour of his head, and three days fits with the prophecies in the Jewish scriptures. Jesus precludes as much doubt as he possibly can.

He also preserves his dignity. No one sees him leave the tomb, clumsy and stumbling in grave clothes. That would undermine the impact of the event. There is one further modification from the earlier resurrection of Lazarus. Jesus disappears immediately.

'He has risen! He is not here' (Mark 16: 6). Matthew agrees, *'He is not here; he has risen'* (28: 6), while in Luke, *'they found the stone rolled away from the tomb, but when they entered, they did not find the body of the Lord Jesus'* (24: 2–3). In John, Jesus tidies up and then vanishes: [Peter] *arrived and went into the tomb. He saw*

the strips of linen lying there, as well as the burial cloth
that had been around Jesus's head. The cloth was folded
up by itself, separate from the linen' (John 20: 6–7).

In Nazareth, as a boy, Lazarus taught Jesus everything
he needed to know. During his last week in Jerusalem,
Jesus is still learning: life can be awkward the second
time around. He exits the tomb and disappears.

In forty days from now, Jesus will ascend into heaven,
his afterlife consistent with the pattern of his friendship
with Lazarus. Jesus lets Lazarus go first. He pays attention. Then he does what Lazarus did, only better.

Cassius summons the soldiers charged with guarding
the tomb. His lips are thin with rage but he lets them
speak. Not one of them can give a reliable account of
what has taken place.

In Mark, there is *'a young man dressed in a white robe'*
(Mark 16: 5) who somehow infiltrates the tomb. Cassius
has the soldiers flogged. They add an angel – *'His*
appearance was like lightning, and his clothes were white
as snow' (Matthew 28: 3).

Cassius seizes the *flagellum* himself and strikes hard
behind the knees. Now there are *'two men in clothes that*
gleamed like lightning' (Luke 24: 4).

'So which is it? One man or two? Angels or men?
Young or old? You will tell me the truth.'

When the story changes to *'two angels, in white'* (John
20: 12), Cassius turns and flails the wall, leaving the
whip embedded in the plaster, at the centre of its own
explosion of blood.

What is certain is that the body of Jesus is no longer
in the tomb. Cassius urgently needs to find either the

body or the man, for his own career and his own safety, but suddenly no one is even sure what Jesus looks like.

He is bearded, everyone agrees on that. But then he is encircled by a bright light, and Mary Magdalene who knows him well mistakes him at the empty tomb for a labourer – *'Thinking he was a gardener, she said: Sir, if you have carried him away, tell me where you have put him'* (John 20: 15).

Cassius has every gardener in the city arrested. None of them are the resurrected Jesus. And then a strange story filters in from travellers using the Emmaus road: *'As they talked and discussed these things with each other, Jesus himself came up and walked along with them; but they were kept from recognising him'* (Luke 24: 15–16). Cassius combines the uncertain descriptions with the consistent cases of mistaken identity. Jesus is in disguise.

Not that anyone knows where he is.

Cassius mobilises every soldier in the garrison to search for an escaped criminal. Whatever his outward appearance, he will be limping and possibly bleeding. Shouldn't that be true? Cassius wants to check with Yanav, but Yanav too is missing.

If in doubt, the man they're looking for will smell of myrrh and aloes.

He won't get far. Checkpoints are double-manned. The sick are stopped at the city gates and searched.

Cassius cancels the Lazarus miracle at Bethesda. Instead he sends experienced legionnaires to raid the porches and turn out the invalids. Jesus is not found hiding among them.

Everyone pretends to be surprised. That's one common thread. Jesus's family and the disciples feign amazement at the empty tomb, but Cassius doesn't trust them. To disappear so efficiently, Jesus must have made extensive preparations. This is a meticulously planned operation, and the work of more than one person.

If nothing else, the story of Lazarus has taught Cassius that Jesus uses his friends to achieve his objectives. Lazarus has questions to answer.

From Sunday morning the Lazarus story begins to fade. Lazarus has the star-bright birth in Bethlehem and the sheltered childhood in Nazareth. He comes from the line of David and enters Jerusalem on a donkey – but not elegantly, nor at the head of a procession, not in a way that three out of four gospel writers will choose later to remember.

For Lazarus, too many of the telling details are absent: the virgin-birth mother and the spectacular public death and the words to explain his experience. Nor does Lazarus ever understand the significance of hide-and-seek – he seeks when he should be hiding, and hides when he should seek.

Over the next forty days Jesus will make a limited number of appearances. The gospels have reports of Jesus with the disciples (behind locked doors, for security reasons), where he shows them his open wounds. In 1 Corinthians 15, Paul states that Jesus appeared to Peter, to the twelve apostles together, to more than five hundred followers at once, to James, and then once more to the apostles.

This last appearance, as noted by Paul, is probably the same as the story Matthew and John tell of Jesus on the shore of Lake Galilee. The disciples have been night-fishing, but as dawn breaks they have nothing to show for their efforts. Jesus appears on the shore, too far away to help. He shouts at them to fish differently, to throw their nets on the unconventional side of the boat. That's where they find what they're looking for.

On the beach Jesus lights a fire. They cook fish and they eat. Jesus offers them bread. On the rare occasions he does make himself known, Jesus, like Lazarus, is hungry.

Cassius attempts to use the disciples as a lure. He allows them their freedom because whenever Jesus appears the disciples are never far away. He has every disciple followed, and the entire garrison looking for a wounded bearded man, but Jesus continues to elude him.

Not so Joseph of Arimathea. He swears he is simply a friend, no more nor less. Cassius spits in his eye. Joseph of Arimathea is never heard from again.

As for Lazarus, it is inconceivable that he isn't implicated. At the very least he advised on how to survive inside a tomb, and Cassius will not forgive him.

In the Antonia Fortress, in a small cell on the third floor, Cassius has the bed carried out. Lazarus will not be sleeping.

'Admit you're a fraud. Why did you pretend to come back to life?'

Cassius uses the whips, the weights, the flames. Lazarus screams like anyone else, and then Cassius has him killed with saws. His hands and his feet are cut off, and he is beheaded. The body parts are kept separate and as far apart as possible on the floor of the cell in the Antonia.

Cassius posts a twenty-four-hour guard, then a double guard. He orders the door to be locked and manned for forty days. The severed hands and feet must be kept in sight at all times.

As the body rots, and begins to stink, this is quickly the least popular job in the garrison. Cassius assigns it as punishment for any common soldier who flags in the search for Jesus.

There is no evidence that Lazarus was killed after the resurrection of Jesus, though as an act of retribution it makes perfect sense. Cassius may, in any case, have by now forfeited the authority to make such a decision. He has recently botched the execution of a dissident religious leader. Even before that he'd underestimated the influence and power of Jesus.

He is a *speculatore* who has failed to identify and prevent trouble. The consuls in Rome will take charge from here on in, using more traditional methods.

The Russian writer Leonid Andreyev and the American Eugene O'Neill both have Lazarus deported to Rome, and neither foresees a happy outcome.

O'Neill's Lazarus, at first, stays relentlessly optimistic − 'There is only life' − but he fails to convince the emperor, who knows of one sure way to test this thesis. 'I am killing God,' he says. 'I am Death.'

In Andreyev's short story *Lazarus* (1925), Lazarus discomforts the sceptical Romans. The immensity of the 'unknowable Yonder' is visible in his eyes, and the governing class of Rome is unable to turn away. Lazarus's cold stare induces a profound indifference to life. He has seen the infinite, and he makes the effort of empire, with its endless strategies and setbacks, suddenly seem futile.

The emperor, who is himself a god, cannot allow this apathy to take a permanent hold in Rome. He summons Lazarus, and by force of will he defies the 'horror of the Infinite' that Lazarus brings to mind. The emperor prefers life as it is, with its limited vistas and occasional fleeting pleasures. The next day a Roman hangman with a red-hot iron burns out Lazarus's eyes.

Compare this to the afterlife story of Jesus. After forty days, as documented in the Acts of the Apostles, Jesus ascends with glory into heaven. Lazarus has shown him the prospects for a resurrected man on earth. He will have to serve a *speculatore*, or be blinded by the Empire, or live in fear of assassins.

The fate of the resurrected is uninterrupted misery, with no reason to smile for thirty years to come.

The disciples recognise the ascension of Jesus as an elegant solution to this problem. Back in Jerusalem, the problem unresolved is better known as Lazarus. For the disciples, Lazarus is god's headache.

They decide to erase him from the record. He appears in none of the gospels written while the majority of the disciples are alive. Nor does he feature in the letters of Paul, who is equally sensitive to the inconvenient fact of Lazarus.

Jesus himself had predicted they would have to act: *'If anyone says to you at that time, "Look! Here is the Messiah! Or Look! There he is!" – do not believe it. False Messiahs and false prophets will appear and produce signs and omens, to lead astray, if possible, the elect'* (Mark 13: 21–22).

There is only one true messiah. Jesus is the son of god and he ascends into heaven. Lazarus stays behind. He increasingly resembles a fake, a trick, an ordinary man. He must be shifted aside. None of his words will be remembered, and if the disciples have their way then like the son of the widow of Nain even his name will be lost. The disciples influence Mark and Matthew and Luke – no one will touch the incredible story of Lazarus. It gives off an objectionable smell.

Besides, Lazarus can be difficult. He knows more than he should, and not just the Nazareth fact that Jesus casts a shadow. The story of Jesus is finding a durable shape. Surprise revelations from his childhood, or from their friendship, are unlikely to be welcomed with joy.

7

Lazarus, however, is not so easy to finish off. He refuses to be first of the martyrs, his life ruined by Jesus, and knowing what we do about the rest of his days, this never appears to be what Jesus intended.

The story of Lazarus will not stay buried. That's a pattern with Lazarus, and it is no coincidence that John, the only gospel in which Lazarus features, is the last to be written (85–100 CE). By this time the other disciples are dead. John can't quite remember why they wanted

Lazarus suppressed, and his story is faithfully revived.

Over the centuries, this process has continued, with information about Lazarus resurfacing at regular intervals. In the oral tradition of the Middle Ages, as preserved by Jacobus de Voragine in *The Golden Legend* (1260), Lazarus and his sisters are 'thrown by infidels into a ship without a rudder and launched into the deep, in the hope that in this way they would all be drowned at once'.

The infidels could be Pharisees, or possibly Romans. The powers-that-be are reluctant to keep the conundrum of Lazarus in sight, and they reach the same conclusion as the disciples: no-one wants this story told. Lazarus is pushed out to sea along with the primary witnesses, Mary and Martha.

Reading between the lines, it becomes clear that after the ascension of Jesus, Lazarus lacks direction. He has no rudder, no means of steering the boat, and de Voragine adds that they are also 'without sails or food'. They do have Mary, with faith enough for three, and she trusts that Jesus is watching. He will not allow Lazarus to perish at sea, by water, not after the fate he sent for Amos.

The ship lands safely on the far side of the Mediterranean, on the coast of southern France. Lazarus has a series of adventures involving the gift of fertility, typically a consolation of the gods, and perhaps a coded affirmation that Lydia has travelled with him. According to Catholic legend, Lazarus saves several mothers and children, before settling in the region as the inaugural Bishop of Marseilles.

*

Alternatively, he is buried in the town of Larnaca on the island of Cyprus. This is more likely, as the south-east coast of Cyprus is closer to Israel than Marseilles, and the rudderless ship may have drifted towards land on the island's volcanic currents.

In 890 CE a tomb was discovered with the inscription *Lazarus, Bishop of Larnaca. Four days dead. Friend of Jesus.* Ever since, the succeeding Larnacan bishops have kept the bones of Lazarus safe beneath their magnificent *Agios Lazaros* Orthodox Church. The Lazarus icon in the church is beardless, incidentally, though his cropped hair is turning grey.

Wherever Lazarus goes, he never escapes his friendship with Jesus, but there is no suggestion in any of the records that Jesus ever appears to him. Lazarus is like everybody else – he simply has to believe.

In Cyprus he settles with his sisters and Lydia in a house fronting the sea. At night, the foreign smell of thyme from the inland bushes can wake him, and he sits up until sunrise for the view across the ocean to Palestine.

Lazarus occasionally receives visitors from Judaea. At first they ask what is beyond, but as time goes by they travel from greater distances and show more of an interest in Jesus.

'What was he like?'

Lazarus describes Jesus on the shore, watching Amos drown. The pilgrims want Jesus on the cross.

'There was no cross,' Lazarus corrects them. 'He died nailed to an olive tree.'

They prefer the cross, and Lazarus is old and forgetful. Christians everywhere can picture the Roman cross.

It is a shared image that unites the oppressed across the empire.

'Tell us about the sign above his head.'

'There was no sign.'

On the island of Cyprus, in the town of Larnaca, the local tradition has a story about Lazarus smiling. He lives here for thirty years, until one day in the market he sees an urchin stealing a pot. He reputedly says: 'the clay steals the clay', and he smiles.

The nature of this smile is not known.

In other Larnaca traditions Lazarus works miracles, including transforming a vineyard into a salt lake. What is certain, because it is preserved in the architecture of the island even today, is that the episcopal thrones in every church of the town bear the icon of St Lazarus, and none of them the image of Jesus.

The early Jesus Christians failed to erase Lazarus from their Church. In addition to the Gospel of John, and the architectural remains on the island of Cyprus, and the persistent imaginative revivals, Lazarus is embedded in the Christian liturgy.

The followers of Jesus repeatedly insist that Jesus is the son of god.

We believe in one Lord, Jesus Christ, the only son of God.

Centuries of theological exposition have misunderstood the emphasis in this memorable line of the creed. Clearly, no one doubted the arrival of a messiah, and in the Gloria there is the same insistence on identity, on who and not what: *For you alone are the holy One, you alone are the lord, you alone are the Most High, Jesus Christ.*

Lazarus haunts the insistent and foundational words of Christianity. Jesus is the son of god, *not* Lazarus. Once upon a time it was necessary to insist that this was so. Think back to the pictures, and the images that survive of onlookers bowing down to Lazarus.

The story of Lazarus resists the pressure of the early Church, and miraculously Lazarus survives. He comes back to life in mosaics and sculptures, on recovered crockery and early decorative lamp covers. He is gilded on countless icons, and carved into the monuments of the necropoli of ancient Rome. All anyone has to do is look.

Lazarus is indestructible.

He may even have been happy.

The Larnaca fragment that made Lazarus smile is less convincing than another story offered by the Chinese mystic Wei Wu Wei, in *The Tenth Man* (1966). Wei claims to know the joke sent by god to make Lazarus laugh.

Ten theology students are travelling from one Master to another. They cross a river in spate, but are separated by the strength of the current. When they reassemble on the other side, the students count each other to check everyone has made it safely across. Each holy man counts nine other students of theology. Alas, they bewail their poor drowned brother.

A passing traveller asks them why they're weeping. He counts the students and assures them that all ten are alive and well. The students count again, and call the stranger a fool. They refuse to be consoled.

In his anguish, one of the trainee theologians goes to the riverside to wash his grief-stained face. He leans over a clear pool and calls out that he has found their brother, drowned at the bottom of the river. Each man in turn tearfully looks down into the water.

They all see him, but he is too deep to reach, so they conduct his funeral at the place on the riverbank nearest the body.

The traveller returns in the other direction. The students amuse him, so he asks them what they're doing now. He bursts out laughing, then tells them they've celebrated their own deaths as well as the deaths of all the others. This means all ten of them must be truly dead, deader than anyone who ever lived, dead twice over.

'On learning this each student was instantly awakened, and ten fully enlightened holy men returned to their monastery to the intense delight of their grandmotherly old Master' (*The Tenth Man*).

Lazarus too must have made significant spiritual progress, if by now he can laugh at a drowning.

Belief is the problem. Some people refuse to believe anything unless they see it with their own eyes, like the students of theology at the river. Even then, what they see may not be true.

Jesus predicted it would be like this, in the parable that mentioned Lazarus by name – '*If they do not listen to Moses and the Prophets, they will not be convinced even if someone rises from the dead*' (Luke 16: 31). There is only so much a god can do.

The disbelievers have endless reserves of ingenuity: a parable by Jesus about a man named Lazarus is unconnected with Lazarus his friend. No one saw Jesus emerge from the tomb, and therefore it never happened. No one saw Lazarus die.

After Lazarus, the spectacular miracles come to an end. Smaller miracles are not infrequent, even today, and people notice but often say nothing. These less flagrant signs and wonders are easier to accommodate. They leave no distasteful smell.

Lazarus dies and he doesn't die. He doesn't die and he dies.

I want to keep him alive, even at the very end, because with the Lazarus story no ending can be stated with certainty. On the frontier between life and death, in his case, all normal rules are suspended.

In his novel *Behold the Man* (1969), Michael Moorcock explains the resurrection of Jesus by giving him the capacity to time travel. This accounts for his adeptness at prophecy, and also for his sudden disappearance from first-century Jerusalem.

If time travel can apply to Jesus, then it may also help with Lazarus. Lazarus and Jesus are time travellers, and their portals are inside the tombs. Lazarus goes first, a detail that never changes, but one of the two friends, tragically, will not return alive.

I can be convinced by this. If there is ever time travel there will always have been time travel, and Cicero will turn out to be right: what cannot happen does not happen. Lazarus and Jesus are pioneering time-travel friends, in the early days of the science. They are far too conspicuous when they arrive in first-century Palestine, not believable as inhabitants of that particular time and place.

Their trip is a fiasco, Lazarus returning to the future with the crucified body of Jesus in his arms. Regulations are put in place to avoid repeat catastrophes of this kind, and since then those regulations have been studiously observed. Time travellers are much more discreet. Though that could always change, from one day to the next.

We need to open our eyes. Life is full of possibility.

Lazarus may never have died.

Everyone owes nature a death, and Lazarus has paid his debt. In five hundred and sixty years from now, in the year 2570 CE, Lazarus will be identified trudging across a desolate, beast-filled desert in the ruined state of Utah. This is how we find him in Walter M. Miller's *A Canticle for Leibowitz* (1959). He is still wandering sixty years later (2630 CE), and rejecting the adoption of the symbol of the cross — he throws rocks at Catholic novices engaged in their Lenten fasts.

With Lazarus anything is possible, but if he were alive today we would know that as a fact. I think.

He colludes in his own second death. He accepts that he has to die twice, an anomaly that his friend Jesus learns to avoid. Lazarus trials the problem so that Jesus can know. In this sense, as in so many others, Lazarus is the teacher.

Lazarus lays down his life twice for his friend. No one else can do this but Lazarus, and genuinely there is no greater love. He is the only named friend of Jesus.

I think he lives at least another thirty years, as Church tradition indicates. He reaches a good age and he comes to know happiness, to the extent that several testimonies insist on him smiling.

And even though Jesus requires his friend to die a second death, Lazarus knows that death is not the end. There is something beyond. The second time, so as not to distract from the story of Jesus, Lazarus will die without drawing attention to himself, far from Jerusalem and Rome. He dies in Cyprus or Marseilles, generously moving aside.

Angels may carry him to heaven, where the prophet Abraham may await. He will be reunited with Eliakim and his mother Sarah and with Amos. He had not remembered that it would be like this.

He returns to what is beyond. Jesus walks forward from the shore.